GALA DAY

The pain didn't immediately register. The hind foot rushing toward his head was far more immediate. But the immense wallop of the fore foot sent him rolling, twisting, unable to control his movement, unable to deliberately avoid the hoof bearing down on him, unable to predict if it would hit him or miss him.

For some reason he didn't blink or shut his eyes. The shining metal held him mesmerised, like a rabbit caught in headlights. He knew, as the foot struck, that it would be that vision that would end his career. Whatever breaks and fractures were about to rain down upon him, it was his nerve that would shatter first. Would he lie in bed at night, still seeing the flash of steel? Would he walk up to a horse and see only the legs and the order in which they struck the ground at a gallop? Would the foot crush his chest? Would the hoof smash down through his skull cap and end such thoughts entirely?

The Georgian Rose Press
georgianrose@eircom.net

First published 2005
2nd edition 2009
3rd edition 2013

ISBN 978-0-9534167-4-5

CHAPTER ONE

The Newbury crowd roared as the thirteen runners sprinted towards the winning post in the penultimate race of the day.

"*And Satin Princess bursts through now to take it up, it's Satin Princess, with Breadline making some headway now in pursuit, but nothing's going to catch Satin Princess, she's going three, four, five lengths clear...*"

From his position on Breadline, Pete Allen was thinking much the same as the racecourse commentator. Resigned to second place, he put in some stylish effort to close the gap; more for show than through any real hope of succeeding. But he already knew – as he had known when pulling out for a challenge deliberately timed too late – that he couldn't win.

In front of him, former Champion Jockey Bob Graham had dropped his hands and was coasting home to an effortless victory. The style that had, in the past, won him three Championships was elegant and distinctive. And yet...

As Pete edged closer he couldn't fail to notice that Bob was in trouble. Cursing under his breath, he watched Bob kick his feet from the irons of the slipping saddle and put his left hand back to try to prevent the saddle slipping down under the filly's belly. The saddle was by now round her loins, Bob riding her bareback.

At least the filly hadn't reacted in fury to the uncomfortable saddle now flapping under her loins. She was within touching distance of the winning post and Bob had already given up the awkward attempt at hanging on to the saddle. Instead, he nursed her towards victory and looked forward to being able to jump down from her less-than-comfortable back.

'Go on, go on,' Pete muttered through clenched teeth, 'go on, *go on*... oh *shit!*'

Flapping on the turf in front of him was Satin Princess' number cloth, normally held firm over the top of the weight cloth by the girth. As she crossed the line and pulled up, ten feet behind her, only just on the wrong side of the line, lay the weight cloth – together with its ten pounds of lead.

'You okay, mate?' Pete asked Bob as he pulled up beside the luckless winner, now being led by her jockey.

Bob pulled a face that said it all.

'Yeah, well, it gets worse, mate. You lost your weight cloth.'

Bob swore loudly and struck the ground violently with his whip.

'Where?'

'Where d'you think – an inch past the post?! About ten foot before the line. Bad luck, mate.'

'Shit! Not bad luck for you, is it, you jammy sod? You're on the winner.' He cursed again. 'You didn't go over it, did you?'

'Can't vouch for the lads behind me, but it was still in one piece when I last saw it.'

Bob snorted in disgust. A new weight cloth was the least of his worries.

Pete left him and cantered gently back to the paddock. Jammy sod. Well that was a matter of opinion. And from where he was sitting he could hardly consider himself lucky.

The stable lad greeted him and led him up to the winners' enclosure.

'That should see us right for York next week, Pete.'

'You reckon? I've got news for you.'

They reached the winners' enclosure and walked straight in to the spot reserved for the runner-up; since, until the weigh-in, they were still officially only second. A miserable Bob Graham followed them in and met his elated connections in the winner's spot. The spectators pressed around the small enclosure within the parade ring clapped him heartily, in the warm August sunshine.

In the runner-up's spot, the young trainer walked forward to give his charge a pat.

'Well done, Pete; an excellent ride. Just not good enough. Still, you did your best.'

At twenty-six, Sebastian Churchill was easily the youngest trainer in Newmarket, in only his first season. As private trainer to Walter Casburg, owner of the soon-to-be promoted runner-up, he was already enjoying a noticeable amount of success.

Alongside them, Bob was explaining to his dismayed owner and trainer that he would be unable to weigh-in with the correct weight. Sebastian, overhearing, listened with a blank expression.

'We've won then?'

Pete nodded. 'No bloody doubt.'

Sebastian's broad smile didn't waver. 'Damn it.'

Bob walked through to the weighing room and Pete made a move to follow him.

'Come straight back out,' Sebastian told him firmly.

Predictably, the official announcement was quickly made of an objection by the Clerk of the Scales to the winner. Pete accepted the few congratulatory pats from his colleagues in the weighing room, then stood in the doorway, watching his trainer before making a move to join him.

Sebastian, chatting happily to one of the racing hacks, betrayed nothing in his demeanour. Dark-haired and attractive, he was every bit the charmer; permanently smiling because he permanently had something to smile about. Pete remembered the time when he, too, had been the charmer, the up-and-coming star. A classic case of too much too soon, leaving him at thirty-two with nothing but a playboy lifestyle and the income of a second-rate jockey to sustain it.

And even the lifestyle he struggled to maintain was only as surface deep as his precious Porsche. At nineteen, with the wealth to be found at the top of his tree, he could have had anything; and wanted everything. He hadn't known then about such alien concepts as the future. Fortunately he'd met Barbara – steady, dependable, non-racing. But the lifestyle was too good to give up; even if he did stop short at taking home his besotted fans. Not that he'd ever let anyone know that…

True, he was still very much a heart-throb to the female racing fraternity. But the joy had quite suddenly gone out of his habitual playful flirtations.

Sighing softly to himself, he went out to join Sebastian. They tucked themselves away where there was no danger of being overheard.

'Not the end of the world, is it?' Pete asked hopefully, 'it's too late to affect the weights for Wednesday's race, surely?'

'Any winner after the fourteenth incurs a seven pound penalty,' Sebastian reminded him calmly, 'certainly something we could have done without.'

Pete considered the weight penalty that Breadline would now have to carry in his race at York in four days time. There was little point in kidding himself that his services were worth an extra seven pound burden.

'I suppose you'll be putting a boy up at York now?'

Sebastian nodded. 'I might try and get hold of a decent five pound claimer, that should be enough. None of the boys claiming the full seven pounds are any damn good. I'll have Sophie go through the race for me; she's pretty sharp when it comes to handicapping.' He grimaced as he spoke of his 'baby' sister, just two years his junior. 'That's if she can find the time to look at the weights for me, in between organising this ruddy gala day of hers. It seems to take up every minute of her time these days.'

'How is she?' Pete asked; as he always did.

'Well enough. Throwing herself totally into this gala day, as I say. Still, it seems to be doing her good. Gets her out of herself.'

'Good. Look, I'd best get back in. Any instructions for the last?'

'Play it by ear. But if it does happen to show some ability, keep it to yourself, would you, so we can have a bit of a punt next time, okay?'

Pete smiled. 'Will do.'

He returned to the changing room, still cursing his luck. As usual, Sebastian Churchill had come up smelling of roses; unlike certain others...

He sat down at his usual peg and tried to put on the characteristic show of cheerfulness. Around him, the talk was of racing at Deauville the next day. Most of his colleagues appeared to have been booked to ride at the French seaside track. He picked up a copy of The Racing Post and studied the Deauville runners.

'You're not riding in France tomorrow, then?' he asked Chris Marsh, sitting alongside him.

'No. Not worth making the trip. The guv'nor can't see ours beating the French horse.'

'Marcel's not listed here for a ride, either.'

Chris shook his head. 'Couldn't get one. But he's going over anyway, just to watch. His father-in-law owns the favourite, doesn't he!'

Pete looked around him. Of the Newbury-based jockeys, only Chris would be spending the following day at home. If Chris turned him down...

He moistened his lips.

'Could I ask a favour of you, mate?'

Chris glanced up. 'Sure. Fire away.'

'I know I've left it a bit late to spring this on you, but something's just cropped up. Would you and

Anne mind if I came back with you this evening?'

'What, stop the night, you mean?'

'If that's okay?'

'Don't see why not. Course you can. What's up, anyway?'

Pete shook his head. 'A bit of personal bother, that's all. It'll sort itself out. But I'll need a lift as well. Maybe we could pick up my car tomorrow?'

'Sure; no problem.'

Terry Jones came in from the weighing room and sat down in his usual place next to Chris.

'What's up then? Coming back with us, did you say?'

'Chris and Anne are putting me up for the night.'

'Why?'

'It's personal, Terry, okay?'

Terry's dark eyes rested on Pete with suspicion.

In silence, they weighed out for the final race of the day, but none of them could finish in the frame. They changed quickly and met Anne and Su Jones outside the weighing room. Much to Pete's relief they made a fairly large group as they walked out to the car park.

'Where d'you park? Did you get here early?' Pete tried to ask casually, hoping his nerves weren't as visible as they felt.

Chris paid little attention. 'Not far in.'

The light blue Mercedes was already within sight; parked a mercifully long distance from a flashy white Porsche which held Pete's attention, beside

11

which two men could be seen waiting ominously for its owner. Fortunately, none of the other members of the group appeared to notice it and Pete shivered involuntarily.

Chris threw the kit bags into the boot and Pete settled himself in the back with the girls, alongside Su. She eyed him teasingly and he played up to her with relish; forgetting for a moment the problems which haunted him.

'What happened to the shades?' she asked, flashing her green eyes wide as she tossed back her long wavy hair. It matched the same silky black sheen of her husband's; although his was natural.

'They got broken.' He didn't tell her how they had been broken; or by whom.

'Someone walk over your grave?'

'I got a draught. Wind your window up a bit, Chris, mate.'

They arrived in Lambourn and dropped Su and Terry off outside their cottage on the outskirts of the village, then continued a little further up the lane to Chris and Anne's more modern farmhouse, bought long after the farm itself had been divided into lots and sold off.

'I like this spot,' Pete remarked, as he retrieved his kit bag from the boot and followed Chris and Anne up to the front door, 'nice and quiet.'

They left their bags in the hall and went straight through to the living room, Chris and Pete flopping down on the sofa while Anne went out to put the kettle on.

'There's a bottle of Moet in my bag,' Chris

called out to her, 'stick it in the fridge would you, love.'

'It's full,' she called back, 'you'll have to put it out in the shed.'

Pete leaned back comfortably and took in his surroundings; feeling the inevitable stab of regret. Anne's touch was everywhere, right down to the matching photo frames that displayed countless horses and Chris' beaming face as he was led back in to a variety of winners' enclosures. His own home was suddenly devoid of such warmth.

'Tea or coffee?' Anne called.

'Better make it a black coffee.' He didn't need to remind her of no sugar. In his profession, it was taken for granted.

She fetched in a tray of mugs and kicked off her shoes, sinking back into the easy chair opposite. A slim and attractive thirty-year-old, her light brown hair cut in a bob and bouncing on her shoulders. None of the thin sharp features of her husband. Soft blue eyes, where his were steely grey. Yet they made an obvious couple, just as Terry and Su could pass for brother and sister. Albeit with an allowance in height. Su towered over those around her, at a mere five foot eight. Pete wondered if he and Barbara were so consciously alike. It seemed to be an odd quirk that came with married life.

He remembered flirting with Anne back in the days when they had been teenagers. She a stable lass in the yard where Terry and Chris were serving their apprenticeships, he already a star apprentice and on his way to his first lucrative retainer with champion trainer Nick Marchant. But, then, there wasn't a girl on the racecourse Pete couldn't remember flirting with, at one time or another. And he had only ever loved Barbara.

'Oh, I nearly forgot,' Anne said suddenly, fishing in her jacket pocket as it hung over the arm of her chair, 'I saw this for Barbara.'

She tossed a little object wrapped in tissue paper across to Pete. He unwrapped it with interest and smiled.

'Another bloody cat!'

'Where d'you get that, love?' Chris asked, as Pete passed the china kitten to him for a look.

'A stall at the back of the grandstand. Su bought herself a lovely candlestick. And when we saw the cat, we thought of Barbara straight away! Sweet, isn't it?'

'Looks like all the rest of them to me!' Pete complained.

'Grumpy old sod! No wonder she wouldn't take you on holiday with her!' Anne teased. 'How's she enjoying it, anyway?'

'Having a ball,' Pete told her truthfully. 'Her sister's got her running her hat shop and she's already selling thousand dollar ostrich feathers to silly women for the Melbourne Cup! Or something like that.'

'It's months away!' Chris objected.

'Didn't know it was a working holiday!' Anne laughed.

'Who but Barbara could go to the Australian Gold Coast and spend her time in a flaming hat shop?!' Pete agreed.

'Well, you did all the beaches and that when you were over for the winter, didn't you?' Chris said.

'Barbara did the beaches. I was working, remember?!'

'Bloody hard work too, I should imagine,' Chris agreed, 'I wouldn't fancy it myself. Different style out there altogether. How d'you find the Aussie jockeys?'

'I thought I'd get cut up and pocketed all over the place, but they were a good enough bunch. But, like you say, a different style of racing altogether. They didn't need to hamper me – I threw away nearly every race! Even when I rode to orders, I got it wrong!'

'Back to Madras next winter?'

'I thought I might stay at home and brave the All-Weather, actually.'

Anne pulled a face. 'Barbara'll love you for that one. Better give her the cat first, eh?!'

Pete smiled and nodded.

'Are you riding at Windsor on Monday?' Anne asked him.

He nodded again. 'Three rides for Sebastian and one for Tommy Carpenter.'

'I was just wondering if you'd like to stay tomorrow night as well? It seems silly to drive all the way home when Windsor's only round the corner from here.'

Pete was taken aback, but much relieved at the suggestion.

'Thanks,' he agreed, 'it's good of you.'

She smiled sympathetically. 'Well, it can't be

much fun at home, with Barbara away.'

They finished their tea and Anne went out to prepare a light supper, which passed for their evening meal. It wasn't often that Chris rode locally and they had so much of the evening to spare, so they took advantage of the occasion and sent Chris in to the village to hire a couple of videos.

'Time for bed – and a merciful lie-in in the morning,' Anne said sleepily, as the last of the blood and gore had flowed. 'Made a change from the usual recording of the afternoon's racing, anyway!'

'You don't get tired of it, do you, Anne?' Pete asked.

She smiled. 'It's in the blood, isn't it? Besides, a video of Newbury races is a lot less predictable than a Jean-Claude Van Damme movie!'

The following morning, Chris and Pete drove into the village to return the videos, then continued on to Newbury racecourse, to pick up Pete's car.

'How's it going, riding for Sebastian?' Chris asked conversationally, as they headed down towards the racecourse. 'He's having a fair few winners. Yesterday's was a piece of luck for you, too.'

'Hardly. It's gone up seven pounds in the weights, so I won't get the ride at York.'

'Really? We've a boy at our yard your guv'nor might be interested in. A smart little seven pound claimer. A good head and nice hands.'

Pete was dismissive. 'Seb doesn't want to put a complete novice up. He's got Sophie checking out five pound claimers for him. Truth to tell, I don't think he's that keen on apprentices anyway. Doesn't trust them.'

'They all ride like flipping Marcel Dessaint these days!' Chris agreed. 'Since Marcel won the Championship our head lad's done nothing but yell at the new boys. "Lower those bloody leathers! Get those knees down!" I've not seen anyone with the talent to carry off Marcel's style.'

Pete grinned. 'It's not that he doesn't trust their ability. More like he doesn't trust their mouths.'

'And boys have this in-built need to win every race, of course.'

Pete shot him a glance. 'It's not like that, Chris. Christ almighty, you know me better than that.'

'I wasn't suggesting that. I just meant they wouldn't go easy on a horse being saved for a better race.'

'Yeah, well, it's a fair cop, guv'. I should really have been saving our horse yesterday; sparing him a seven pound penalty. But what can I do, Chris? I wouldn't actually stop a horse. But I have to put bread on the table.' He sighed. 'Life's bloody unfair, sometimes. There have been days when I've said, this is it, I'm going to pull my socks up and ride like the best of them. Get noticed, get back in the big time. And the horses I've gone out on have been absolute bloody stinkers! No one notices the guy riding a blinder somewhere out the back of the field! This job with Sebastian, it was meant to be my chance. But I should have known why he'd really picked me.'

'Be fair, Pete. You've always had a bit of a short, fancy style. You're as close to Marcel's style as any of us will get. Now that he's flavour of the month, so should you be.' He laughed. 'Every boy in every stable is trying to mimic a style you mastered years ago! Maybe Sebastian doesn't want you for your stopping power alone.'

'Stopping power. Whether you believe it or not, you said it.' He waved off Chris' protest. 'Everyone knows I'm not crooked; and they all know I'm not quite straight. And it's too late in the day to shake it off.'

They sat in silence for a while.

'Do you see much of Sophie, now that you ride for her brother?' Chris asked, as they approached the racecourse.

Pete shook his head. 'She rides out for her Dad. Seb gets her to check out weights and book apprentices, but we don't see her at the yard very much.'

'The girls miss her. Do you think she'll ever go racing again?'

'Maybe; once this gala day of hers is over.' But Pete didn't sound very hopeful.

'Being on a racecourse again, seeing everyone gathered together, maybe it'll do the trick,' Chris agreed. 'It's taking her out of herself a bit, anyway.'

Sophie Churchill was the main driving force behind the gala day, which was hoped would raise an incredible sum for the Injured Jockeys' Fund.

Everyone within the racing fraternity had been called upon to play a part and Anne and Su were very actively involved in its organisation.

They both sat quietly for a while, each wrapped up in his own thoughts. After nearly two years, Chris had finally stopped blaming himself for the death of a young colleague. It wasn't so long ago that he would have ended any conversation connected with the late Dominic Marchant with the words, 'I really couldn't have done anything to avoid him.' Now, at last, he was resigned to the truth in those words.

An unfortunate accident, a typical race fall, and there had been nothing that he could do. One moment they were galloping safely towards the top of the hill at Epsom; the next, Dominic – a promising young apprentice of just seventeen – was on the ground, beneath the feet of Chris' mount.

Chris had ridden and re-ridden that race a thousand times in his mind; and each time the result had been the same. Sophie had been a spectator that day, as on every other. Her father David trained at Newmarket and it had been his horse from which Dominic had taken that fatal fall. She and Dominic had been friends from the cradle. And, just that season, live-in lovers. It was little wonder that she could no longer bear to go racing.

They rolled slowly into the racecourse car park.

'Sticks out like a sore thumb,' Chris said; breaking the heavy silence.

Pete's sparkling white Porsche sat alone in

the empty car park, with no lurking dangers in sight. As Chris drove nearer, so a few startling changes in the bodywork became apparent.

'Christ almighty!' was Chris' only comment, as he pulled up alongside it.

Shaken, Pete climbed out slowly and stared at his pride and joy. Every window had been smashed, the leather interior slashed to pieces. The exterior of the car was scored with scratches and dents. The tyres had been slashed. An indescribable amount of fury had been unleashed on the car; fury that had, in all probability, been intended for a different subject.

The most likely alternative now leant weakly against the Mercedes, his face white.

'Was this the spot of bother you couldn't tell me about?' Chris asked unnecessarily. He could think of nothing else to say.

Pete climbed shakily back into the Mercedes and Chris followed suit.

'I'll take you back home and call a garage to have it picked up.'

Pete didn't reply. If he had gone back to his own car after racing, instead of travelling home with Chris...

'Christ, I feel sick, mate,' he said with feeling.

'I take it you know who and why?'

'I could take a fair guess. But I won't be reporting it to the Jockey Club.'

'Do you think all that damage is enough to let you off the hook?'

Pete closed his eyes. 'I bloody hope so.' But

he had his doubts.

They drove back to the house and Chris made arrangements for the Porsche. Recovering his spirits a little, Pete also spoke to the garage and arranged to hire a car until his own was ready. While Chris finalised details, Anne took the opportunity to have a quiet word with their houseguest.

'The men who smashed up your car, would they be the same two who were waiting by it last night when we left the racecourse?'

'You saw them?'

'I know you did – you went as white as a sheet. Whatever they used on your car, was it meant for you?'

'I don't know; but I'm bloody glad I didn't find out the hard way. I owe you both big time, Anne.' He swallowed. 'Thanks for not saying anything, when you saw them.'

'Just count your blessings that Su didn't notice, or the whole world would know by now.'

'Are you certain she didn't?'

Anne smiled. 'It would have been a miracle if she had. She was draped around Terry's shoulders at the time, chewing her way through the back of his neck, if I remember rightly!'

'There's something to be said for young love after all.'

CHAPTER TWO

Pete woke up early, trying not to listen to the rather obvious noises of an enjoyable wake-up call drifting across the hall. He'd had a fitful night's sleep, too filled with thoughts of smashed up cars and weapons of destruction; and following on too many nights lacking in the kind of activity that now woke him. Bloody Barbara and hat shops and Australia. Bloody Bob Graham and his slipping saddle.

He dragged himself out of bed and sought sanctuary in the en-suite bathroom, enjoying a refreshing shower and grateful for the clean clothes to change into. He'd slobbed around in Chris' bathrobe for much of the previous day, while Anne put his own clothes through the wash and the tumble dryer. He had been ill-prepared for a weekend away.

He picked up the emptied contents of his pockets from the dressing table, a chilling reminder of just why the unplanned break from home had been so necessary. His sunglasses, nearly as expensive as the car, as he used to joke, were now every bit as worthless. Broken.

Just as his hands would be, if he didn't clear his account.

It was a pathetic threat, of course. His hands were his livelihood. And his account was less than a few thousand. Even a bookmaker as shady as Dave Bisley, the type of bookie who'd risk both their licences by offering an account to a jockey, wouldn't stoop to such criminal methods. For just a few thousand.

That's all it had been when Bisley had

stopped him in the car park on the way into Newbury racecourse. Gently removed his glasses; reminded him of his financial commitments; crushed the glasses underfoot.

Mere menacing with words or not, it was pretty frightening stuff and Pete had been forced to think on his feet. Had thought of Breadline, for whom there would certain to be plenty of financial interest, but on whom his instructions were 'whatever you do, *don't win.*' And so he told Dave Bisley, with all his usual cocky confidence, that he didn't know any winners, but he knew for a fact Breadline was a loser.

On the way into Newbury racecourse, he'd only owed Bisley a few thousand. Now, the price of a Porsche could scarcely be a dent on the amount of liabilities Breadline had just cost the generous bookie. All Pete could hope was that it was punishment enough for his part in the flawed scheme. With his presence at Windsor races that afternoon well advertised, it had to be.

Downstairs in the kitchen, breakfasting with Chris and Anne, he picked half-heartedly at the barely-buttered toast. Anne watched him with concern.

'More butter?' She offered tentatively.

'I wish!' He grinned. 'This is more than enough for a man hoping to do eight three today.'

'Eight three?' Chris remarked. 'I thought your one in the handicap was off eight two?'

'It is. But we can afford a pound overweight. We're well in as it is.'

'Never mind a pound overweight,' Anne cut

in, 'if the butter's not a problem, what is? Your name is printed quite clearly against four runners in every daily paper. Is that going to be a problem?'

Pete gave up trying to eat the toast. 'I really don't know. I hope not.'

'They don't know how he's getting to the course and once he's in, what can they do?' Chris pointed out. 'It's Windsor racecourse, for Christ sake, not a dark alley.'

The wise words of wisdom were hardly reassuring, but at least seemed to end any further speculation. Conversation drifted to lighter topics as the morning progressed and they got ready to leave for Windsor races.

'I suppose Sophie has roped you into the gala day?' Anne enquired. 'Donkey Derby or show jumping?'

Pete grinned and raised a finger theatrically to his lips. 'Sshh. So far I've got off scot-free.'

'Bloody hell! How did you manage that?!' Chris demanded, 'I'm signed up for everything! I think kids are even going to pay fifty pence to throw wet sponges at me!'

'Before you get your cheque book out,' Anne warned, 'he is joking.'

Chris grinned at her. 'Put the idea in Sophie's head and I won't be! As it is, I'm in the Donkey Derby *and* the show jumping team.'

'Any good?' Pete asked with interest.

Anne smiled. 'Terry's our ringer. Bob and Marcel are on the team just to draw the crowds; Chris is on to cover Terry's presence. And Terry won just about every gymkhana going as a kid! So if you were contemplating a bet on the National Hunt team – forget it!'

'I'm not contemplating any bet on anything ever,' Pete said firmly, 'but when it comes to Them and Us, I take a strong partisan interest!'

'So do Them,' Chris said, 'so don't let them know about Terry!'

'We'll hammer them anyway,' Pete said with confidence, 'we've got better balance, better timing...'

'They jump fences daily for a living,' Chris interrupted.

Pete grinned. 'Not with style, though!'

'There's five-a-side football,' Chris suggested, 'the National Hunt boys versus us. And the Northern boys versus us Southerners. I think some trainers are getting teams together, too. And cricket – Newmarket Eleven against the Lambourn Eleven.'

'You're not talking me into any of it,' Pete insisted.

'Riding lessons?' Anne suggested cheekily.

'Darling, you couldn't afford me!'

'The one big crowd-puller is the show jumping,' Chris said, 'a chance for us to beat them at their own game. Sophie says the interest it's generated, she'll have to book us into the Millennium Stadium, just to accommodate everyone!'

'Yeah, well let us down, mate, and she'll have to book you into a Siberian salt mine, for your own safety!'

They laughed and began to gather up their

things for the afternoon, as though nothing out of the ordinary had ever happened. Pete found their silence on the Newbury incident privately amusing, wondering if they were merely being polite, embarrassed or as much in the know as he was. Perhaps when tempers had cooled he might give Bisley a ring and find out exactly where he now stood. But until then, he was grateful not to have to answer questions, when he didn't have any answers himself. Unless Bisley was already planning a meeting at Windsor…

'Okay?' Anne asked gently, as Pete lingered over his kit bag.

He picked it up and swung it over his shoulder. 'Me, I'm hunky dory. Just wish I could say the same for the Porsche!'

Chris peered out of the window impatiently, then turned to pick up his own bag.

'It's no Porsche, but our chariot's here.'

They made their way outside and Anne and Chris joined Su and Terry, who'd fetched their own car for the day. As neighbours, it was usually their practise to pool the tiring driving duties. But the perfect system often ran aground on work mornings, the two days a week that the horses from their respective stables were given serious gallops. Terry's stable was first out onto the gallops, Chris' yard working a little later, enabling the two jockeys to ride out together for both trainers. The ensuing arguments as to which jockey had the better horses generally led to a minor fall-out for the day – and separate cars. The childish squabbles had never improved with maturity, but at least kept the rest of the racing fraternity entertained.

On very best terms now, the two couples roared off in the ubiquitous Mercedes, leaving Pete to follow in his own hired Merc'. Even if he was seen arriving in it, he reflected grimly, at least it would quickly be lost in the sea of Merc's that was the Jockeys' Car Park. Nevertheless, it was with a sense of dread that he approached the racecourse and entered the car park.

Such dread was new to him. Despite his reputation, he had never actually been in trouble. He might have occasionally saved a horse for a better race, but keeping a horse's ability unexposed was not a flagrant breach of rules. Holding a betting account was a definite disqualification offence, but his bets were never large and his debts cleanly cleared without pressure to bend further rules. Until now...

A new, uglier, peril reared its head. Supposing Bisley made alternative arrangements to pay off the sudden massive debt? Deliberately lose the two thirty or else... or else what? He'd go to the Jockey Club and lose his own licence along with him, Pete? No, he was safe from that, at least. But supposing Bisley knew of other 'or else' scenarios? A shady bookie would have a fairly big repertoire of 'or else' threats, Pete imagined. He decided to keep his imagination firmly in check.

He parked and crossed the bridge over the river into the racecourse itself. It was a big bridge to cross, he thought with a grin. And his grin increased as he strolled safely to the weighing room without seeing Bisley or his henchmen.

Depositing his kit bag by his peg, he returned outside and surveyed the paddock area. All the regular faces, but no unwanted visions. Perhaps his Porsche had paid the ultimate price after all.

He spotted a group of regular race-goers, teenage girls, sheltered under the shade of the trees at the far end, watching the runners for the first. He shot them the perfected smile, throwing them into an instant flurry of indecision. It usually took only a second smile to defeat the horses hands down, but Pete retreated instead to the weighing room, lacking the heart for the usual playful flirtations.

He settled at his peg in the changing room and changed into his breeches, polo neck top and body protector, pulling on his thin tight boots with effort. His valet fetched him over the silks he'd be wearing for the first race and the trainer responsible for his first ride handed him the weight cloth, its pockets filled with seven pounds of lead weights. He walked through to the scales and weighed out at the correct weight, the routine of the day displacing any lingering thoughts of Bisley.

The trainer was given back the weight cloth, together with Pete's saddle, and disappeared off to saddle his two-year-old colt for the first race of the day. It was one of the few horses in the twenty runner field to have had the experience of a previous race and Pete's services were much in demand from his colleagues, whose own mounts were seeing a racecourse for the first time.

'Wait for me in the paddock, would you, and

give me a lead down,' Chris asked, 'my filly's a little madam at home.'

'Join the queue, I'm leading down three!'

The large group of jockeys walked out together to the parade ring as soon as the horses were all led in, saddled, and the paddock resounded with the usual ringside gossip, parade ring discussions between the connections of the runners, and the horses themselves, squealing with excitement and calling out.

A bell rang to signal for the jockeys to mount and most were legged up onto their mounts as the horses walked past, the trainers unwilling to upset the fractious juveniles further by making them stop and stand still. Some horses gave excited bucks and pulled hard at the lead rein to get out onto the track; others became mulish and reluctant to leave the newly familiar territory of the ring. There was a general melee of horses at the exit, some waiting for a lead, a horse to canter to the start with, a relaxing companion; others waiting to give a lead; none finding it easy to sort themselves out into any order.

It was here that accidents could occur, harmless falls as horses reared and kicked out at one another, unseating their riders. If they happened at all, more often than not the jockey would simply be legged back up again. It was out on the track, during the race itself, that falls became more serious. The turf failed to offer such a cushioned landing when a rider took a spill at forty miles an hour. Nor could horses so easily avoid a stricken body, their half tonne weight thundering by, closely packed, intent only on the winning line.

On this occasion there were no misadventures, the horses eventually finding suitable companions and cantering down the full length of the virtually straight track to the six furlong start, hidden from the grandstand by a slight kink where it was crossed by the longer figure eight track. Pete's mount gave him the opportunity to ride an impeccable race up to the dogleg; at which point the inability of the colt kicked in. By the time they came in view of the stands, Pete was scrubbing along uselessly at the rear, his style and effort once again going by unnoticed.

The runners returned to the unsaddling area, sides heaving with effort, heads high and ears pricked with the sheer thrill of it all. This time the sounds filling the air were of the breathing of each horse, coming in deep, loud snorts; the hearty pats from their lads and owners resounding off their broad sweat-soaked necks, with words of 'well done, good boy!' echoed across the paddock, regardless of whether the recipient was a winner or loser. And explanations by returning jockeys of defeat or victory; while all the time the gathered race crowd buzzed with conversation.

Added to the heady mixture of sound came the ever-present aroma of the racecourse – hoof oil, fresh dung, leather and horse. Pete could think of no better environment as he walked back to the weighing room, without need to weigh in because he had no prize to lose should he fail to show the correct weight. He would have been perfectly content, had only he not tasted the thrill of real success. Three brief years as a star had left him with a perpetual longing to be back up there again. Not for the money or the status or the groupies, but for the type of horse that now stood beside him as he walked through the winners' enclosure. He desperately yearned to get back up on good horses again.

And so the afternoon passed, like every other afternoon spent on a racecourse, Pete scrubbing around at the rear of the field, unable to showcase the talent he had never lost. His colleague, Marcel Dessaint, able to take his pick of good horses, had as usual picked right and ridden a treble. The two contrasting trends looked set to continue, without hope of reversal.

Pete found himself glancing round for Sophie Churchill, despite the fact that she hadn't been racing for two years. Perhaps it was talk of her efforts with the charity gala day, earlier that morning, which had triggered old memories. But he missed her presence, quite suddenly. Especially here, on an uninspiring Monday afternoon, with a crowd made up virtually entirely of professionals. And the walk back to the car park loomed ominously.

And then there was home… no Barbara… no real home at all.

'Pete Allen? Silent? And no shades?'

The jovial enquiry broke his reverie. Danny Western, journalist, barred his way into the weighing room.

'Any quote for me on why you're not in shades? And no dolly bird dangling from each arm?'

'Bugger off, Westy!' He tried, half-heartedly,

to edge past the tall burly hack.

'It was the shades! I always knew it was the shades!' Western grinned, but his tape recorder was held up and whirring, as usual. 'What about the car? I hear you're in a Merc' today – any story in it?'

'It's why they all drive Merc's, isn't it?' Pete smiled, 'more reliable.'

'The Porsche was left abandoned at Newbury Saturday.'

'Yeah. And the mechanic towed it Sunday. What is it, slow news week?'

'York week, sunshine. Any tips?

'I'm a jockey, we're lousy tipsters.'

'So your retained stable has a runner in all the big handicaps and you're not riding any of them – any tip in that?' Western persisted.

Pete couldn't resist the opening. He eyed Western's noticeable paunch. 'A very good tip, Westy – watch the calories!'

'You bastard, Pete Allen! So are any of these horses any good? You got them into the races at a low mark.'

'Here's your quote, Westy, you fat bastard – and be sure to quote me verbatim on that! – I rode them in their prep' races and they didn't really feel ready yet. Seb's done a bit more work with them at home, they're in off a good mark, so we're pretty hopeful they could pick up some prize money. Satisfied? And verbatim, remember!'

Western grinned and stepped aside, taking away on his tape no more than the form books had already told him. A handicap, ideally, saw every horse entered given an equal chance. Good horses therefore carried heavy weights, less talented horses carried less. And a talented trainer and jockey combination, such as Sebastian Churchill and Pete Allen, could quite easily see that their good horse slipped in with a low weight. The problem to a journalist and tipster being, which were the carefully concealed good horses – and which were the genuinely untalented?

The problem would have been quickly solved had Pete mentioned the fact that he was desperately wasting down to the lowest weight he could manage in order to ride in the races in question. And he wasn't about to endure such suffering for the genuinely untalented, a fact that would quite comfortably have paid off his former debt with Bisley, had only Bisley been prepared to wait a few days.

He returned to his peg and stretched out his legs, enabling Dave the valet to pull off his boots, inching each one in turn down a fraction at a time.

'You've grown into them again!' Dave complained.

'I blame me Mum,' Pete told him, 'she was always buying me clothes to grow into.'

'Well, no wonder!' Dave moaned, as the first boot slipped off, 'you're wearing ordinary socks, you plonker!'

'Plonker yourself. Barbara's away. Do you think I'm going to mince into ladies' wear and buy a packet of pop socks?'

'I'll buy your flippin' pop socks. You could've just asked. And there's hundreds of them in the spares bin, anyway.'

'Oh yeah, right, hundreds! When I rummaged through I found one packet. I think Sir Gordon Richards left it there, he'd swapped his sugar ration for it with a Yank!'

'He swapped more than that,' Bob Graham remarked, overhearing, 'have you any idea how hard it probably was to get nylons off a Yank in the war!'

'Not as hard as it is to get you lot to cough up for pop socks,' Dave moaned, 'tomorrow you can pull your own bloody boots off!'

'I bet I could get nylons off a Yank!' Pete told Bob, winking. 'Although if it's stockings, I prefer them left on!'

Boots removed, Pete stripped for the shower and was soon changing back into street clothes once more.

'Westy's outside,' Dave warned, as Pete threw his kit bag over his shoulder and said his goodbyes.

'It's okay, he nabbed me earlier.'

'The man's wasted in the racing press,' Bob said, following Pete out, 'the tabloids would sink to greater depths of sleaze and depravity if he ever switched interests!'

'Speaking of sleaze and depravity,' Pete laughed, 'I hope some of the girls are still outside!'

'Dirty sod! No wonder Barbara needed a holiday! When's she due back?'

'Oh, I told her to stay on an extra few weeks, give her sister a hand in the shop. Makes a nice break for her, really.'

Bob smirked at him. 'Thank Christ for groupies, eh?'

Pete grinned.

They separated outside the weighing room, Bob to give Danny Western his views on York, Pete to walk out to the car park and cross his big bridge again. But any misgivings about walking out to the car park alone came to nothing. He made it to the hire car unmolested and was soon speeding his way back to Newmarket.

The journey home passed quickly, the phone hopping with last minute bookings for the week ahead. Sebastian himself rang more than once, finalising details for the important York festival. His main concern was with Pete's weight and Pete had no qualms in assuring him that he could do eight stone two, privately hoping that the final pound would magically vanish before he was called to scale.

'How's Sophie?' he asked Sebastian finally, as always.

'Really well, actually. Out with Roddy this evening, third night in a row.'

'Roddy? As in your assistant Roddy?' He wasn't sure if the news hit him with surprise or disappointment.

'The very chap. He took her out Saturday night to discuss the Newmarket Cricket Eleven.'

'Some discussion!'

'So it would seem!'

'Good to see her back out there, enjoying life again.'

'Good to see her with a decent sort at last,'

Sebastian agreed, 'not wishing to speak ill of the dead or what have you, but young Marchant was a sullen little B.'

Pete said nothing. He hadn't much liked Dominic Marchant either. But the boy had been a jockey and a bloody good one. One of their own. As was Sophie…

'Anyway, you'll see her yourself tomorrow morning,' Sebastian continued, 'she's riding out for me. Dad might have the better horses – but I have Roddy!'

'See you in the morning, then.'

CHAPTER THREE

Work mornings at Sebastian's yard began at five in the morning. Most horses in Newmarket stepped out from six onwards, but Sebastian Churchill was as keen to conceal his horses from work-watchers as he was to keep their ability covered on a racecourse. Nevertheless, the Newmarket work-watchers had quickly missed the presence of his string and merely started their own days earlier.

Sebastian had instead tried to retain the advantage by sending his horses out in bandages and blinkers. Noticeable markings on legs and head were hidden beneath cloth, the skilled work-watchers hard-pressed to identify his horses, even though they could comfortably put a name to each of the other two thousand horses in Newmarket. The slender advantage wouldn't last for long – markings could be hidden, but posture, traits and build were quickly learnt give-aways. But Sebastian persevered, because the owner of the thirty-five horses in his care insisted upon it. Walter Casburg had no intention of sharing the odds.

Walter himself, tall, slender, late-fifties, stood with Sebastian halfway up Warren Hill, waiting for the rumble of hooves as the horses galloped up the Hill in pairs, Sebastian's finger poised on the button of his stopwatch. Walter also held a stopwatch; working horses against the clock a time-honoured tradition in his native America.

Although he had a sizeable home in Suffolk, Walter rarely stayed for long. His visits were frequent, brief and influential. The care of the horses was Sebastian's domain; the operation of the stable strictly Walter's. For him it was just an extension of his gaming businesses in America, the forthcoming York results on a par with the spin of a roulette wheel.

'I've seen enough,' Walter announced quite suddenly, after half his string had passed by, 'too damn early for breakfast this morning, but I sure as hell could go some now.'

Sebastian held out the car keys.

'No problem, Walter, I'll walk back with the string.'

Walter ignored the proffered keys.

'Nonsense, son; we've business to discuss. No better place than over a breakfast table.'

'Work hasn't finished yet,' Sebastian protested, 'the two-year-olds will be setting off shortly.'

'You've an assistant, haven't you? Damn it, son, designate! You don't keep a dog and bark yourself.'

Sebastian sighed privately and hurried across to Roddy, mounted on a hack and watching the exercise nearer the top of the Hill.

'Rodders! The old boy is insisting on breakfast and yours truly must play the good host. Keep an eye on proceedings for me, would you, there's a good chap.'

'But what about the juveniles?'

'My sentiments entirely, but the old boy favours egg and bacon over the possibility of seeing next season's Derby winner breeze past!' Sebastian looked back towards the old man in question, reluctant to tear himself from the prospect. 'What the hell, Rodders, I saw them all breeze by Friday and there wasn't a hint of a Derby winner then. I can afford to hold my breath until Friday, don't you think?!'

Roddy grinned.

'You'll let me know, all the same?'

'Sebastian, if something comes up that Hill like Shergar, you'll be the first to know!'

'Quite. But in the meantime, just keep an eye on the work riders, would you? Mike will be watching them keenly enough, but just double check we're matching horse and rider appropriately; it makes a vast difference to the youngsters.'

Roddy nodded and Sebastian headed briskly back to Walter, secure in the knowledge that events would be noted and reported by both his assistant and head lad.

At the foot of the Hill, potential Shergars waited for their turn to gallop. Most were already fairly experienced, Walter preferring precocious, quick-maturing two-year-olds who could reimburse their hefty purchase price during their first season. The true potential Derby winners tended not to race until the autumn, if at all at two.

Pete had the mount on a colt who had so far shown no potential whatsoever in his three racecourse appearances. Having failed to take any interest in a racing career, the young colt now bored of the morning exercise, too, and amused himself instead by trying to unship his rider.

'Steady, steady,' Pete soothed, impatiently waiting his turn to begin the gallop. He called across to the lad beside him without looking away from his own mount. 'We'll follow straight up on the heels of the fillies, I can't keep this little bugger waiting any longer.'

Two fillies set off up the Hill and Pete immediately kicked after them. But not even the opportunity to chase the opposite sex sparked any interest from his mount. He galloped in fits and starts, determined to slow if Pete kicked him on, but equally keen to grab the bit and run away with his jockey if Pete relaxed and allowed him to slow. His erratic stride was interspersed with little bucks and fly-kicks.

Not surprisingly, the working companion quickly left them behind. Pete cursed and wrestled the colt, relieved to bring the awkward ride to a close as they approached the top of the Hill. His style of riding had been developed more to aid a horse naturally in the speed of a race than to perform an uncomfortable balancing act, and he knew that if the bucks and kicks persisted, gravity would win.

He rode, as always, with just a toe in the iron. There was less strain on his calf, better balance for him, better balance for the horse. So much better balance, in fact, that it was as though his own body weight had been lifted from the horse beneath him. Except this horse beneath him was only too well aware of his presence and was intent on removing the offending weight. They had only to pull up with the rest of the string a few yards away for the ordeal to be over for both of them.

As Pete 'steady, steady'ied, his voice becoming less steady with each repeat, so the colt reared and jinked more furiously, grabbing at the bit, snatching the reins, arching his back and dropping his shoulder. It was a miracle Pete succeeded in staying on for so long; a miracle he prided himself in even as he began the inevitable descent to the floor.

He kicked his feet free effortlessly, the irons never holding more than his toe anyway. But somewhere in the battle between propulsion and gravity, his feet pointing skyward, the irons flapping wildly, the slender foot and treacherous iron met. Even before his head smacked down onto the ground – even before that awful moment, suspended in the frozen second, that he knew his head was *about* to smack down onto the ground – he realised his foot was caught in the iron.

Time stopped. Each piece of dirt, passing beneath him at thirty-five miles an hour, was visible, unmoving. His head still hadn't cracked down onto the turf. He knew his foot was caught, knew the consequences, twisted it hopelessly in search of escape. Failed. Waited for the impact. Watched the shining, razor aluminium plates reflect the sun from the soles of the colt's feet. Watched the foreleg directly in front of him, the off-fore, come down onto the ground; then lift again; the colt suspended in the air, just as he was.

When all four feet were off the ground Pete was well aware of which would be the first hoof to touch back down. All the weight, all half-ton thoroughbred, all thirty-five mile an hour propulsion, would come down on the off-hind foot.

The one directly above his head.

His shoulders thudded to earth, snapping his head back viciously.

His head smacked down; bounced; smacked down again.

Time continued to pass in microseconds, frozen; allowing him vital time to think, time to save himself; time to realise there was no hope, no salvation. But time enough to twist himself away from the hoof bearing down on him, to watch it land, the plate glistening with malice, digging into the turf millimetres from his face, ripping up the muddied blades of grass, digging in deeper as it pushed the colt's body-weight forward...

The off-fore would follow, stretched out to cover the ground somewhere ahead of his ragdoll body that trailed across the turf shoulders first; and then it would lift, curl back, strike up into the empty space beneath the belly.

Except there was no empty space.

He dangled beneath the belly, waiting for the impact, the blow of hoof, the laceration of plate.

It hit, just as the hind hoof gathered forward once more. The pain didn't immediately register. The hind foot rushing toward his head was far more immediate. But the immense wallop of the fore foot sent him rolling, twisting, unable to control his movement, unable to deliberately avoid the hoof bearing down on him, unable to predict if it would hit him or miss him.

For some reason he didn't blink or shut his eyes. The shining metal held him mesmerised, like a rabbit caught in headlights. He knew, as the foot struck, that it would be that vision that would end his career. Whatever breaks and fractures were about to rain down upon him, it was his nerve that would shatter first. Would he lie in bed at night, still seeing the flash of steel? Would he walk up to a horse and see only the legs and the order in which they struck the ground at a gallop? Would the foot crush his chest? Would the hoof smash down through his skull cap and end such thoughts entirely?

It missed; chipping his shoulder, tearing through his arm, sending him bouncing off away from the bulk of the body, sparing him the taste of shredded grass kicked up in its wake. Time was rushing forward, regaining some of its normal speed. Pete no longer had time to think of the sequence, of the forefoot up front about to sweep back up under the belly...

He felt the second blow, deep in his thigh. Felt the razor edge of the plate drive forward into his skin; felt the toe start to turn down, ripping away the flesh. Felt sick and dizzy and no longer aware of where he was, which way up he was, at what speed he was being dragged.

A shocking force struck him in the stomach, such a shock to the system that it brought him back to reality with the speed of a light switch. His first rational thought not 'I'm alive' but 'where the hell did that come from?' He knew at once he was free, no longer trailing beneath the belly of a galloping horse.

The ground felt no more stationary than it had done. But he knew the rhythm of a gallop and knew there were no feet within the vicinity of his stomach if he still remained suspended from the iron.

So he was rolling, rolling away from his landing point, conscious enough to be aware of it. Suddenly quite conscious enough to be aware of his rides that afternoon.

He struggled to keep his mind on the incident. How many kicks? How many strides? How lucky could he expect to be? How quickly could he expect his first saviour to arrive? Too bloody quickly. He'd been dragged three, maybe four strides? A hundred yards, if that.

'Shit!'

He sat up with urgency, head reeling, trying to pretend it wasn't.

'Oh shit.'

He leant forward, got up onto his knees, could get no further than all fours.

Someone was with him.

'I'm fine, I'm fine,' he announced, not quite sure how his voice sounded and how successful the lie. He focused on the feet, the ankles and the calves of his rescuer, just about all that were in his current visual range. The relief of recognition engulfed him at once.

'Oh Christ, Soph', thank God it's you! I've got to ride at York...'

'Sshh... I know.' She dropped down on her haunches beside him and took off his hat. 'I gave Mike my filly to hold and ran straight over, she's a

44

double handful, I've bought you a couple of minutes' grace.' She glanced up quickly to check. 'He's on his way over, you've got about four deep breaths to fake fitness. Any breaks?'

'Shit!' He used up two deep breaths and struggled to compose himself. 'No, bit cut up and bruised, maybe.' He forced himself up onto his haunches and felt Sophie's arm tighten around him and haul him up quickly to his feet.

'You're a pro', Soph'!'

'Dominic never lost a ride through injury! Start poking about at the minor cuts for damage, he won't notice the rest.'

She tore open his jacket and unzipped his body protector, calling out,

'He's fine, Mike, he must be made of rubber!'

Pete kept his head down and felt tentatively at a raw cut on his back, thankful that his guardian angel had turned up in such a guise. She might be just a kid, but she'd covered for her late boyfriend regularly enough in the past. Barbara would be fretting over him and insisting on doctors…

'Hardly made a dent on the protector,' Sophie continued, 'there must be an angel watching over him!'

Mike was distracted by the shouts of two lads, who between them had caught Pete's colt and were now fetching it back over.

'Keep a hold of my filly, I'll give him a leg back up,' Sophie said breezily, not giving the head lad a chance to respond.

She bustled Pete over to the colt and legged him up into the saddle once more.

'Definitely no ribs?' she verified under her breath, reluctant to be an accomplice to a pierced lung.

'I can't do this, Soph'…'

'Just stay on.'

The lads responsible for the colt's capture read the signs instantly and squeezed up on their own mounts, either side of the now deflated miscreant. With the colt safely sandwiched between them, Sophie left Pete reasonably secure in the saddle and hurried across to her own filly, who was successfully keeping Mike's hands full. He eyed her suspiciously and gave her a grudging leg up.

'The colt's got a stiff leg,' she lied, 'probably pulled a muscle dragging Pete's great hulk along. Pete's going to take him straight back and put a heat pad on him.'

Mike looked up at her. 'Now, why does that not surprise me?'

She smiled sweetly at him. 'I'll go with him, if you like? Make sure everything's okay?'

He shook his head in defeat, but raised a hand as Pete walked alongside to join Sophie.

'You want a word?' Pete asked.

'When people aren't hurt,' Mike said pointedly, 'they tend to lie there for a bit before they realise it.'

Pete grinned broadly. 'I'll bear that in mind for next time!'

'If we lose any races this afternoon,' Mike warned, 'I'll personally tell Sebastian you're not fit.'

Pete said nothing and walked his colt forward after Sophie.

'I'm going to come off,' he said shakily as soon as they were out of earshot, 'and maybe throw up and faint, not necessarily in that order.'

Sophie smiled at him. 'Mike was right. The quicker to your feet, the worse the injury you're hiding. On the other hand, the worse the injury, the less you're able to say!'

'And you're the expert?'

'Dominic often fainted, threw up or fell off. But he never mentioned it first.'

'Yeah, well, maybe the nausea's passing. But I swear I'm going to come off. It's like I've no balance at all.'

'And if he was really hurt,' Sophie persisted, 'I called an ambulance – not popped him back in the plate trying to save his rides for the afternoon!'

'Christ, Soph', I never knew you were such a hard bloody taskmaster! I am actually hurt, here, and struggling to stay upright.'

'Keep talking, stop thinking about staying upright, and maybe you will actually stay upright long enough to get back to the yard! I can't carry you and I can't manage both horses on my own.'

'Ulterior motive, eh?' Pete teased. 'How the hell did you ever keep Dominic talking? I knew him two years, which is the same number of entire sentences I ever heard him say.'

'He was never concussed. You've no broken bones, so stop grumbling and keep yacking. The yard is within sight.'

Despite the cheeky tone, a hint of desperation crept into her voice. Pete wondered if it was because she could hear the waver in his own voice.

The two horses pulled up in the main yard. Sophie jumped down quickly and stood alongside Pete.

'You can stop talking and pass out, now,' she told him gently.

'We're back already?'

'Time flies when you're having fun. Are you able to jump down?'

'I'm thinking more of a scramble and slide down.'

He managed the inelegant dismount and succeeded in remaining on his feet, despite the renewed rush of nausea. He held the colt while Sophie put away the filly, but was ready to collapse by the time he relinquished the reins. He sat on the ground in the middle of the yard and watched as Sophie dealt with his former mount.

'That's a very humble little colt!' she grinned, rejoining him at last. 'He's not certain quite what he did, but he's sorry for it anyway!'

'Good for him,' Pete complained, 'sorry for the discomfort of eight stone dragging down on one iron and tangling up his action.'

Sophie stood with him in silence for a while.

'Do you feel up to walking back to the house?' she asked, eventually.

'Could you just drive me home? I want a bath and bed.'

She smiled and held out a hand, which he grasped, and hauled him to his feet.

'You've done this before,' he said.

'Umm. Too often. But not for a couple of years; it's just like old times!'

'Sorry, Soph'.'

They made slow and steady progress across to his car, not needing to fish for keys. They'd been left in the ignition. Security men stalked the yard twenty-four hours a day, even though few of the horses were valuable enough to warrant their wages.

Pete's flat was virtually within walking distance, but, as with the ride back to the yard, he didn't see the time pass in normal scale. Things came and went in waves, non-descript, fuzzy. One moment Sophie was on his right, driving; the next, she was opening the door on his left, helping him out. He gazed up at her, his heavenly saviour, so angelic and wise. And he wondered when it had happened; when she had stopped being the pretty little kid tagging along with her dad. And why hadn't he noticed?

'I'll come in and run the bath,' she said.

He imagined that his appreciative gaze probably looked more like the dazed expression of an imbecile and he raised a grin as he edged slowly out of the car.

'I can manage. But, if you insist.'

His door key was on the chain with the car keys and it was Sophie who unlocked the front door and ushered him inside. He recalled Barbara often saying Sophie had popped in for a coffee, though now it seemed odd to see her in their flat, finding her way round with ease. He'd only ever seen her at the races, with Dominic or her parents.

He sat down on his bed, the duvet still half thrown back from that morning; Barbara's absence painfully evident in this room more than any. Sophie was already bustling out into the hall; into the bathroom; running the bath. The steam and scent of antiseptic drifted into the bedroom.

Sophie returned, with a glass of water and two painkillers. She really had done this before.

'What was it with Dominic?' Pete asked; they'd often speculated, in the weighing room. Never asked. 'Collarbone?'

'Dominic? Kidneys. Too many diuretics. He never actually carried an injury. How about you? Why the hire car?'

Pete grinned. 'Thank Christ, I spent all bloody weekend with Chris and Anne and they never once asked why! You're all busy speculating and thinking the worst.'

'Like collarbones.'

'Exactly like collarbones. Except maybe the truth is probably worse than your guesses!'

Sophie sat down on the edge of the bed. She may have been Sebastian's kid sister, but she struck Pete as far more sensible and mature. That same Churchill charm, though, oozing from every pore.

'I haven't been racing, of course,' she told him, 'but the general gossip is that you backed Satin Princess. Her win should have covered some heavy losses, but her disqualification simply added to them. A bit like collarbones, really – unimaginative.'

'Yeah, I do always back odds-on. It makes sense.' Pete nodded to himself, relieved that his dubious reputation hadn't been sullied still further by the gossipmongers. He caught Sophie's eye and grinned sheepishly. 'Trouble is, I never really have big bets. Not enough to wipe out losses with odds-on shots. They weren't heavy bloody losses. A couple of grand. But my bookie decided to put on a bit of pressure for payment, before I ran it up any higher. He caught me on the hop, Soph'. Next week, after York, I could pay him off with cash, but he was there bloody Saturday, in the car park, with a couple of blokes who should have stopped off at Twickenham. I told him to lay Breadline for as much as he liked.'

'Oh Pete! Satin Princess was odds-on!'

'I would imagine he took a fair amount of bets on it, yes,' Pete agreed grimly, 'but at the same time, I was right, wasn't I? How could I be held responsible for the bloody result getting overturned by the Clerk of the Scales? Smash up my car in fury, maybe, yes… but that's got to be it; hasn't it?'

'You think it might not be?' Sophie was horrified.

'Do me a favour, Soph' – don't tell your brother.'

She smiled. 'He thinks it's hilarious, your precious car; serves you right for backing Satin Princess, he said!'

'Bastard!'

'He can be at times. But Pete, on his behalf, don't share stable information again. Telling your bookie his winners will damage the odds, but telling your bookie his *losers* – think what it will do to his reputation. He's just starting out.'

'I didn't pull Breadline, Soph', I swear it.'

'I know that. I went through the handicap myself, made sure there was at least one better than us, so he wouldn't pick up a penalty for York. But what must your bookie think? And all his cronies? If Seb found out, he'd be there smashing up your car himself.'

Pete looked suitably apologetic. It hadn't occurred to him that Sophie didn't yet realise her brother was running a crooked yard. He hadn't realised it himself, when he'd first accepted the job as stable jockey. He'd stupidly believed in the Churchill charm and seen it as a lift up out of the gutter.

Sophie stood up. 'I'd best let you get your bath. I'll ring you in plenty of time to catch your flight up to York, in case you sleep through.'

'Cheers.'

She stopped in the doorway, but didn't immediately turn back to face him.

'What's it like, hanging upside down beneath a horse?'

Pete hesitated.

'The sun reflects off the shoes.'

'That's the most chilling thing I've ever heard.' She turned away again and disappeared into the hall.

Pete heard her open the front door and called out quickly.

'If you're expecting me to volunteer for a trick riding show for your gala day, you've another think coming!'

'Great idea!' came the reply, 'I'll be in touch!'

CHAPTER FOUR

The phone rang.

Pete sat up groggily and reached for the receiver, aware that he had slept long enough for the affects of the painkillers to be wearing off. He studied the taped cut on his outstretched arm for signs of seepage, suspecting that stitches might have been more appropriate, but all seemed well. Which assumedly went for the gash on his thigh as well.

'Pete Allen,' Pete said cheerfully, frowning at the effort and fumbling for the drawer of the bedside cabinet in a one-handed search for more painkillers.

'It wasn't an accident.'

Pete had barely responded with a confused 'pardon?' as the phone clicked off and purred innocently. Nevertheless, he spoke into the dialling tone, as though the noise was a mistake.

'Hello? Who is that? Are you there?'

Clearly, no one was. He hung up, puzzled, and rooted through the drawer for the tablets.

The phone rang again and he snatched at it. 'Pete Allen.'

'Only me, you're awake then.'

'Sophie, hi!'

'Feeling better?'

'Bit sore, but fit and able. Hey, listen, Soph', ever heard of a horse called It Wasn't An Accident?'

There was momentary silence. 'No,' she said doubtfully, 'Dad used to have one called No Accident. Any relation?'

'No idea. Anyway, thanks for the wake up call. No chance of seeing you at York, I suppose?'

'No, but I'll be on the gallops Friday, for sweeping up duty!'

He laughed and said goodbye.

'Bye. Oh, and that horse? The name's too long. Too many letters.' And she was gone.

Pete replaced the receiver and scrambled out of bed, clutching his tablets and desperate for a glass of water. He walked fairly steadily to the bathroom and pushed open the door, the sudden burst of light reflecting back at him from the mirror, blinding, like the flash of steel. He froze with sudden fear.

Too many letters.

He all but ran for the basin, filling the glass to over-filling, his hands shaking so badly he could barely turn off the tap. He gulped down pills and water, choking, and dropped the glass into the basin. He looked at his terrified face in the mirror and shook his head in disbelief.

There was no way. No bloody way.

'Shit, it's ridiculous!' he said to himself, aloud; and hurried back to the bed, sitting down to dress. He stared at the phone. Who had called before Sophie? And how could his fall that morning have been anything but an accident?

'Shit!' He cursed his own doubt. The colt had been bored, mischievous. It had never been bored and mischievous before. No one could have predicted it. Couldn't have caused it. How could they? Stinging darts shot at it? Ridiculous! Electrodes or buzzers or something in the saddle cloth, irritating it, zapping it, making it lash out and buck... equally ridiculous...

Pete allowed the doubt to creep in once more. And yet there was no justification. Even if some lunatic had upset the colt, so what? He may, or may not, have fallen. And the odds of catching his foot in the iron! Even now, he couldn't believe it had happened, couldn't see how it possibly could have. He didn't even push his foot home in the iron. He'd kicked his feet well clear... just a freak act of God that the loose iron had hooked back down over his foot...

How? Surely not even God could conjure up freakish incidents like that. How had the iron come back down onto his foot? Magnets? String? Glue?

'Oh shit, this is stupid!'

Pete glanced impatiently at the clock and snatched up the phone, tapping in a long number with urgency.

'Hello...'

'Helen, it's Pete, I need to speak to Barbara.'

'Sorry, Pete, she's not here.'

'Not there? It must be nearly midnight?'

'It's not just a little holiday, Pete. She needs her own space. She's staying in the flat above the shop.'

'Well can I have the number?'

'There isn't one. The phone's down in the shop. She wouldn't go down there to answer it at this time of night.'

'Helen, please... I need to speak to her.'

'I'm sorry, Pete, what can I do? I'll tell her you called; get her to call you first thing in the morning.'

Pete hung up uselessly, then tapped in the speed dial number for Bisley Bookmakers.

'Nikki, it's Pete,' he said at once, before Nikki on switchboard had even greeted him, 'did Dave ring me a short while ago?'

'Your account's closed, sweetheart. Persona non grata.'

'But did he call me? Can you find out?'

'He's driving up to York, he left in the early hours. I doubt he'd even use his mobile. And he hasn't been in the office.'

'And my account's closed? Deleted, off the records, no outstanding?'

'You're not on the collection list, sweetheart.'

'Cheers, Nikki, you're an angel!'

He hung up and got dressed, unconvinced that the fall had been deliberately arranged. And not certain it had been an accident. Maybe just Bisley putting the frighteners on for a sick joke. Maybe Bisley actually putting the frighteners on.

He swung his arms, testing the muscles and shoulders for aches and pains. Nothing that a few minutes on the Equicizer in the York changing rooms wouldn't put right. The safe, predictable, mechanical imitation horse. No one could really cause a deliberate fall from a real horse.

It was the possibility that they could that haunted him.

He stood, at last, at the corner of Hamilton Road, kit bag slung over shoulder, one eye out for Bob Graham, one eye out for... he didn't actually know. And as the World and His Uncle knew that he would presently be flying up to York races in Bob's plane and staying for two nights at The Black Swan, that put him at a distinct disadvantage.

Bob duly pulled up at the kerb and Pete climbed gratefully into the passenger seat, keeping his bag on his lap. He peered over his shoulder at his two unfortunate colleagues, crammed into the ineffective back seat.

'Hear you took a fall this morning?' Bob remarked, as they sped off up the Cambridge Road.

'Nothing serious. Did you hear anything else?'

'Such as?'

'Some bloody prankster rang me up and said the fall wasn't an accident! A little two-year-old threw me, for Christ's sake!'

'You're joking me?! Sick bastard.'

Grunts of disapproval were murmured from the back.

'Was it Sebastian?' Bob asked with a grin.

Pete laughed.

'He must be pretty pissed, hearing you took a fall hours before York!'

'I'm telling you,' Pete assured him with feeling, 'this bloke was serious.'

Within ten minutes they were pulled up at the private Cambridge airstrip, home to Bob's plane.

'Hope you fly better than you drive,' Pete joked, flipping his seat forward and releasing his colleagues from their contorted positions in the back. He allowed himself a careful glance around the airfield as Bob unpacked the three kitbags from the boot. No visible signs of malice. And the little plane appeared to have its full compliment of engines attached.

Pete and the two other Newmarket jockeys climbed aboard while Bob made his routine checks. Then they were off, the three day meeting at York one of the highlights of their season – televised, publicised, and a chance to showcase their talents on horses of the highest calibre. For Pete, it was make or break time.

He arrived at the racecourse in a far better frame of mind than earlier that day and set off in search of Sebastian and Walter, who'd flown up together by helicopter. He located them with ease in the bar and joined them for a glass of champagne, leaving his untouched.

'Sophie assures me you enjoyed a miraculous escape this morning?' Sebastian checked with Pete, 'And Mike insists that you couldn't possibly have walked away from a fall like that without injury?'

'Both correct, it was a miracle!' Pete grinned.

Sebastian smiled. 'It's a damn good job that I trust Sophie, because I certainly wouldn't trust you as far as I could throw you – which, incidentally, should be quite a distance, now that you've wasted down to ride at eight one! Trusting that you have, of course?'

'I'll be weighing out at eight stone one pound to the dot for the last,' Pete assured him. Privately, he wondered if Sophie might have any of Dominic's diuretics left.

'Now that you boys have gotten over the niceties, maybe we can talk business?' Walter suggested.

'We'll win the last, possibly the fifth and probably the first,' Pete predicted.

Walter shook his head. 'A win in the fifth would be icing on the cake, if you can manage it, but I'll drop you from my horses for the rest of the season if you come home in the first.'

Pete stared at him.

'I mean it, son, I'll drop you as easily as that little horse dropped you this morning – and perhaps just a little more painfully, too.'

Sebastian looked on with obvious anxiety. 'There was no mention of this on the way up,' he protested.

'The need hadn't arisen,' Walter explained.

'I can look after a horse, but I can't lose on a good one,' Pete insisted.

'A thirteen runner nursery? Son, if you can't keep a horse covered in that company, you're no damn loss to me anyway.'

'What exactly are we supposed to be saving it for, anyway?' Sebastian asked. 'Today's race is worth three times the purse at Newmarket next week. That's why we came here.'

'The purse is peanuts. I've just seen the opening show. Our horse is among the fancied runners. Five to two is the best on offer. He isn't guaranteed a win, so I can't back him seriously. I'm looking at no return at all. Next Saturday, an easier race, the odds will be longer, and I can lay down some serious money.' He smiled at Pete menacingly. 'Providing he doesn't win today.'

Pete looked to Sebastian for help. 'I won't go out there and contravene the rules, Mr Casburg. Replace me, if you must.'

'And I can't give him those kind of instructions,' Sebastian agreed.

Walter smiled, without humour.

'You, son,' he said, directing his words at Pete, 'already contravene the rules as you see fit. You have an account with a bookmaker. That's enough to get you warned off.' He turned to Sebastian. 'And you, son, know exactly why you have to do as you're told. I'm guessing you wouldn't like it spelled out to your employee, here, so we'll say no more, huh?'

'Look, Walter, I'm happy to arrange coups; Pete's happy to ride to instructions. But this isn't a coup. The plan was to win if we could. The horse is able. The race is too high profile for deliberate mistakes. We're not simply refusing your request. We simply can't do it; it's too late.'

Walter sat back in his chair, assessing the situation without betraying any thoughts in his expression. Finally, he simply nodded.

'It's good to establish ground rules, on both sides.'

He picked up his glass and finished his drink in swift gulps, then stood up.

'Excuse me, boys, but I've people to see.'

The trainer and jockey watched him leave.

'Phew!' Sebastian said with exaggeration.

'Thanks for sticking up for me, Seb.'

'I could do damn all else, Pete.'

'But next time? I'm not stopping horses for

you.'

'And I'm not asking, believe me. Walter doesn't know racing. He only knows gambling. As of today, he hopefully understands a little bit more. We run horses over the wrong distance, in the wrong ground, over unsuitable courses. But we don't stop them. And he doesn't damn well ask it of us.'

Pete stood up. 'Don't tell me, Seb – tell him.'

He left Sebastian in the bar and sought sanctuary in the weighing room, hoping the many and multiplying demons of the day would be lost outside. The only demon to greet him within the restricted area was the scales and he quickly set to work appeasing it with ten exhausting minutes on the Equicizer. Not only did his stiffened muscles limber up, but a few vital ounces fell from the pound he still needed to shed before five fifteen. The remaining obstinate ounces would hopefully be ridden off in the August heat of the two o'clock and four-ten races; which only left dehydration to contend with.

'Okay, mate?' Chris asked, sitting down beside him.

'Absolutely hunky bloody dory!' Pete admitted. 'If you thought Sunday morning was a bad day, you should have woken up in my shoes this morning!'

'One of those, eh! Bob said you took a fall.'

'A fall, the first and least of the day's instalments.'

'Oh well, the day can only get better. I'd fancy yours for the first.'

'Well that was instalment three or four, or

possibly even five, it's been such a stinker,' Pete complained, 'I told my admiring owner he might get the opening winner and he bloody near ate me alive! As if it's my fault he can't get better than five to two about it!'

Terry, sitting to the other side of Chris, looked at him with disapproval.

'Is it?'

'What d'you mean, *is it*? What, did it open at ten to one this morning until I got here and laid down my hard cash?! Bloody hell, Terry, if you want to kick me in the nuts, join the queue.'

Chris grinned at them both, but Terry failed to see the humour.

'Did you blab? Why would your owner blame you for the shortened odds?'

'Because he's a treacherous yankee bastard! Bloody hell, you're like the Spanish Inquisition, I can't even make casual conversation with you around!' Pete shook his head, tired of the continual jealousy and suspicion. 'I'm off to weigh out.'

He joined Sebastian in the weighing room, wishing some of the Churchill charm would rub off.

'Christ, I hope we win,' he told Sebastian with feeling, 'then I can relax and start to enjoy the meeting. Have you seen any more of Casburg?'

Sebastian seemed lost in thought. 'His behaviour was strange, wouldn't you say? Quite threatening.'

'I wouldn't know him as well as you. He runs casinos, doesn't he? Mafia?'

Sebastian smiled. 'I hardly think so! But that

quip about the colt this morning, dropping you. It was very out of order.'

'Maybe he'll apologise in the winners' enclosure.'

'He came back to the bar afterwards. Bought me a drink, actually. No more said of the matter.'

'For now.'

'Yes. That's what's worrying me. Still; more to life than minor worries! How are you planning on winning this nursery?'

They discussed the first race, a handicap over seven furlongs for two-year-olds, Pete growing more confident with each word.

'Well, you've convinced me!' Sebastian agreed, as they settled on the usual 'play it by ear' tactics, 'unlike our good friend, I'm not too proud to accept five to two – in fact, I shall gratefully take two to one, if that's all I can get!' He lowered his voice. 'Would you like me to deal you in?'

'Best not, Seb.'

Sebastian took the saddle and weight cloth and disappeared out to saddle Windwaker for the first. A short while later, Pete joined him in the parade ring, touching his cap courteously to Walter and silently cursing him under his breath.

'You're hopeful of a win, then, son?' Walter said, without enthusiasm.

'The top weight might beat us, but I think we're better than the rest,' Sebastian assured him, 'Pete's hoping to hem in the top weight and steal first run. If we can get the run of the race, it's ours.'

The bell rang and Sebastian gave Pete a leg

up onto the colt. Windwaker was experienced and calm, giving Pete no trouble at all going to post. In the race itself, they were quickly away and able to take up a rails position, settling just ahead of the top weight, who posed the biggest threat. After two furlongs, they began the gentle left-handed bend into the straight and Pete allowed Windwaker to move slightly off the rails. As he hoped, the top weight edged up on the inside, aiming to slip through and steal the rails advantage. Pete straightened Windwaker back up and forced the rider behind him to snatch up. The sudden loss of impetus made it hard for his rival to get back into stride and would, with luck, make the vital difference between winning and losing.

The runners thundered up the straight towards the winning post, the pace picking up as they entered the final two furlongs. Pete kicked for home and urged Windwaker on, seeing off each of the horses who moved up to challenge and quickly drawing away at the line to win by a length and a half.

Pete was led in to a round of applause, and greeted by the television crew and cameras for the all-important interview. York had got off to the promising start he had hoped for and he made the most of every minute, the shocks of the morning absorbed by the success of the afternoon.

Without rides in the next three races, he relaxed in the sauna for half an hour and worked out on the Equicizer, looking with longing at the bottles of water lying on the benches. Even a sip could replace the pound he had fought all day to lose.

He weighed out at a comfortable eight stone four for the Melrose Handicap and rode with energy throughout the gruelling mile and three quarters, even though his mount never felt like winning and eventually faded to fifth place. But the three minutes from start to finish did more for the shedding of excess weight than either the Equicizer or the sauna, neither of which he bothered with as he sat out the Acomb Stakes. By the time he weighed out for the last on the card, a five furlong sprint handicap, he barely tipped the needle over the eight one line.

It simply remained for him to make the sweat and tears worthwhile and win. A double would put his name back on the television at start of viewing the following afternoon and build on the publicity of today. Pete Allen, sporting pin-up, was on his way back.

The sprinter beneath him was an old man in comparison with the young three-year-olds who topped the handicap. But his old man, at five, was a tough and experienced battler, receiving weight all round from his younger rivals and ready to take advantage of the handicapper's disdain. He may not have won for eighteen months, but he hadn't raced off a weight as low as eight stone one for two years. This was his afternoon, his starting price tumbling from sixteen to one down to fifteen to two, because Walter had put on his serious money.

On the off, Pete scrubbed him along at the rear. The old horse liked to wind up his pace in his own good time, picking off his rivals as the furlong poles flashed by, waiting for those ahead to tire and drop back to him, making his task easier. He hated to sit in front and get caught, and pulled himself up to a standstill if ever he had the misfortune to find himself in the lead anywhere before the winning post. So Pete pushed and urged and prayed, hoping the winning post would appear just in time, and not too soon. With one horse still in front and not slowing, the post loomed large. There was nothing more that Pete could give, but he felt the horse swell with extra effort and quicken pace fractionally, pushing himself to the limit, straining his head forward to edge his nose over the line.

They won by a short-head.

As Pete leant forward to throw his arms round the gelding's neck in gratitude, he remembered the successes of old, in the type of prestigious races he'd had to sit out that afternoon. He hugged the gelding warmly and tugged its ear. Next season, he felt certain, he would be riding not in the day's three handicaps, but in the Group One events. Sebastian Churchill had thrown him a lifeline after all.

CHAPTER FIVE

Pete sat alone in his room, reluctant to face the crowd in the bar downstairs. Chris and Terry had fetched Anne and Su for the meeting and there was a host of other jockeys booked in for the two nights, ready to drink Perrier into the small hours. There were even those, for whom the scales posed no threat, happy to get enjoyably drunk on stronger liquids. Pete could face neither dinner nor the company of cosy couples. It was a first; and one of many firsts he'd been forced to endure in Barbara's absence. And still she hadn't phoned.

He studied the form for tomorrow's racing, without a ride in the first because Breadline had earned a penalty for his accidental win at Newbury. He thought of that win and its repercussions and wondered if there were any further surprises awaiting him. The only repercussion currently bothering him was the sore matter of an apprentice now taking the ride on Breadline, costing him the certain winner of the first race and an opportunity to return to the television screen and discuss his double of today.

In the second, he was no more than hopeful. A two-year-old colt had been showing enough promise at home to warrant a debut in a fairly valuable maiden race. But the prize money had attracted other well-regarded maidens and only one would be able to lose their maiden tag and become a winner.

The third was the prestigious Ebor Handicap and once again Pete was more hopeful than confident. Sebastian was confident to the point of allowing

Casburg to lay down serious money, but the trouble with races like the Ebor was that every trainer from Findon to Perth was secretly laying out his horse for the race and in truth anyone of them could win.

His mobile rang and he forgot the form books in his eagerness to tell Barbara the excitement of the day.

'Hello?'

'Just me,' it was Sophie's cheerful voice, just as welcome, 'no need to ask how you are, a double is as good a disguise of soreness as I've ever seen! The interview was great, four million pairs of knees must have weakened nationwide!'

'Still got it, eh?!'

She laughed. 'By the way, you'd pull in a bigger audience than Chris if you signed up for the jumping team.'

'Yeah?'

'Yes; and a little bird told me you did just as well as Terry on the gymkhana circuit.'

'Bloody hell. Shut the little bird up before it sings some more, would you! It'd do my street cred' no good if that got out!'

'It wouldn't have to get out, if you were on the team.'

'That's blackmail.'

'Is it? How about your street cred' come gala day, when you lead our team to victory over the National Hunt boys?'

'And that's tempting.'

'Think about it, though, Pete; Chris is happy to step down.'

'And who is your little bird?'

'The chap who picked up some of your trophies a couple of years later.'

'Terry! Bastard!'

'As it stands currently, he's going to be the hero come gala day.'

'Is he hell! Sign me up! No, wait, Germany. I'll have to check we've no runners in Germany first, I seem to be riding there almost every Sunday.'

'No, you're okay, I made certain we'd lose no one to France, Italy or Germany that particular Sunday, when I set it all up.'

'Fine, then, you've left me with no get out clause.'

'At least I didn't request the trick riding display!' Her tone changed and she grew sombre. 'Incidentally, that horse you asked me about this morning…'

'It wasn't an accident?'

'Was that what I think it was?'

'A threat?'

She sounded horrified. 'It wasn't, was it? Who would do such a sick thing?'

'No idea. But, Soph' – it was just an accident, wasn't it?'

'Well of course it was! How could it not have been?'

'You untacked the colt – anything odd? Something sharp in the saddle cloth? Glue on the irons?'

She was staggered. 'But that's just so absurd. The call was a sick joke, but the fall was an accident.'

He breathed a sigh of relief. 'I kind of thought so. But it was a bit unnerving.'

'My God, I should say so.' She was silent for a moment, trying to take it in. 'That bookmaker, Dave Bisley?'

'I wondered that myself. Chances are, we shall never know.' His turn for uncertain silence. But he needed to talk. 'By the way, Soph', my day got steadily worse from there.'

'Worse?'

'Don't say anything to Sebastian. But Casburg didn't want me to win the nursery. Nearly bit my head off when I said I was hopeful.'

'*Why?*'

'The odds weren't good enough. Never mind twelve grand in prize money, that's just small change.'

'Your day did get worse, didn't it? And was he any happier after the race?'

'Happy wouldn't be the word. Resigned.'

'Well you've runners in Germany this Sunday, I was helping Roddy with the final declarations. The prize money *and* the odds will be small change, so don't expect any thanks if you win!'

'Have you seen who's declared?!' Pete laughed.

He could almost hear the smile in Sophie's voice. 'I have to admit, I thought Roddy was heading for an early dismissal, but it seems Walter's insistent on the horses running. Maybe they're just there for experience. But the distance won't suit either of them, and the filly hates soft ground, which it's certain to be. But there you go, they're his horses and he's the boss.' As an afterthought, she added, 'You know, they do a lovely pasta salad supper there, you can have it sent up to the room.'

'Cheers, Soph'.'

He hung up, grateful for the advice. How had she known? She'd watched him on television riding at eight one. Pretty obvious, really, that he wouldn't be down in the restaurant. And if Dominic had been able to eat a pasta salad supper, so could he.

He lay back comfortably on the bed and phoned through his order, happy to rely on Sophie's knowledge. Menus had never been worthy of his consideration, until Barbara had left him to fend for himself. He wondered if he should call Barbara, but there seemed little need. Little need... he wondered if he could get through the night without reaching for her. Bloody, bloody Queensland.

No one, it seemed, had bothered to come down for breakfast. Pete sat alone with a glass of orange juice, thinking of bacon sandwiches.

'Where the hell were you last night?' a familiar voice demanded, 'I didn't think they let groupies into the rooms before ten!'

'Bugger off, Westy, can't a man enjoy an orange juice in peace?'

Danny Western settled himself down at Pete's table, together with his plate of full English breakfast.

'Didn't know a man *could* enjoy an orange juice,' Western quipped, 'not wasting, are you?'

'Hangover.'

'Celebrating the sprint handicap? So would I be, if anyone had bothered to let me know the stable jockey had sweated down to eight one for it.'

'Follow the odds,' Pete advised, 'you ought to know ours is a gambling yard.'

'It did plummet a bit. Sebastian?'

'Sebastian?' Pete shook his head. 'Casburg.'

'So Casburg's the player? I thought someone who owned gaming joints would know better.'

'He thinks he knows better. That's always their downfall,' Pete agreed, taking an interest. 'What do you know of him?'

'He owns casinos. Owned a few horses with Dean Hadlay. Now owns many more with Sebastian. Presumably they met at the roulette wheel.'

'Met at Hadlay's. Seb was his assistant for a couple of seasons.'

'And which came first, the job of assistant or the intro' at the roulette wheel?' Western mopped up fried egg with a piece of toast. 'The only reason Seb got packed off to the States was to cut him loose from his accounts with Ladbrokes and William Hill and a hundred and one independents! Old man Churchill couldn't afford to keep bailing him out, the air ticket was cheaper! Didn't you know?' He made rapid inroads on a sausage. 'He'd run up more than a full term's school fees before he was legally allowed to even have an account! Had he not been at the right school, they'd have turfed him out. But he was at the right school, weren't we all, old boy, hence I know these facts and you, clearly, don't. Bit of bacon?'

'Your figure would kill any appetite.'

'Well at least I've got one, Skeletor. You've not touched your orange.'

'I did eight one yesterday, it takes a while to get back up to normal.'

Western downed cutlery and rifled his pocket, producing a race card. He flicked through until stopping on the last race of the day. 'The Falmouth Handicap. There's an apprentice on yours at eight one.'

'Well, maybe there'll be a jockey change,' Pete conceded.

He watched the journalist, with only partial interest, the bacon too great a distraction. But something slipped in beside the aroma. He recalled, just in time, the tape.

'You're not recording this, are you?'

'Me? No.'

Western took up his knife and fork once more, ready to clean the plate. Pete quickly leant forward, his hands under the small round table, and snatched the tape recorder from the journalist's jacket pocket. It whirred guiltily. It always whirred.

'Give me that!' Western made a grab at it, as Pete held it aloft.

Pete pushed a button and listened to it rewind rapidly, but before he could locate a record button, Danny Western reclaimed his property.

'For fuck's sake, Allen, I've interviews on this from yesterday.'

He fiddled with the tape with urgency and it clicked off at once, beginning to play. The recognisable accent of Marcel Dessaint purred out across the breakfast table.

'Fucking hell, is this before or after?' Western cursed, listening to an unenlightening string of words. It didn't help matters that the background noise of cars and passers-by occasionally drowned out Marcel's words. 'Fuck, it must be in the car park, I got him on the way in *and* on the way out!' He gave a look meant to kill and Pete grinned back. 'It's not bloody well funny, messing about like a bloody kid, I had it cued up for the next interview, thank you very fucking much.'

Marcel started to express his hopes for the forthcoming International and Western sat back, in relief and exasperation. 'Well thank you, Pete Allen, you've rewound it back to the start! And your bloody horse in the Falmouth isn't even in with a God's chance in hell anyway!'

Pete leaned forward sharply and tried to take back the tape. Western jerked it away instantly.

'Not so fast, sunshine. I'm not going to quote you anyway. You're wasting for a loser.'

'No, you bloody idiot, you can quote me all you like – I want to hear that!'

'Marcel telling us how he planned to win the International? You're too late to get a bet on, you know!'

'Shut up and give me the tape,' Pete snatched it from his grasp and rewound it fractionally, pushing 'play' once more. 'Where were you?'

'Car park on the way in yesterday.'

Pete listened intently, then rewound the tape

and handed it, playing, back to Western.

'Do you remember that bit? Did you see who said it?'

Western listened with interest. Marcel Dessaint paused to think of the correct English word for 'slaughter' and somewhere alongside him a voice said clearly, "it wasn't an accident." Marcel then resumed his prediction of a one horse race.

'Think back,' Pete urged, 'was it Bisley or one of his henchmen?'

'Henchmen?!' Western laughed, 'welcome to the twenty-first century, Allen. Bookies nowadays employ *aides*.'

'Aides, henchmen, their knuckles still do as much damage. Who said that?'

Western thought about it. 'I can't remember,' he said truthfully, 'but I know it wasn't Bisley. I've seen him around on the track, but he hasn't got a pitch here and he wasn't there yesterday morning.'

'Not one of his men?'

'How the hell would I know? Not one that I'd recognise, no. But he could have dozens. It was no one I recognised or paid any attention to.' He stopped the tape, ran it forward, then listened to intermittent snippets of sentences as he cued it back up. Satisfied, he pushed 'record' and set it down whirring on the table. 'So,' he asked, 'what is it to you anyway?'

'Yesterday morning some joker phoned me up,' Pete explained, feeling that he owed Western something, at least. 'I'd taken a bad fall on the gallops, got dragged by an iron a few strides…'

Western winced.

'Exactly. Not nice. And some bastard rings me up and says,' he paused for effect and mimicked the voice on the tape as best he could, ' "it wasn't an accident".'

Western sat back and reconsidered the previous morning. 'It was the Owners And Trainers' car park,' he said, after considerable thought. 'Marcel was saying how it would be a slaughter, a procession, and I remember seeing Lady Hamblett's Jag' going backwards and forwards as she tried to park it. She was crunching the gears and the slaughter bit just reminded me.' He nodded, now certain of his facts. 'Owners And Trainers'.'

'Owners And Trainers', with a jockey and a hack just passing through. So my friend was probably also just passing through.'

Western frowned in concentration. 'No, I don't think so. There was someone leaning against a car. Loads of people getting out of cars. No one just walking along, like ourselves.' Again, he nodded to himself, convinced of the accuracy of his memory. 'When you're with Marcel,' he explained, 'you notice people walking along. They generally veer off and make a b-line straight for him. Autographs, photos, the usual iconic worship.'

'And mobiles?'

'That's asking too much. Everyone walks along with phones pressed to their ears talking to themselves. I couldn't tell you if they all had mobiles or if none did.'

'Well, cheers, Westy, anyway. If I ever ask you to turn that bloody thing off, remind me why I shouldn't.'

'Last sausage?' Western offered generously. 'The horse won't win anyway.'

The horse didn't; in fact, none of them did, though Pete did manage third in the Ebor. He was interviewed on television prior to the big handicap and took the opportunity to announce his place on the gala day show jumping squad, hoping it would draw in a few more paying punters. When asked if he'd ever competed in anything like it before, he replied truthfully, 'no'. Gymkhanas and charity gala days were poles apart, after all.

Sophie phoned to thank him for the added publicity and he decided to go down to dinner, accepting Chris' invitation to join them at the table he and Anne shared with Terry and Su.

'You told Sophie, then?' Pete said amiably as they ate.

Terry nodded. 'Had to. Chris was all over the place!'

'It wasn't me,' Chris complained, 'those show jumpers are potty! You watch them on TV, they have all sorts of rubbish in their mouths to keep them in check.'

'Yeah, he's right, their bridles look like the contents of an ironmongers!' Pete agreed.

'It wasn't a show jumper!' Anne complained mildly, 'it was a kid's pony!'

'It was no thoroughbred,' Chris reminded her, 'and I couldn't pull it up or turn it.'

'You were up its ears every time it landed,' Terry told him, 'at which point, I remembered seeing your name, Pete, on the lists of honours whenever I won anything.'

'Well, cheers, mate – now I'm roped in with the rest of you poor saps!'

'Barbara will be home in time for it, won't she?' Anne asked, 'It would be a shame for her to miss it.'

'He can't take his wife with him!' Chris interrupted, 'his adoring public will be there! Do they even know you're married, Pete?!'

'He's right, you know,' Pete agreed with a grin, 'now Marcel's married I'm their last chance!' He fired a seductive wink at Anne, to prove the point, and she choked on her wine.

'Most girls don't laugh,' Pete complained, 'they swoon.'

'You'll be swooning when the back of Barbara's hand has dusted your ear!' she warned.

They finished dinner and spent the remainder of the evening in the bar, whiling away the final evening of their stay in amiable conversation. Even Terry relaxed in Pete's company, no longer quite so afraid of losing his licence by association; although Pete had always recognised the hostility as jealousy. He'd thrown away the career that Terry could only dream of having. And it hurt; hurt them both.

But the first two days of York had done much to amend things and the final day was still far enough away to appear promising. Pete had a ride in the Group One sprint, though little chance of actually winning. Success, if there was to be any, looked more certain in the Rose Of York Handicap, and he was not without chances in the final two races of the day.

Intent on increasing that slight chance in the last race by studying the form, Pete said his goodnights reasonably early and headed up to his room. The mile and a half Great Yorkshire Handicap was full of tried and tested old handicappers, their ability known to all. Knowing as he did their quirks and preferences, it wouldn't be hard to come up with a battle plan that would put him in the frame. The frame, of course, into which the numbers of the first four horses home were put. It would be nice to be in the frame. And much nicer still to win.

He smiled to himself, eager to find flaws in his rivals and plot his victory around them. As he walked up the stairs he decided on the even better idea of giving Sophie a call. She was a whiz on handicaps and knew the formbook inside out. Between them, he felt certain, the race was at his mercy. At his door, he fumbled hurriedly in the lock with the key, turning it one way and the other until the door finally swung open. Flinging the key onto the bedside cabinet, he sat on the bed and spread out the relevant page of The Racing Post, tapping in Sophie's number on his mobile as he did so.

The bathroom door swung slowly open and he made a move to go and push it shut, but Sophie answered at once and he ignored it, leaning back on one elbow to examine the form page laid out before him.

'Hi, Soph', are you busy?'

She breezily waved off any former commitments and he set about picking her brains for the perfect race tactics. To his surprise and delight, she also came up with some interesting tactics for the Rose Of York Handicap.

'You studied my horse's form?' he asked incredulously, flattered.

'I do follow Sebastian's horses, you know,' she pointed out, the smile ever-present in her voice.

He privately kicked himself. 'Any gems for the sprint?'

'It's between Marcel and Bob, isn't it. But if anything goes wrong with the two Group horses, any one of the handicappers could spring a surprise. Walter can afford the entry fee, so you may as well be in there.'

'Cheers, Soph', it's much appreciated, you know that.'

'A pleasure, you're more than welcome.' She broke off for a moment to call out to someone. 'Just Roddy,' she apologised to Pete, 'we're going to the late showing at the pictures, I'd best be off.'

'Have fun, then. And thanks again.'

He put the mobile on the cabinet beside him and began to fold up The Racing Post. He was aware of the bathroom door slowly opening further, but this time ignored it, grateful for the breeze from the open window, breaking the muggy evening.

He sat round on the edge of the bed, his back to the bathroom, and pulled off his shoes, stretching out his toes and wriggling them with the pleasant satisfaction of release. They'd spent the long hot day wedged first into tight boots and latterly smart Italian shoes. He studied their movement with all the interest of one who faced the boredom of a night alone in a hotel room, then leaned forward and stripped off first one sock, then the other.

He half twisted, to lay back on the bed and draw up his legs, but instead found himself twisting the opposite way, pushed face down onto the bed by an unknown force, his legs caught up under him, a heavy hand grasping the back of his neck and thrusting his face down into the pillow, muffling his cries and stifling his breath.

He struggled frantically to free his legs and kick out at the unseen assailant, but only succeeded in twisting his injured muscles still further. Yesterday morning's fall was suddenly fresh in his mind as unhealed cuts and bruises screamed their reminders. He could barely breathe, never mind put up any sort of fight, and quickly opted to lie still and avoid any further pressure.

The initial shock rapidly faded and the who's and why's flooded just as rapidly into his mind. The 'or else' scenario had apparently reared its ugly head.

Someone heavy seemed to be sitting on his hip. His legs still partially hung from the bed, crushed painfully beneath both body weights. Thank God his own was still only eight stone, despite the meal, he found himself thinking. He was desperate not to allow his thoughts a freer rein, such as What Next?

The 'what next' revealed itself to be a sudden wrenching of his left arm, his right arm still safely crushed beneath his ribs, if safely was quite the word.

The discomfort beneath him nearly matched that from above, though the arm twisted high up into the shoulder blades took some beating. Next was dislocation, if the assailant intended to go that far. He waited calmly, because he had no option to do otherwise.

A hand remained on the back of his neck, another clasping his arm. Only two. That had to be good. The weight above shifted somewhat, a knee now driving into the small of his back. Not so good. Suffocating though it was, he was grateful for the pillow. More shuffling of weight. The hand on the neck became a forearm, the impossible stretching of his own left arm suggesting that it was the same hand and forearm that now pinned him down. Leaving one hand free. Not so good at all.

Then his captor spoke.

The voice was familiar, recognisable, terrifying. He'd heard it yesterday morning. And again, on tape, this morning.

'In future, tow the line.'

Tow the line? Do as instructed? Lose to order? Recoup Dave Bisley all his losses and some generous compensation to boot? Having ridden all meeting like a bloody champion on the comeback road and been on telly?

Pete wriggled in protest, the words 'not bloody likely' soaking into the pillow with his tears. Perhaps fortunately they got no further than the duck down, but the knee in the back brutally dealt with the wriggling, all the same. He opted once more to lie still.

One thing reassuring in the words 'tow the line' was that he had to be riding to do so. No career-threatening injuries, then. Nor a beating worthy of keeping him from York tomorrow. But the knee in the back continued to cause ever-worsening pain and deflate any optimism raised.

The knee moved, but the pain remained. Like the ghost of skating boots, Pete imagined the knee would remain with him in spirit for at least a few hours. Meanwhile, the body above ominously appeared to be in need of two hands and was shifting with brutal disregard for the body beneath. A backside replaced the hand clamping his left arm, though it made little difference to his inability to move. It did, however, make a vital difference to his inability to breathe and he struggled furiously to move his head, just sufficiently to allow oxygen back to his nose and mouth. Where it went from there was anyone's guess, as his lungs had long since given up the ghost beneath the crushing weight of his assailant.

And now came the else factor, the culmination of the implied threat. Being sat upon was never really going to be the punishment, though Pete had clung to the hope tenaciously. Now the seating arrangements were proving to be no more than the means to the end, and his left foot was the target.

Pete yelled and choked into the pillow, though he knew the sound got little further. He couldn't tow the line with a broken foot. He rode on his toes, were they aware of that? Oh God, supposing they weren't? Supposing they didn't care? He thrashed now violently with any limb or muscle that could still move, snatching his foot away, feeling it snatched back, his knee ligaments on fire with the unnatural strain. And through it all, through the noise of inner pain and scrunching duck down and sobs and gasps of breath, he heard a physical sound, something real and out there, something slight and insignificant, like…

…Like the sound of a match striking.

CHAPTER SIX

The cigarette burned into the sole of his foot, the arch, leaving him free to ride on his toes, use his heels for encouragement, tow the line if he chose, and no choice not to. All movement stopped. He just wanted to lie very still, very quiet, make it go away, pretend it had already gone, wasn't there...

The burn came again; he jerked away involuntarily, hurting everything from knee to ribs to shoulder, and still nothing could detract from the searing pain in his foot. Nor the next. Nor the next...

Biting silently into the pillow, he didn't notice the foot go free. He felt the weight lift awkwardly from his back, but he used the freedom simply to hug the pillow tighter to him, to draw his legs up, to curl into a ball and wait for it all to go away...

Sometime later, perhaps minutes, perhaps seconds, he began to be aware that maybe he should have withdrawn from the pillow, just once; just enough to catch a glimpse of his assailant. But he didn't want to withdraw just yet. And, listening intently, it was already too late.

Just five words spoken. In how long a length of time he couldn't even begin to guess. No more than five minutes; maybe less. A lifetime. In Future Tow The Line. It Wasn't An Accident...

He needed cold water. And brandy. And a bar of chocolate.

The other aches and pains subsided and he felt as though he could venture a move. But he didn't try. Just lay very still, in a ball, imagining the heat of brandy in his throat, the soothing chocolate, the icy water dissolving all pain… Imagined them until he so desperately needed them he could slowly uncurl and lift his face, for the first time since the attack, from the pillow.

He hopped to the mini bar and ripped open a chocolate bar as though he hadn't eaten in a month, savouring the first bite before opening the miniature bottle of cognac and gulping it down like water. Another bite of chocolate and he hopped across to the bathroom. The bastard must have been hiding in there, waiting for him. He sat on the toilet and placed his foot gingerly into the bidet alongside, turning on the water. He withdrew his foot sharply, with a yelp and a curse, and sat for a moment squeezing the instep, trying to ease the pain from the arch. Blasting water onto the wound was not the answer.

He stood up and lifted the toilet seat, flushed the toilet, and studied the clear contents for traces of bleach or cleanser. Then rolled up his trouser leg and dipped in his foot. It stung momentarily, but he persevered and the cold water began to make inroads on the soothing of the burns.

Someone tapped hesitantly at the door and he jumped, his heart racing illogically. The attacker wouldn't come back. Or knock first.

'Pete? Are you there? Are you okay? It's me, Terry.'

It was certainly Terry's voice. But Pete didn't immediately answer. Or remove his foot from the toilet.

'Are you alright, can I come in?' Terry asked,

coming in anyway.

Pete heard the door and hastily withdrew his foot, hopping out to meet his second unwelcome guest of the evening.

'Sorry, mate, I was in the loo.'

'What's up with your foot?'

'Cramp.'

Terry looked down at it briefly, accepting the lie, then turned back to the door.

'He's okay, come in if you like.'

Danny Western joined them, looking around the room with interest.

'You're okay, then?' he asked, without too much concern.

'Why shouldn't I be?' Pete asked in return, mystified by their appearance.

'Remember at dinner I saw this guy going upstairs?' Terry asked Pete, who could only shake his head in denial. 'Well, I did mention it. Not one of the guests. Well I saw him again, up on your landing, on his way down. Only a while ago. Made me wonder what he'd been doing up there. I was by Westy's door, which was handy, so I gave him a knock. When the guy passed us, I asked him if he knew any nightclubs.'

Pete stared at him. 'Nightclubs?'

Western interrupted, holding out his ubiquitous tape. 'Voila!'

He pressed the play button and the tape purred into action. There was a general muttering of excuse me's and apologies as various people seemed to get in each other's way. Then Terry, "Are you just

off out? Can you recommend any good nightclubs?"
And the chillingly familiar voice, "Don't know any."

Western turned off the tape. 'I thought of you right away,' he told Pete, 'Did the voice ring a bell?'

'Alarm bells. And the face?'

'I didn't recognise him from yesterday. But he's someone's henchman, if not Bisley's. Whacking great bloke.'

'Don't you mean aide?' Pete teased.

'Bookies have aides, thugs have henchmen. And this bloke was a thug. Wasn't he, Terry?'

Terry nodded. 'When Westy said who he thought it was, we came up here, expecting to find you in pieces.'

'Well you took your bloody time about it!'

'I didn't know!' Terry protested.

'I had to explain to Terry,' Western said in defence, 'and then listen back to make sure, then we were wondering first who he was and where he'd been. Besides, you're not in pieces, anyway.'

'Was he in here?' Terry asked.

'Possibly snooping or eavesdropping,' Pete lied, 'I don't know. But I've only just finished with The Racing Post. I was on the phone, going through tactics and form. If he was looking for info', he got plenty.'

'Paid for?'

Pete shook his head, despairing of Terry's perpetual suspicion. 'Not paid for, not offered, not forced. I bet, small amounts, never against myself. I don't stop horses, I don't sell info'. Happy?'

Terry shrugged. 'You get followed around by

thugs and have your car smashed up, though.'

'Car smashed up?' Western smiled.

'Leave it whirring if you like, it's my licence, your conscience,' Pete told him, 'but whatever reputation Terry here has saddled me with, it's common knowledge. Some poor misguided thug actually believes all the tales he's heard, all the dirt dished, 'cause we all love kicking the fallen hero. So he hangs about, hoping to employ my services. Uses some thug-like encouragement. And you can say I've brought it on myself, if you like. You can say what you bloody well like. You will, anyway. And when I turn up at the races with a black eye and a broken nose, just consider that it's more likely because I *didn't* sell info' or stop a horse, not because I did. Even if it doesn't sell papers.'

Western held up his hands in surrender. 'Okay, okay, I've got a conscience! And you're as honest as the day is long. And I need to top the tipping list to keep my job, so I'm never going to get off your backs. So can we all fuck off back to bed now, please?'

'You'll look out for this guy and dig for me?' Pete asked him.

'I'm a journalist, it's my moral obligation.' Western followed Terry out, then stopped, and turned back. 'Is your saddle here or in the weighing room?'

'Weighing room.'

'Check the leathers before you mount up, anyway. Better safe than sorry, eh?'

'Shit!'

'It's the way of the world, sunshine. First,

they let you know what they can do to you. Then they let you know what you can do for them. Watch yourself, eh?'

All too late, but it was the thought that counted. Pete warmed to him. 'Do me another favour, Westy? Include Casburg and Seb in your dig.'

Pleased to see the back of them, despite their good intentions, Pete locked the door securely after them and hopped to the window, closing it against the refreshing breeze. Then he collapsed onto the bed, not relishing the thought of hopping around for the next day as well. At present he couldn't even put the ball of his left foot to the floor, the tightening of the skin on his arch excruciating. He wondered if he could simply put his weight on his heel, but couldn't be bothered to try it. Instead, he phoned down to reception and asked if they knew of any all-night chemists, despatching a member of staff out for a tube of burn cream, if such a thing existed. He hoped to God it did, the thought of spending the night with his foot down the toilet didn't exactly thrill him.

The thought of spending the night alone didn't thrill him, either; tonight more than any other night. He briefly wondered what his chances would be with the receptionist who would shortly be delivering his order. After the past two days he'd already endured, it would be a sharp slap in the face, in all probability. But at least he'd thought beyond Queensland...

The cream finally arrived, brought up to his room not by the receptionist but by the manager. Still, there was such a thing as instant relief in a tube, so the day wasn't a complete write-off. He studied the instructions cautiously, hesitant at putting anything on or even near the burns. Just in time, he remembered to undress first, sparing his trousers a heavy dosing of gel. Taking a deep breath, he squeezed out the gel liberally, directly onto his foot. He wasn't going to aggravate the injury by poking and rubbing. This ruled out the gauze supplied by the chemist, so he slept instead with the duvet pulled up over his ankles, hoping the morning would bring with it some improvement.

Sleep came to him intermittently, snatches of relief between the longer periods of discomfort. He rode the third, fifth, sixth and seventh races of York's final day a hundred times over in his head; remembering to check his leathers each time...

The pain woke him, the relentless searing, and he hobbled to the bathroom on his heel, an unsuccessful idea quickly abandoned. The ball of his foot proved easier, and less painful than the night before, and improved the awkward hobble to a limp. He washed and dressed, then reapplied the gel, less liberally this time, tentatively adding the gauze and going so far as to pull on his socks. Shoes could wait.

He went down to an early breakfast in stockinged feet, his limp noticeable enough not to provoke comment on his lack of shoes. By the time Western joined him in the empty breakfast room, his own bowl of cereal was almost gone and his feet hidden securely beneath the table.

'Eating again?' Western remarked.

'Nothing below eight three today. Even that

can be a struggle, but eight one was really pushing it,' he admitted.

'Won't go there again, then?'

He grinned. 'I would for a winner.'

'Duly noted!'

Pete glanced round the empty room. 'You've not got the tape on, have you?'

Western fished in his pocket and pulled it out, placing it on the table and turning it off.

'Not now.'

'I'm in over my head, Westy. I don't know who I'm hiding from or where the next strike is coming from. I did Bisley a favour at Newbury, let him know Breadline wouldn't win. It was no secret, we couldn't beat Satin Princess at those weights. He was badgering for info' and I just fobbed him off with the obvious.'

'You fucked up there.'

'And he smashed up the Porsche.'

'You were lucky!'

'Okay, so next up, one of my owners tells me to lose a race I was expecting to win. I refused. And I won.'

'Enemy Number Two.'

'Enemy Number Two, as you say. So, which one is Mr Henchman working for?'

'You had a run-in with Mr Henchman last night, didn't you?'

Pete said nothing in reply.

Western nodded. 'I thought as much. First the car, then the physical pressure. Then the pay-off. I think you owe your bookie big time, sunshine.' He smiled. 'Cut me in on pay day, won't you?'

Pete shook his head. 'If you dig for me, it's for free. There isn't going to be a pay day.'

'Your funeral.'

Pete allowed himself a rueful grin. 'Probably.' He stood up to leave. 'You can turn the tape back on if you like. I'm in with a bloody good chance in the Rose Of York. And the Great Yorkshire's in the bag.'

Western nodded and Pete limped out of the breakfast room and up to his room.

This time he was more careful with the key, making certain the door was still locked before unlocking it and entering. Western was right. No demand had yet been made, but it had to come. Tow the line.

He gathered up his things and slowly packed his bag, leaving his shoes until the last possible moment. It took some cursing, and no little sweat, but eventually he was fully dressed and ready to leave.

And determined not to tow the line.

His determination didn't displace his nerves. He shared a taxi to the racecourse with three of his colleagues and remained securely in the changing room, checking his leathers.

'That saddle's only eighteen months old,' Dave reminded him, watching.

'Any excuse for a new one!'

His grin faded at the sight of the medical officer, stalking the weighing room in search of someone. And unfortunately no one else had limped in that afternoon.

'Ah, Allen,' the doctor said ominously, finally standing in front of him, 'can I see you in my office.' It was a statement, not a question.

Pete limped through to the medical room, wishing Mr Henchman had called for him instead. The tactics of the night before had been plotted in vain, if the dreaded red ink appeared in his medical book. Unfit to ride. Stood down. Six and a half minutes of race riding hung in the balance.

'What did you do to your foot?'

'I stood on a dog-end.'

The silence of the medical officer suggested a need for further clarification.

'I ran along the hall of the hotel, barefooted, and trod on a cigarette butt. I jumped, as you would, and stepped on it a second time. And it bloody hurts.'

'We'd better take a look at it, then.'

Presumably the look revealed four burns, not two, but the doctor was gracious enough not to remark upon it.

'And how do you propose to ride?' he asked.

Pete's insistence that he didn't use that part of his foot was also deemed worthy of further clarification. They walked back through to the weighing room and stopped beside the Equicizer.

'Just give me a couple of minutes burst on that, would you,' the medical officer told him. It was uncanny how he could take the words of a question and form them into a demand.

'A couple of minutes?!' Pete protested, 'The Derby is only run in two and a half minutes!'

'Just show me how your foot will be

affected,' the doctor explained, his patience strained, as always, by his patients.

Concentrating on a clean medical book, Pete mounted up and proved the burns to be no hindrance at all. The fearsome red pen remained in the medical officer's breast pocket and Pete's medical book was returned to him intact.

After that ordeal, changing into his riding boots proved a piece of cake.

The effort was a wasted one in the third race, his first ride of the day, but paid dividends in the fourth on the card, the Rose Of York Handicap. Sophie's formbook knowledge also helped in no little way. She had predicted that the main danger would be a colt particularly well-handicapped and not the favourite at all. Pete followed tight on that colt's heels, allowing the favourite to steal a run, trusting that it would tire before the closing stages.

Meanwhile, after just three furlongs, they began the turn into the straight and the colt Pete so carefully tracked drifted off the rails, uncomfortable with the left-hand turn. It was a trait he'd shown at Doncaster and Ayr, when Pete had ridden behind him, and Pete was ready for the move. They straightened for home, Pete now ahead of his main danger and picking off the leaders with ease. His own gelding was happy enough to lead and Pete allowed him to hit the front with two furlongs still to run. He opened up as wide a margin as he could, hoping it would be sufficient to get him home.

Both the favourite and the colt who'd given him a lead came at him in the closing stages, but he'd stolen the vital first run and kept them at bay, scraping home by a neck. Walter Casburg appeared to be every part the delighted winning owner and was in the best of humour throughout the afternoon.

Unplaced in the next, Pete went out for the final race with great expectations, the two left-handed turns again featuring in his well-laid plans. Most horses were happy to gallop in any direction, but a surprising number had preferences. And a dislike of left-handed courses figured high on their lists. His own mount was an experienced older horse, lacking in pace and ability, but more than making up for it in courage and cunning. Sophie had wondered how well he could thread through a large field and Pete seemingly lost the race a dozen times, running from one pocket to the next. But as those around him did the same and failed to get out, his brave old-timer went for every opening and came flying from out of the pack, cutting down the leader just before his acceleration faded. It was another narrow victory, but a win nevertheless. Pete very nearly forgot to look over his shoulder in the euphoria of a successful meeting.

But he didn't forget his fellow conspirator and rang her as soon as he could, to offer dinner that night in Cambridge by way of thanks.

'It would be lovely,' Sophie agreed, her tone already betraying the next word, 'but I'm having dinner with Roddy tonight.'

It was just one of those weeks.

Sitting on the plane, flying home with Bob Graham, he still had reason to congratulate himself on a successful meeting. A double on the opening day and a double on the closing day. Never mind the disasters in between.

They made good time back to Cambridge, Bob praising favourable tailwinds. But Pete had been content for the journey to go on indefinitely. He hadn't been safe in a hotel. What demons awaited him on home ground hardly bore thinking about.

'Let Hopalong have the front seat,' Bob insisted, swapping airplane for Merc'. The back seat victims protested heartily, but contorted themselves with practise and left Pete to nurse his foot safely in the front. His limp even earned him enough sympathy to be dropped directly at his door, preventing him from checking the shadows as he would have liked, for fear of being seen and ridiculed by his colleagues.

There were no hidden menaces; for that evening, at least. His answer phone held a wealth of offers, no doubt as a result of his four wins at the high profile York meeting. Marcel Dessaint had topped the champion jockey table for the meeting with just six wins, so he had much to be pleased about. And much not to be. Including three missed calls from Barbara.

He cursed her bad timing. Was it so great in bloody Queensland that she'd forgotten York? Mind you, it was his first season for many a year to actually ride there. It was a meeting where the big guns plied their trade, leaving him to pick up their dregs at such lowlier venues as Hamilton, Lingfield and Folkestone. And now, here he was, just two wins behind Marcel himself.

He went through to the bathroom and ran

himself a much-deserved bath, with steam and bubbles in equal and abundant measure. Now that the preoccupation with race tactics had ended, there were a million and one aching muscles calling for attention. The gash on his leg, picked up on a now long-distant Tuesday morning, had been aggravated by being sat upon. The burns on his foot were just plain aggravating, without need of excuse. He carefully lowered himself into the hot bath and rested his left foot up beside a tap. It might as well have been kissed by Kylie Minogue, the amount of washing it would now miss out on.

Thinking warmly of Kylie, he sunk his head beneath the soothing bubbles.

CHAPTER SEVEN

It was gone eleven when the door-knocker sounded. Pete, slumped in an armchair watching dull late-night offerings on TV, stiffened instantly.

It came again; a gentle, hesitant tap. Unthreatening. The momentary fear subsided and he rose slowly, surprised at how set he had become. Out in the hall, he allowed himself a quick glance through the spy-hole, but already had the door unlocked as he recognised his visitor.

'Sophie!'

'Pete, I'm so sorry, it's far too late, I shouldn't disturb you...'

'Don't be ridiculous.'

He ushered her in and she stood uncomfortably in the living room, suddenly more convinced than ever that she had made a mistake. Pete watched her patiently, unable to guess at the reason for so unexpected a visit.

'I don't really know what I'm doing here myself,' Sophie admitted, as though reading his mind. 'I've just had a bit of a barney with Roddy. I thought I might be able to come and tell you about it. But I feel a bit of a lemon now.'

'Sit yourself down and tell me all about it. I could use the company.'

She smiled. 'Of course, footloose and fancy free for a while. Not all it's cracked up to be, is it?'

'Tell me about it! I have to make my own tea in the morning!'

'Oh well, you'll appreciate it all the more when she gets back. Any postcards on that yet?'

Pete shook his head.

'I'm thinking of joining her! But Australia isn't quite far enough away!' The joke hid her nerves, but Pete wasn't fooled.

'What's happened?' he asked gently, 'is he there? Do you want me to go round?'

'Oh, no; nothing so dramatic. In fact, it's a bit pathetic, really.' Much more pathetic, she felt now, than she was ever prepared to let him know. She blushed at her own stupidity; and Pete smiled.

'Just a tiff?'

'I suppose so. Dominic and I didn't have tiffs.' She smiled. 'We didn't talk. I suppose I'm not very used to relationships yet.'

'Don't trivialise it. You wouldn't have come round if it wasn't important to you.'

It was very important. But Pete couldn't offer the escape she had sought.

'It seemed so at the time,' she admitted sheepishly. 'Roddy wants me to go to Deauville with him for the weekend. And I refused. And he issued an ultimatum.'

'Well, it might not be the most original advice in the world, but is he worth it?'

'That's the trouble. I think he is.'

'Then why not go? You can't stay faithful to a memory forever, Soph'.'

'I can't go racing, Pete.'

'Roddy's not insensitive. He won't expect you to. There's the Sales and the beach and the night clubs. You'll have a great time, believe me; it'll do you the world of good. And if you hate it, it's just for

101

a weekend, after all.'

She gave a laugh, in agreement; and wished that she could tell him the truth. She didn't need this caring confidante. What she needed was the public persona. It had been a final straw to clasp at. But no more than that.

Relaxing visibly, she began to take in the room, aware that it was somehow different. The shelves were bare of the usual clutter of ornaments.

'The cats!' she exclaimed with sudden realisation. 'Have you taken them down to clean? You'd better have them back up before Barbara gets back!'

Something in Pete's expression made her bite her lip. Immediately, her own troubles were forgotten.

'She isn't coming back, is she? Oh, Pete. I'm so sorry; I had no idea...'

He made a gesture, as though to say it didn't matter. But it wasn't so simple to put into words.

'I've told no one yet. Can't face it...'

He stood up, for the sake of it, and went out to the kitchen; offering tea as an excuse and not waiting for her to decline it. She followed him out and stood to one side as he went to the fridge.

'Shit! No milk, I'm afraid. Forgot to get any in. I've been doing some low weights lately.'

'It's completely empty, Pete,' Sophie said with concern, 'it shouldn't be empty. I know you've been riding winners.'

He smiled ruefully. 'Somebody must have drunk it, then, eh?'

He grinned, suddenly, at her dismay and a

little of his former façade crept back, despite himself. He winked at her.

'Come on, Soph', I'm not such a sad loser yet. I gave it to the neighbours. Honest.' He could see that she remained unconvinced. The brashness faded once more. 'Okay, so I am a sad loser. I came in; and her things were gone; and there was no milk in the fridge and I really didn't want to look at bottles of Cliquot and Lanson. So I took them next door. Leave the rest in the weighing room. Sit here at night, sober and miserable and doing my best not to go upstairs to bed...'

'Oh, Pete...'

'You don't take milk anyway, do you?'

'I tried to keep everything out of the house. I learned to live without it.' She smiled. 'I still go without, though there's no need, really.'

'Yeah? I can't handle it myself. I didn't forget, by the way. But if it was there, I'd lash it in! Black tea and coffee? Urgghh!'

They both laughed and sat down at the table, waiting for the kettle to boil.

'Actually, there are a few crates of bubbly still down in the basement, if you'd prefer a drink?'

Sophie shook her head.

'The buggers never give us scotch, do they?! Now there's a drink I could do with right now.'

'Then it's for the best, Pete. What are you wasting for, anyway? Anything specific?'

'More bloody rides!' He laughed. 'Your brother keeps laying them out for handicaps and I'm doing the donkey work, getting them in at the lowest

103

possible weight, and losing the ride that matters as a result! So I reckon if I can ride at, say, eight two, I'll get to keep the bulk of them.' He stood up. 'Tea or coffee?'

'Whichever. Tea, in preference.'

'It all tastes like boiling water to me! Tea it is, then.' He poured two mugs and stabbed at the teabags carelessly. 'I've always done eight four, no problem. You wouldn't think those last two pounds would be such buggers.'

'You're fairly stocky, can't you sweat it off?'

'That's how I kept at eight four!' He set the mugs down on the table and sat back down. 'There's a natural minimum, Sophie-Suds, and we can't do a thing about it.'

'You haven't called me that for too long.'

'Yeah. I did think you were taking an awful long time to get your life back. Two years; seemed a hell of a time. And now... I can't see myself ever getting over this. Two years, twenty years... it doesn't mean anything any more.'

'Do you want to talk about it?'

'No.' He smiled. 'You know, anyway. Been there, done that. A bit harder for you, too. No gradual progression towards the end. Just, bang!' He turned the mug around a couple of times. 'Just bang...'

'Did you see it coming?'

'Not really. We were comfortable. Like an old married couple. Well, I guess it has been ten years; but I mean like an *old* married couple. And then, when we came back from Queensland, it was gone. Knowing what she was going to say before she'd said it; knowing what she was going to do before she'd done it. Gone. Like living with a new person. Still Barbara; but not my Barbara. I think I knew I'd lost her. I still can't fathom why it's come as such a surprise.'

'I think that's harder than your sudden bang theory. I never lost him, you see. I didn't have to say goodbye.'

'Oh God! This is morbid, Soph'! Did you want to look at the tape of this afternoon's racing?'

'I saw the replays on Attheraces. You really out-rode everyone in the last.'

'Thanks. You played your part!' He picked up a video tape, left on top of the television set in the kitchen. 'Here's Friday's.'

'Where were you?'

'Pontefract. Tell me you miss it!'

'I miss them all. But I couldn't watch again; not knowing what I could see...'

Pete raised a hand in protest. 'Morbid again!'

She laughed, and followed him through to the living room.

'This one's safe. Vetted it and everything. The three fifteen's a bit of a nightmare; and the four forty-five was a bastard. But no spills.'

'Any winners?'

'None; unless you count morally. I should have had the seller. The infamous four forty-five. Terry and Chris worked a blinder on me and I didn't see daylight till the winner had pulled up! The bastards had fallen out and rode to beat each other all afternoon.'

105

'I used to love it when they did that!'

'Oh yeah, great stuff. Specially if you're caught in the firing line. Terry was on a no-hoper. Any day but a work day and he'd have let me through. But he wouldn't get off Chris' heels!'

'We used to check the car park religiously on a work morning,' Sophie reflected. 'One car, no arguments, no cat-and-mouse tactics. But both cars there and we'd know we were in for a treat! Dominic would alter his entire riding plans on the strength of it.'

'Wish I had. Anyway, see for yourself.' He stuck the video in and settled back to watch it.

'We shouldn't be doing this,' Sophie said guiltily, 'it's far too late.'

'Better than going to bed. Does it get any easier?'

'No.'

'Thought not.'

'Did you know; when she actually left?'

'Kind of. Wouldn't admit it, I guess. She kept going on and on about it. Her whole family were there. Nothing worse than the recently converted. Zealous. Why don't you come over? Why don't you come over? It's not like we hadn't tried. But honestly, Soph', could you see me riding permanently out there? Look at the bloody video. That's me, the little European guy balanced on the withers. I stuck out like a sore thumb in Queensland. Not my style; not my scene.' He grinned. 'Not even any decent racing! Sydney has the best races. All they were offering us were the bloody beaches! I'm a jockey, not a beach-bum. I don't ever want to retire. I certainly don't want to retire while I can still ride.'

'Not even enough to ride out there for the winter?'

'Well, I thought so, at first. We'll see them every winter, I said. More than what most families get to do. And then she kept saying about her sister's shop. How she'd always wanted something like it herself. A chance to do something of her own. If she wanted a job, I wouldn't have stopped her. No reason why she had to stay home each day.'

'Except to sit by the phone,' Sophie pointed out.

Pete grimaced. 'Umm. You tend to forget, sometimes. Anyway, I said I wasn't going to talk about it.'

'Who's that chestnut on your inside? Is that Bob, riding?'

Pete studied the screen. 'Yeah; Bob... sorry, Soph', I'll have to look it up.' He fumbled on the coffee table beside him for a race card.

'It's running through for third,' Sophie said.

'Oh, that's right. That's that colt of Tim Bradley's. The one out of that good racemare he used to train. Bob rode that for third. Can't think of the little beggar's name. He ran a nice race though, didn't he?'

'Certainly. He caught my eye. He'll win next time out. Tim would put you up, if you asked?'

Pete looked at the screen with renewed interest. 'Yeah, I guess he would. I have ridden for him, from time to time. Never ridden a winner for him yet. And Bob wouldn't necessarily be available again. Not at poncey little tracks like Pontefract.' He made a mental note. 'Thanks, Soph', I'll give him a ring when I see it going again.'

'Old habits die hard.'

He smiled at her. 'You miss it.'

The tape ended, an evening's racing condensed into twelve minutes of action.

'I do miss it,' Sophie admitted.

'She said it was just a holiday,' Pete said, 'I knew it was a reccy'. We'd only been back a few weeks, but she booked up for another trip over. Chester week. And you talk about sitting by the phone! The one time she could have really got the call and she was in bloody Australia!' He smiled. 'It's not funny, is it? She only came back to get her things. And that's it. Ten years down the pan.'

'At least you can start again, in a while, when you're feeling better,' Sophie remarked, as though to herself. Conscious of the fact, she blushed and smiled. 'Well, you've always been a ladies' man, haven't you?'

'When it was pretend, yes. And there's no reason why you can't, either, Sophie-suds. You're nearly there already. One little bit of commitment and the new life beckons. Go for it, eh?'

'I really can't.'

'So you're going to go home to him, refuse Deauville and watch him walk out the door? If I'd known I was contagious I'd never have let you in!' He grinned, the old Pete still there somewhere. 'On the other hand, though, Soph', if he gives up on you that easily, maybe he's not worth grieving over?'

She sighed. 'Believe me, it's not easy. He's given me more than enough chances. It's just reached the point when he can't make excuses for me any more. How often can I give him the cold shoulder before he draws the conclusion he's beating his head against the wall?'

'Okay, so why are you giving him the cold shoulder? Maybe you don't like him as much as you'd like to kid yourself?'

'I'm afraid of sleeping with him.'

She'd said it. Against the odds and her own better judgement, the thing she had rushed round to tell him was suddenly out.

'If you laugh at me, Pete Allen, I shall leave.'

'I wouldn't dream of laughing. I haven't even crossed that choice bridge yet. Can I tell you a secret of my own?'

She nodded her assent.

'I've never actually slept with anyone other than Barbara. Until you just brought it up, I hadn't considered it. But now... I guess it's going to be a bit... scary, if you like. Not only can I sympathise, but you've just opened up a whole new can of worms for me. Cheers, Soph'!'

'This is turning in to a hell of an evening,' she admitted. 'The real reason I came round was specifically to tell you that. And more. I had such a stupid idea in my head and now you've just dispelled all that.'

'Okay then, let's make a pact. You try it first and if it's really no different with someone else I'll give it a go!'

'No. I'm scared of sleeping with Roddy because I've never slept with anyone.'

'I'm in exactly the same boat, Sophie-suds – and you know something else? I don't think it's so very unusual. Own up to Roddy instead of me and you might start getting somewhere.'

'No; you don't see at all. I really haven't slept with anyone. Not anyone at all. Not even Dominic.'

Pete stared at her, without comprehension.

'You had separate rooms, you mean? He was a snorer and you're all elbows?'

Sophie shook her head. 'Same bed, no sex. He was gay and I was too infatuated to care.'

'*What?*'

'Just the sort of reaction I'd expect. Except that you worked with him and respected him. Roddy never knew him and owes him no favours at all.'

'Oh God, I'm sorry, Soph', I never meant it like that. It's just so... well, a bloody shock. He used to have all the girls swooning over him. Whenever I was outside flirting and he turned up, I'd just pack up and go in!' He shook his head. 'I can't believe it, I really can't. You were such a perfect couple.'

'And Roddy is going to know, isn't he? You're polite now, but I can hear the laugh in your voice. Roddy will be straight into the first racecourse bar and telling everybody, whatever he promises.'

'Not necessarily.'

'Would you?'

'No.'

'And why not?'

'I can't pretend I liked him. But he was a bloody good jockey and that's how we'll all remember him. No one dared mock him to his face and I don't know anyone who'd like to mock his memory, either.'

'That's what I hoped, from you. But Roddy will only see the joke. How do I get round it, Pete?'

It was a night of revelations. And the revelation of exactly why she had called round hit Pete with excruciating embarrassment. He couldn't dare voice the obvious solution, but once it had surfaced he couldn't suppress the appeal of her childish quest. And she wasn't a child; wasn't the little Sophie-suds of old; anymore than he was the playboy of the paddocks.

'You could always stay here for the night... no strings attached,' he ventured.

Just as she had planned, had hoped, had feared. And couldn't immediately voice an answer.

'Shit! This is awkward!' He said lightly. 'Tell you what, I'll make us more tea. While I'm escaping out the kitchen, you can escape out the front door. If you want to.'

She smiled with relief. 'I don't want to.'

'I'm glad... I think. I suppose this is sort of adultery. I'm still married; you've got Roddy. It's okay for us to feel guilty and uncomfortable.'

'Maybe I should go.'

'No, don't,' he said quickly, the sense of urgency surprising him. 'Even if we just sit up all night watching tapes of races.'

'I'd like that. And that tea you promised.'

She followed him out to the kitchen and perched on the table while he turned the kettle back on and put teabags in the mugs.

'While we're being all honest and open,' he said, 'I'm glad you told me about Dominic. I was in awe of him. Everyone was. Not awesome, like the bloody yanks! But that mix of admiration and fear. I wouldn't have wanted to get on the wrong side of him. You've kind of cushioned that now. Not that it really matters now.' He poured the boiling water into the mugs and stabbed once more at the teabags. 'But when I remember him, it won't be with awe; just admiration.' He handed her a mug and grinned broadly, stifling a laugh. 'But bloody hell, though! Him, of all people!'

They walked back through to the sitting room and slumped together on the sofa.

'D'you fancy a film?' Pete asked, 'I taped one the other evening. Can't remember which one; I was waiting for it to come on and started nodding off.'

'I'm beginning to nod a bit myself already.'

Pete started the video and fast-forwarded through the adverts.

'Oh no! It's bloody sub-titles! I didn't know it was bloody sub-titles.'

'Ah, leave it on. It's Il Postino; it's a lovely film, you'll enjoy it.'

He turned to her, with raised eyebrows. 'I've never yet enjoyed a film described by a woman as lovely!'

By the end of the film he had to privately concede that that was no longer the case. And the surprisingly enjoyable slush had given rise to other benefits, too. Sophie's tears had started long before the sentimental ending and she hid herself gratefully within his arms, sniffing apologetically.

'It's just that I know what's coming.'

'You mean someone's going to die? Way to blow an ending, Sophie-suds!'

She laughed and sobbed, all at once, and snuggled against him all the harder, as though her tears were something to be ashamed of. Barbara had loved soppy films; she'd cried so openly and frequently... He hadn't expected to feel comfortable with someone else in his arms. He kissed Sophie gently, easing the pain of the screen death. And they were still kissing as the credits rolled.

The tape played on, unnoticed, through the titles of the next programme, until clicking off, rewinding and ejecting noisily. They sat up, somewhat startled.

'It's not too late for me to run you home...' Pete suggested tentatively.

Sophie smiled.

'Oh yes it is.'

CHAPTER EIGHT

The morning brought with it only one regret.

They barely had time for any awkward embarrassment, flying round trying to use the bathroom at once and be ready to ride work by five-am. Sophie had the added disadvantage of having to return home first for her riding clothes, leaving them short of time and short of sleep.

'Did we get any sleep at all last night?' she asked, pouring two black coffees while Pete faced up to donning his boots.

'Late films and early mornings don't mix,' Pete agreed, 'on top of everything else!'

She smiled, without embarrassment. Radiantly, Pete thought. Then she was gone, back to her own flat, before he had even picked up the coffee she'd poured. Her own sat, barely sipped, beside his. Two mugs, just like old times. That radiant smile, in her eyes, in her voice... and his one regret of the night before. No strings attached.

Shit. Life just dealt him one blow after another. Physical, mental; no strings, just bloody great chains. She might as well have used super glue, the attachments he'd formed last night. If he'd told her... who knows? But it was no use breaking his heart again when it hadn't even mended first time around. If he had told her, she would have spent the rest of their lives avoiding him. He was eight years her senior, hadn't gone to Harrow, didn't ride ten Group winners a season, scraped a living at the minor meetings; while she was a girl of means, who didn't have to scrape a living of any sort. And was pretty and young...

Shit.

He arrived at the yard before she did, mounting up and circling with the others, hoping to be spared the sight of her appearance and good morning kiss with Roddy. As he circled back in front of the entrance, Mike was already giving her a leg up onto a filly. He watched, in passing, then kicked his feet out of the irons, just to be sure. No glue or magnets. And his colt was calm and relaxed. Which was more than could be said for him.

They filed out of the yard at last and headed for the Limekilns, the morning's work ending without any misadventures. A pity, really, he couldn't help but think. The last spill had turned an acquaintance into a... he edited his romantic thoughts, replacing 'lover' with 'one-night-stand'. Worse had happened, if it was any consolation; which it wasn't.

'Casburg gone home, has he?' he asked Sebastian, jumping down in the yard and handing his mount over to its stable lass.

'Not as far home as you'd like,' Sebastian told him, 'he's staying over for a few weeks, Deauville, Baden-Baden, maybe even the Leger meeting.'

'Oh joy of joys. Has he said anything?'

'We've found races we want to win and horses we want to win with and routes from A to B,' Sebastian confirmed.

'So he's clear on not expecting any wins along the route and about not springing surprises on the morning of the targeted race?'

'No surprises. You'll come in for breakfast?'

'A light one, Seb. I'd like to stick at some lower weights, if I can.'

'Great stuff! I won't have to send Sophie off in search of apprentices and lightweights. What is it, steamed mushrooms?'

Pete grinned at him. 'And the rest!'

They walked together to the house, Roddy and Sophie joining them in the kitchen. Sophie took charge of cooking and serving, any tiredness either blown off on the gallops or well hidden. Roddy and Sebastian were too busy discussing that morning's work for more personal conversations and Pete relaxed, already willing, if not happy, to wipe recent memories from his mind.

'Not having any yourself?' Sebastian asked his sister, as one plate short appeared on the table.

'I'll grab something at Mum and Dad's.'

'Let me know if he's taking any owners down to Sandown. He can give Pete and me a lift, if not.'

Sophie pulled a face. 'You could always offer *him* a lift, you know!'

'Certainly! If he likes! Just buzz me from there, would you?'

Sophie grinned. 'He'll pick you up from here straight after we come in off the gallops. The owners will all be down tomorrow. Variety Club Day.'

'Oh of course. And your Gala Day next weekend. It's a month of digging deep, it seems.'

Sophie hurried out, the early start enabling her to also ride work for her father. There were no miss you kisses or see you laters exchanged with Roddy, who continued with his bacon sandwich, unconcerned. The pair would have the whole afternoon ahead of them, while everyone else was at Sandown. And then Deauville.

'I'll nip home and change,' Pete told Sebastian, finishing his cereal, 'pick me up en route, would you? Save me hobbling back.'

'Will do.'

The two day meeting at Sandown Park passed without winning rides, but Pete maintained his high profile, rarely off the television screen throughout the high-jinx of Saturday. Hauled out before the cameras time and again to face an endless succession of game show hosts and comedians, his good looks and natural clowning perfect for Saturday afternoon entertainment, but no doubt grating for those who had tuned in purely for the racing. He could only hope that the children's charities would benefit as much as he had.

The sparser crowd and picturesque, antiquated facilities of Baden-Baden the following day offered a stark contrast to the Variety Club invasion of Sandown. Though Casburg shared the flight over with Sebastian and Pete, he didn't trouble them with conversation and instead they discussed between themselves the events of the forthcoming gala day. Pete's sudden enthusiasm had waned just as rapidly and he remembered now the hundred-and-one reasons why he had not initially volunteered. Sophie just had this way of sweeping him along...

The German foray proved fruitless, Pete again drawing a blank for wins, though none had been expected. He had become such a regular visitor to the German tracks that he invariably picked up at least one local ride and these, in the past, had proved more successful than his stable's attempts. His retained rides for that afternoon had apparently been sent just for the plane trip and failed to show any promise whatsoever.

'I don't know why you fetched them over,' Pete complained to Sebastian, as they packed up for the day and headed off to catch their flight.

'Walter enjoys coming here, he likes to have runners.'

'You could at least try to send him over a winner!'

Sebastian shook his head. 'The prize money's not good enough.'

Pete looked theatrically behind the young trainer. 'Thought he was working you then, pulling your string!'

'His words, yes. I'd personally opt for any prize money, however small, just to finance the day out.'

'I think he's got a bimbo over here, some busty little fraulein!'

Sebastian laughed at the notion. 'Could be. I never see him, he just comes into the parade ring for the race, then vanishes. He uses the track for all his German business contacts. They probably own all the casinos here.'

'And he's not flying home with us?'

'Deauville. Staying for the week. Relieving Omar Sharif of his hard-earned at the backgammon tables, no doubt.'

'Are you going over for the sales, or are Sophie and Roddy checking out the yearlings for you?'

'He won't buy from Deauville. Sends everything over from the States. I told him they have the choicest bred yearlings at ridiculously cheap prices. Not interested.'

'You should take out a public licence next season,' Pete advised, 'get shot of Casburg altogether.'

'Love nothing better. But there's a bit of a delicate problem.'

'You owe him money?'

Sebastian looked at him, startled. 'I do, as a matter of fact. We've come to an arrangement, the stable pays off the debt. But he's a good owner, Pete, we can run this stable lucratively long after the arrangement ends. He's assured me of his future support.'

'When he's willing to throw away twelve grand in prize money because he can't get a bet on?' Pete argued. 'What use is that to us? We need the prize money *and* the winners.'

'A few well-planned coups and we can have all three. Of course, as a public trainer, I could aim for a better class of horse than Casburg keeps. Start looking to the Classics.'

Pete laughed ruefully. 'I can't even walk! Let's not run yet, eh?'

The next few days passed uneventfully, with doubles at Windsor and Brighton compensating for the lack of winners elsewhere. Tuesday morning on the gallops, Sophie was no more than a rider in the distance, but Friday morning she made a point of seeking Pete out.

'What are you doing with your spare free hours this morning?' she asked him, as he waited with his colt for a lad to take charge.

'I don't know, what am I doing?' he asked warily.

'Practising for Sunday? Dad's got your ponies at the yard and Terry and Marcel are coming up early, to get a few jumps in before racing.'

Racing that afternoon was at the town's July course and the first race was not until two thirty.

'Count me in, then,' Pete agreed. He wanted to ask how she was; how had Deauville been. 'What are these ponies like?'

'Serious jumpers. But the NH boys have got the equivalent. All eight are of the same grade, so it's all down to you boys on top.'

A lad came over and took the colt, Pete slipping it a polo mint as he handed over the reins.

'What time, then?'

'Whenever you're ready, the earlier the better.'

'Great, see you later, then, Soph'.'

She turned away, with some regret, and headed across the yard for the gates, a second string of horses awaiting exercise at her father's. She wished Pete had shown more interest in her weekend. If he'd asked, she would have told him... but the last thing he needed was a silly little innocent who didn't know the meaning of a one-night-stand. On top of all that she had lost, she didn't want to lose him as a friend. Far better to bite her lip and keep her feelings to herself. God knows, she'd managed it for long enough with Dominic.

At David Churchill's paddocks, fences had been laid out, hopefully in exact representation of the arena to be used on Sunday. Bob Graham was there already, taking first pick of the ponies, chatting to them amiably about their prospects as he fed them polos. Their responses told him very little.

'May as well just pick the nicest colour,' he told Sophie, unaware of any additional audience.

'Bloody girl!' teased Pete, joining Sophie as she leant on the paddock rail, 'what about the chap on the end? He's wearing such a pretty pink sheet!'

'Bugger off! And it's a filly.'

'A mare,' Sophie reminded him, 'they're older and wiser than what you're used to.'

'What, in the weighing room, you mean?!'

'They all look alike,' Pete marvelled, 'not even feminine or masculine. Funny how you forget other breeds.'

Bob chose a slender bay pony and mounted; Pete hopping over the rail and making his own way along the line.

'The pink sheet does it for me every time,' he joked, nearly losing a finger with his polo mint to the grey pony on the end. He mounted up and circled with Bob.

'Do you know what you're doing?' Sophie asked.

'No, but the pony does,' Bob assured her.

An hour later, they not only knew what they were doing, but were getting very good at it, too. Their audience had increased to David and Angela Churchill, and now Marcel and Maddy Dessaint arrived. Pete watched Marcel embrace Sophie warmly in welcome, then walked his pony across to them and jumped down. Bob followed suit.

'Let's see how it's really done,' Pete remarked to him, as Marcel chose his pony and mounted up.

'Lower them,' Maddy advised, as Marcel adjusted his leathers and pulled them up to what he felt was a more reasonable length.

He shook his head, disconcertedly. 'I'll come off.'

'Shit, we're going to get hammered,' Pete moaned.

Nevertheless, Marcel put in a more than decent performance, his natural horsemanship compensating for his inexperience over fences. His clear round raised the hopes of the spectators, who now included Chris, Anne, Terry and Su.

Terry watched with approval and then genuinely showed them all how it should have been done, matching their clear rounds, but with the addition of speed. The mood became one of high expectation, the girls screeching with delight and bouncing around excitedly, much to the amusement of their partners.

They all went back to the Churchills' house for a light lunch before leaving together for the races. Sophie sat quietly on the kitchen windowsill, as the jockeys and their wives went upstairs to change from riding clothes to suits. Pete joined her.

'Okay?'

She shrugged. 'It's been a long time since we were all together.'

'You should come with them this afternoon.'

She shook her head; though that thought had driven her to the window, away from the enticement of the old gang.

Pete instinctively reached for her hand and held it gently.

'The girls upstairs are afraid to stay at home and get that phone call,' he told her. 'Barbara was afraid to watch me ride, she was one of those who preferred to wait at home and hope the phone never rang. Until last week, no one had ever picked me up off the floor and held my hand in the ambulance.'

The contact was almost too unbearable. She withdrew her hand, friendship too poor a second best to accept.

'I couldn't wait at home. If he was still riding, I'd have to be there.'

Pete withdrew into his familiar façade, trying to shrug off the pain of rejection. She was Roddy's partner; no strings attached, he'd set the ground rules himself.

'How's this, then, Sophie-suds – you promise to hold my hand in the ambulance and I'll promise not to come off? Just for this afternoon.' He grinned, raising a smile in return. 'Come on, Soph', you know what bitches they can be! They'll only talk about you all afternoon!'

'I don't know…'

'I've to go and change, but give it a thought, eh?' He slid off the wide sill. 'I'll make a pact with the others. None of us will come off. Can't say fairer than that, Sophie-suds!'

She laughed and watched him go, wondering whether now was the right time to venture back; wondering if there really was anything behind the playful flirting. She knew that the girls would be happy to sit with her by the weighing room, without going out to the grandstand. And their company was so badly needed.

Her decision made, she went upstairs to change.

Sunshine, warmth, cane furniture and panama hats set the July course a world apart from the bitter, windswept Rowley Mile course adjoining it. The girls, in cheerful sundresses, settled themselves in what could have passed for a Caribbean beach hut and drank Pimms. Their partners donned the stifling body protectors and helmets of their trade and drank bottled water sparingly. The afternoon drifted leisurely by with frantic ninety second bursts of contests and thirty minutes of Pimms, Taittinger and gossip between each.

Pete cantered down past the steel band and thatched summer huts for the first race of the day and galloped back on the first winner of the day. He followed up with second place in the sprint handicap, then joined the girls to sit out the third race, reserved for apprentice jockeys only. Marcel, Chris and Terry were already with them, arguing the merits of their mounts in the last on the card, the Blue Peter Stakes for two-year-olds and, hopefully, those illusive future Classic winners. With no ride in the race himself, and no Classic prospects in his yard, Pete could only sit and listen.

He amused himself by catching the eye of the women at the next table, enjoying their reaction and carefully raising his sunglasses to deal the final cut. It was all so easy, and so unnecessary. How successful would he be if it was suddenly for real? And how much longer before it would be?

Sophie watched the women opposite, amused, as always, by the familiar reactions. She caught Pete's eye and returned his grin, as he lowered his glasses and turned back to their own table. She'd seen girls get hooked by that grin on countless occasions, laughing at their weakness, their gullibility, never once considering that she might be as susceptible. And now she was an even bigger fool than they – knowing it was no more than a game, but still sucked in.

'Never mind The Derby,' she said, stepping in to end the escalating arguments around her, 'that's next June. What about this afternoon? Which of these super horses will win today?!'

The raised voices decreased to murmurs. No one, it appeared, was confident.

'Bloody marvellous, isn't it?' Pete remarked, 'three certainties for a race next June, but not one bloody chance between you today! Well, chaps, I'm going to win the seller and the Bahrain Trophy, so you may as well all stay here!'

But, as the result was called for the apprentice handicap, they all returned to weigh out for the next, the seller, which Pete failed to win. Neither could he finish closer than third in the Bahrain Trophy. He drifted back out to look for the girls, after showering and changing, and found them in front of the saddling boxes, looking over the two-year-olds in the last race.

'Three future Classic winners?' he mused. 'Twenty-one, sixteen and, knowing how hopelessly optimistic your other half is, Su, that pig-ugly irk over there!'

'Sixteen is Chris',' Anne told him, 'Terry's on eight and Marcel's is the twenty-one. Nice sort, isn't it?'

'So's Terry's. What's your verdict, Soph'?'

'For today, or the future?'

'Both!'

'Ante-post on Marcel's. It's nice, isn't it?' Nice was just about as great a term of praise that could be bestowed upon a racehorse. The press were the only members of the racing fraternity willing to delve deeper for accolades. Sophie looked over a colt being led past as they spoke. 'And that for today.'

'It's fit,' Pete conceded, 'which is more than can be said for the rest of them. Anything I can phone up and beg a ride on next week, do you think?'

She smiled, pleased to be back within the world she loved. 'I'll watch the race and let you know.' Even as she spoke, she realised the enormity of her words. For a moment, it had been second nature.

'I'll watch with you,' Pete suggested calmly, 'and see what I should or should not be doing on my prospective winner!'

He could almost physically feel her backing away, but he ignored it, as though unnoticed. 'Shall we watch from the rails?'

The others nodded, eager to see the race, but careful to appear not to care either way.

'The view from the stable lads' stand isn't bad,' Maddy suggested, waiting for the denial that never came. 'We'll watch from there, then.'

They moved across to the parade ring and watched the young horses under saddle. When the jockeys mounted up, they moved off again, down to the rails and the crude wooden steps that had somehow earned the name of 'stable lads' stand', and watched the horses canter to post. Marcel's 'nice' horse impressed enough to earn an additional 'very nice'. The two words were enough to ensure its Derby credentials.

The lads responsible for the runners began to reappear from the betting ring and filled the wooden tiers. There was the usual tense mix of hope and anticipation, Sophie's own tension lost in the crowd.

Pete painfully recalled over-stepping the mark that morning by taking her hand, though it seemed now the right thing to do. Instead, he rested an arm around her shoulder, taking the weight off his throbbing foot. She accepted the friendly imposition and even went so far as to slip an arm around him in return and offer him a gentle, sympathetic hug. But that's all it was.

On the off, Pete felt her stiffen, but as quickly relax and lose herself in the sight that now held them all enthralled. Marcel's mount, backward, unfit and immature, came home two lengths ahead of its closest rival.

'Bloody hell,' was Pete's comment, which pretty much summed up the feelings of all.

Sophie watched the colt pull up, mesmerised by the performance, as they all were. She gave Maddy a congratulatory kiss, then planted one just as sweetly upon Pete's cheek.

'Thank you,' she told him simply.

The girls made their way at a fast walk to the winners' enclosure, Pete, limping heavily, left behind.

'Hey, I'll head straight home!' he called after them, veering off towards the car parks. They waved their farewells, sprinting now to see the winner come in.

Pete's limp increased as his pace slowed, the activity between races taking its toll. He could nearly put his foot to the ground, but not nearly enough for the walk-abouts entailed in watching races. And now here he was, alone in an empty car park once more, his departure hailed across a crowded paddock, and he couldn't even run.

It was an unfortunate thought to have, coming, as it did, just as a heavy hand clamped down on his shoulder.

He jerked away and swung round, only to be confronted by Danny Western's smiling face. The smile dissolved as Western saw the reaction caused.

'Shit! You scared the life out of me, you bastard!'

'Yeah, well, maybe with good cause,' Western apologised, 'can we hobble a bit quicker to your car? You can give me a lift into town.'

'You're out a bit sharpish? Not taping quotes from the winning trainer?'

Western produced his tape. 'Got them. And more.'

The car park was beginning to fill up, racegoers pouring out now that the latest star had retreated to its stable.

Western watched them all, as Pete stopped beside the hired Mercedes and unlocked it. He slipped smoothly into the passenger seat and cued up his tape, as Pete backed the car out.

On the tape, a trainer told them, from a distance, that he'd always thought the colt was a bit special. The voices buzzing around him were more foreground than background. Pete could visualise Western somewhere near the back of the group, arm raised with all the others, a multitude of tapes whirring away above the heads of trainer and hacks.

"...he'll probably go straight to Doncaster for the Champagne Stakes..." the trainer's voice, his quotes a repeat of every hopeful trainer's, every year, every special horse. Pete paid little attention, listening, instead, to the more interesting snippets drifting in from the crowd, the aside comments between hacks, even his own voice, shouting a goodbye. Too faint to be recognised by anyone other than himself, but a chilling reminder of the tape's omnipotence.

'Bloody hell, does it pick up everything?' Pete asked, pulling out into the slip road that would lead them down onto the main road into town.

'It picks up the loudest noise. Such as last week, when Marcel paused and it homed in on your pal – what d'you call him?'

'Mr Henchman.'

'Mr Henchman. And speak of the devil.'

A general mix of voices, competing with the trainer as he confirmed The Derby as the target.

"...got twenty-fives this morning...prefer the Johnson horse...leave now, before the traffic...he's heading for the car..."

Western paused the tape.

Pete looked into the rear-view mirror searchingly. His foot throbbed more painfully than before.

'Me?'

Western inclined his head, a non-committal nod. 'Presumably. I heard Maddy Dessaint coming up behind me, I turned to maybe grab a quote and saw you heading off. Just as Mr Henchman spoke. I swung round quick, as soon as I heard the voice, but I couldn't spot him.' He clicked off the tape and returned it to his pocket. 'I'll have you know I snubbed the First Lady of racing to come rushing to your aid.'

Pete said nothing.

'Where're you headed?'

'Not home.'

'No. Wise choice.' He withdrew The Racing Post from under his arm and thumbed through it to Saturday's declarations. 'Goodwood or Newmarket?'

'Me? Back here again. We only had one at Goodwood and I couldn't guarantee making the weight.' He tried not to think of Mr Henchman.

Western turned to the list of Newmarket entries and studied Pete's rides. 'So,' he asked, 'which one would the pressure be for?'

Pete flicked on the indicator and pulled over. He leaned his head back against the headrest and tried to unmake a decision. And failed, in spite of the sore foot and bruised limbs and pulled muscles.

'I'm not doing it,' he said with renewed certainty. 'Whatever they want, I'm not doing it. I have to go home. Face up to it. Get it over with.'

'At least come back to The Golden Lion first?'

Pete indicated once more and waited for a gap, pulling out. 'I'll drop you back, of course.'

'I'm not looking for a lift. Come back for a drink.'

Pete grinned, surface deep. 'I'll leave you something in my will.'

'I'd do likewise, if you weren't going first. So here's a little something upfront. Mr Henchman doesn't belong to Bisley.' He folded up The Racing

Post and tucked it back under his arm. 'I told you I'd dig, and I dug.'

CHAPTER NINE

They sat in Western's room, away from the regular clientele, which suited Pete. He was known to be a regular himself. Western busied himself on a laptop, emailing more urgent copy, then set it to one side.

'Are you ready?' he asked Pete, who had declined a drink or a bar snack.

'As much as I'll ever be.'

'Okay. Bisley, he couldn't give a fuck about you. Bookies don't go broke in one day. Big race doubles, favourites clearing the card at Royal Ascot, they dent the annual profits, not one race at Newbury. You want to know his verdict? Win some, lose some. Simple as that.'

'He smashed up my bloody Porsche!'

Western shook his head. 'He closed your account. That's as extreme as he got.'

Pete let it sink in. Only the thought of retribution had kept him from returning to the car that evening at Newbury. Nothing more than sheer luck had kept him from an earlier encounter with Mr Henchman...

Western watched him. 'Bisley closed Seb's account, too. Seb had a free account with him. You know the sort, all losers written off. Perfect for Seb, he can't run up any debt and therefore Old Man Churchill can't find out. For Bisley, a nearly legal way of buying info'. Seb backs a horse, Bisley knows it's a possible. Seb backs it wholesale, it's a cert'. Seb doesn't back it, it's a loser. A window straight into the stable. So why would Bisley shut the window, I asked? Because someone insisted upon it. Presumably Walter Casburg, who objected to sharing the odds. Bisley asked no questions, you already had an account anyway.' He grinned. 'Any of us could have told him what a crap tipster you are!'

'Yeah, yeah. But if Bisley doesn't own Mr Henchman, who does?'

Western's smile remained, but all trace of humour had gone. 'He's on Seb's payroll.'

'*Seb*?'

'Twenty-four hour security. Mr Henchman is a guard by the name of Paul Smith. Walks the yard by night. Beats you up by day. Now exactly whose payroll he's on during beating up hours, I don't know. I dig only so far. No point in burying myself in a hole I can't get out of.'

'So although he's employed by Seb, he could be moonlighting?'

'It's a possibility,' Western agreed, shaking his head to belie his words, 'but so is this: Seb needs you to be more compliant. He needs a few healthy coups, he needs you to lose a few along the way. When you told your owner that you wouldn't throw a race, was Seb within earshot?'

'No, no, no,' Pete insisted, 'you're way off the mark. Seb heard, and he stood up for me. He told the owner straight that neither of us were going to throw any races.'

'Yeah? So that owner was Casburg? Not that it really matters. What matters is, on a racecourse, with an owner present, what were you expecting Seb to do? Threaten to have you beaten up if you don't ride to orders? Or quietly back you up?'

Pete shook his head. 'It's not Seb's way.'

'All I know is, Seb ran up a fuck of a massive bill at Casburg's casino,' Western told him. 'It seems Casburg has an arrangement, he gets his horses trained for free, gives Seb a small allowance instead of a wage. The debt is paid off only partially by prize money – largely by bets. So Seb is a pretty desperate chap.'

'He wouldn't threaten me.'

'He'd just ask you nicely, as a friend?' Western's tone was lightly mocking. He had a point. 'Casburg is not the type of chap you'd want to remain in debt to.'

Pete recalled their meeting at York. 'Nasty?'

'I don't know yet. Seems the perfect businessman at present. But casino owners invariably know good debt collectors.'

'He threatened me. When I refused to throw the race, he threatened to hurt me more than the colt who'd thrown me that morning.'

'Ouch.'

'I held my ground, he backed down. For all his words, nowhere near as scary as Bisley.'

Western looked thoughtful. 'Bisley does his own scaring. Casburg has to hire it. Such as Paul The Henchman Smith. Or maybe your friend Seb would like you to think someone else was piling on pressure, rather than personally making demands.'

Pete shook his head emphatically. 'Not Seb. He's a good kid at heart.'

'Maybe. But there are some bad kids out

there, Pete – what are you going to do?'

'Go home,' Pete said decisively, 'face the music.'

'Admirable heroism. But it's the cowards who survive.'

Pete shrugged. 'I can't keep running. They'll just get me in the end.'

'Fuck that! The end could be a long way off yet. You've already got a limp.'

'That was the threat. Next comes the demand; you said yourself. How hard can that be?'

Western grinned. 'It depends on how convincing you are when you pretend to agree.' He reached into an overnight bag beside the bed. 'Best take this.' He tossed over a small cassette recorder to Pete. 'Might come in handy. I always keep a spare.'

'Thanks, mate.'

Pete turned to leave, nearly convinced by his own words of bravado. How hard could it be? Easier than running away, wondering...

'Watch yourself,' Western called after him; at once shattering the delusion.

He didn't drive straight home, but slowly circled the town, stopping in at a newsagent, picking up a paper, putting it back, leaving empty-handed. The Deauville Yearling Sales supplement had somehow put him off. Which deterred him from his second option. Sophie might have welcomed him into her flat, no strings attached, but after her weekend away it was unlikely he'd find her alone. So; home it was, then...

He thought of Westy's advice and of his own bravado. Facing the music was a bad choice. He couldn't agree to their demands and worry about the consequences later; he lacked the necessary courage. Already he knew that he wasn't going to do that.

His mobile rang, on the hands-free kit, the call accepted without option. He waited hesitantly for the caller to speak.

'Sunday – lose the jumping.'

He laughed, despite himself. 'Piss off, Westy! Jesus Christ, are you deliberately setting out to give me a heart attack today or what!'

'You're home safe, anyway?'

'Not yet. Called in for a paper. Just parking now, as it happens.' He was telling the truth, neatly settling the car outside the flat.

'Yeah, well, I had a thought. Better than the tape idea. Don't hang up. I'll listen out for you, do whatever I can this end.'

Pete pulled the key out of the ignition and looked up at the flat. It was a good offer. But he didn't want Westy listening in.

'Thanks, mate. But I'll manage.'

'Fair enough. But fucking sound convincing.'

Pete smiled ruefully as he hung up. There would be no need to lie convincingly. He got out and locked up.

No one lay in wait in the shadows.

As he walked unmolested up the steps to his front door, the fear now raising the hairs on his skin merely paled in comparison with the perpetual need to look over his shoulder. The limp was a physical reminder of just how bad it could be, but, as he'd told Westy, he wasn't prepared to keep on running. That constant dread took more courage than he had. Merely facing up to them, refusing their demands, once and for all – that was a surprisingly easier option.

He unlocked the front door and stepped forward to meet his demons.

There were neither demons nor humans laying in wait. Breaking and entering seemed to be beyond Mr Henchman's abilities. In all probability, Pete reflected, the York hotel room had been left unlocked. He carefully bolted the door behind him; but without relief. It seemed unthinkable to have to gear himself up for this encounter all over again.

He made himself a tea, with a merciful dash of milk, and wandered into the living room to view the afternoon's racing. The video had been set up for the review of the meetings and he settled back to pick himself a future winning ride from the last race; a task Sophie had overlooked in the euphoria of witnessing a great horse in action. He rewound and fast-forwarded the video to and fro, until finding the race required. He had barely got as far as noting the promising individuals trailing in the wake of a better horse when a car alarm screeched into action.

Remembering the Porsche, Pete ran at once to the door, taking the steps down to the street two at a time in his haste to save the hire car. He stood out on the pavement, the Merc' flashing and screeching and unharmed. Various curtains in various windows fluttered and closed out the scene, the neighbouring motorists no doubt relieved that it wasn't their own car disturbing their evening. Pete envied them their lack of nerves. How long before he could casually look down through the curtains at a cat jumping down from the bonnet?

Nevertheless, he took time to check the car over before returning to the flat, once again securing the door against the marauders he had, in his own mind, welcomed. He went straight through to the kitchen, for more tea, less milk, promising himself to forego it altogether next cup; then back to the sofa and video.

He stopped in the doorway, staring at the space reserved for the television in disbelief. The television was still there. Presumably the video and DVD were still there, too, somewhere beneath what was now no more than a pile of shattered glass and plastic. As the scene registered, he backed away instinctively, taking in the rest of the room, the pictures on the floor, the shelves bare of books and trophies, all now strewn across the floor. The fury last unleashed upon the Porsche had swept through the living room with devastating effect.

He listened, keenly. Then stepped forward, into the hall, into the bathroom; checking the small space carefully for intruders, York still too fresh in his memory. Then the bedrooms; back to the sitting room; through to the balcony. All clear.

'Bastards!'

He sat down heavily on the sofa, the cushions still bizarrely neat and orderly, amid the destruction.

The coffee table had been swept clean of whatever rubbish had been left on it... except a cutting, from The Racing Post. And he'd never cut anything from The Racing Post.

He leaned forward to pick it up, but in the end didn't bother. The closer view was all that was necessary. He looked at his phone for a moment, uncertain which number to call.

It was Western who answered, when finally he'd tapped in a number.

'Still with us, then?'

'Oh, I'm fine, hunky bloody dory. But I've a flat to match my car, the bastards.'

'Fuck.'

'They set off the car alarm. Two minutes I was gone, if that.'

'Lucky you were gone at all,' Western pointed out.

'I *wanted* to see them, confront them. I was going to say no. Bring it to a head. I mean... this... shit.' He stopped, lost for words. Her cats. Her precious bloody cats. If she hadn't taken them; if he'd seen them, a part of her, smashed up on the floor...

'Christ, mate,' he told Westy, 'I told you I was sick of running. I wasn't going to accept their demand. I was going to stand up to them, here and now. And I can't. Bloody bastards.'

'What about the demand?' Western asked. 'It has to be made. What was it in aid of, if not to enlist you for something?'

'It was made. There's the declarations for the sprint handicap on Monday left on my table. I take that to be a hint.'

'Epsom?' There was a laugh in his voice. 'You've to lose on a horse that stands no chance anyway?!'

'We fancy our chances, actually. But mine isn't the one highlighted.'

'Oh fuck. Oh fuck, Allen, that's serious.'

'This had better be off the record?'

'Oh, come on! We've gone a bit past that point. Trust me.'

'Sorry, mate. And you can trust me – I'm not doing it. I'd better go. Heavy tidying to do.'

He hung up, and immediately called Sebastian.

'Seb, you've a guard in the yard called Paul Smith. What time does he start?'

'Who?'

'Smith. Paul Smith. Big bloke, well built.'

'I don't know their names, to be perfectly honest, but three of them should be coming on duty...' he evidently paused to check his watch, 'five minutes ago, actually. Why?'

'I need to speak to him, it's urgent. Can we use the office?'

'It's all yours. Anything I ought to be informed about?'

'Plenty. Either Smith, or someone he knows, left me a message to get the favourite beat in the sprint on Monday.'

'To get the favourite beat?' Sebastian repeated the words carefully. 'Not merely, beat the favourite?'

'No.'

'But you're not even on it!'

'All the better to get in its way, box it in and generally hamper its chances.'

'Good God, man! And Smith left you that message?'

'Not exactly. I think he might know who did. He moonlights as a heavy.'

'A *heavy*? Hired muscles and all that nonsense? For whom?'

'That's what I'm hoping to find out.'

He met Sebastian several minutes later, by the stable yard gates. Seb unlocked and let him in, the car left outside, hopefully safe from harm.

'I'll come with you,' Sebastian insisted, highly agitated by the situation.

'There's no need. And he might be put off, you being an employer.'

Sebastian nodded. 'But what about Monday? What are you going to do about it?'

'Nothing. Except pray the favourite wins.'

'I'd been praying on our own behalf, actually,' Sebastian told him wryly.

Pete grinned. 'My tactics had been to get in the way of the favourite and hope for the best. I suppose now our little horse is on his own. I'm steering well clear of Dessaint and his hot-pot.'

Sebastian looked at him, deeply concerned. 'I had already been assuming that. By what are you going to do about Monday, I was rather meaning *after* the race?'

'I'd prefer not to think that far ahead, Seb. That's what this little chat might resolve.'

'Ah, yes.' Sebastian remembered the errand in hand and pushed a button on his walkie-talkie. 'Would that be Smith?... Well, look, could you tell him, please, someone is waiting for him in the office? If he could go straight away, it seems to be fairly urgent.' He pushed a button and the walkie-talkie went dead. 'Best of luck, Pete. And pop up to the house after, I've a jolly decent cognac waiting.'

Pete nodded his acceptance and walked off toward the office. His only hope was that he didn't meet Paul Smith at the door; other than that, he had no firm plan. He pushed open the door, the lights already on, and found it mercifully empty. He opted for Sebastian's chair, behind the wide desk, and settled back, thumbing through the clutter on the desk and Racing Calendar, defaced by pencilled entries. Almost at once the door swung open again and Paul Smith entered.

He stared at Pete, the recognition instant and an obvious shock. He remained where he was, just inside of the door, and asked suspiciously, 'You. What do you want?'

'You delivered a message,' Pete told him, amiably enough; though anger seethed quietly within, 'but you forgot to wait for a reply.'

Smith weighed up the words and tone and relaxed somewhat, stepping forward to one of the chairs in front of the desk and settling himself down.

'No idea what you're talking about.'

'Okay. But as I haven't got many enemies,

the same person who sent you to deliver a message to me at The Black Swan in York also sent me a message tonight. Maybe you'd be good enough to take back the reply for me?'

Smith stood up and walked back to the door.

'I'm not a messenger boy,' he said, without looking back, and opened the door to leave.

'Fine. But if you and your mates have any money invested this Bank Holiday, the favourite for the big one at Epsom still looks a cert'.'

Smith turned round, smiling. 'Yeah? I'll have a few bob on, then. Buy a few packs of smokes – light one up after the race.' He winked; and left.

'Shit.' Pete stood up, no further forward than he had been. But presumably the message would get back. Maybe more threats. Certainly some confrontation after the threats proved worthless. At some point, it would have to boil over and fizzle out.

He pushed the chair in under the desk and walked up to the house for a cognac he had far from earned.

'Should I dismiss him?' Sebastian asked, after hearing the full details of the attack on the flat.

'It depends who's paying him,' Pete pointed out. 'Who hires and pays security here? You, or Casburg?'

'Casburg. But it's still my yard. I can dismiss him if I choose.'

'There's no need. Chances are, Seb, it's Casburg paying him to deliver messages. And Casburg's horses he's paid to protect. So you're safe enough in that respect. If it was you paying for

144

protection, while he's taking outside orders, I'd worry.'

'Get your point.'

Pete set his empty glass down on the side table.

'I'd best be off, Seb.'

Sebastian merely nodded a farewell, preoccupied. But as he rose to show Pete out, he voiced his own doubts.

'It's Walter, isn't it? Not content with our own coups, trying to pull off outside coups.'

'Probably.'

'But knowing a favourite won't go in, isn't that bookie territory?'

'Perhaps he's selling the info'. Or running his own book.' Pete shook his head. 'I don't know, Seb. Whatever you owe him, he's looking for quicker returns.'

'Umm. That was very much what I was afraid of.'

Pete was shown out by his trainer and they walked together down to his car.

'Still got the Merc', then?' Sebastian observed.

'I told the garage to sell the Porsche for me. I'm getting too old for it. I like the reliability of the Merc'.' He patted the bonnet, as he would the rump of a horse. What he actually liked was the anonymity, though he wasn't quite ready to admit that yet. The Porsche and the groupies had been fun, but only while they were a façade. Now that he was genuinely single it was all too real and too shallow. So shallow it had won him and lost him Sophie in one brief fling, even though he'd told her the truth. It seemed not even the truth was as convincing as the lie he had created for himself.

'Mind how you go,' Sebastian said in parting, as Pete climbed in and started up the engine.

Pete raised a hand in farewell and drove back home, for yet another night of wondering.

CHAPTER TEN

'The only person this incriminates is you!'

Western switched off the tape and rewound it, as they sat under the trees on the July course. They were both dressed casually, Western in jeans and t-shirt, Pete in an Italian linen suit, just about as casual as he ever got. It was Gala Day, the usual air of the racecourse absent, as unusual crowds streamed through the gates, mixed with the regulars.

'If you and your mates have any money invested this Bank Holiday, the favourite for the big one at Epsom still looks a cert',' Western repeated Pete's words, just heard on the tape. 'I'll erase that immediately. Let's hope your Mr Henchman didn't come armed with a tape – that's pretty damaging fucking stuff. The Jockey Club would have you over a barrel.'

'Who'd think of a tape? Anyway, I was the last person he was expecting to meet Friday night.'

'Just as well. But for fuck's sake, Allen, tread more carefully. They threaten to break your legs, you can tell them to go get lost. But they threaten to take your licence…'

'Yeah, yeah, I'm an idiot, give me nightmares, why don't you. How do *you* usually deal with blackmail?'

'Point taken. Want to hear about Goodwood yesterday?'

'Not really; I'll read about it tomorrow. Haven't you got a cricket match to compete in?'

Western shook his head. 'Not me. Football, five-a-side. Racing Post versus the tabloid tipsters.'

Pete grinned. 'My money's on them.'

'Cheers, and I'm backing the NH boys in the show jumping!' Western raised the whirring tape in salute, now recording over all previous indiscretions. 'Hadn't you better go find Sophie and your team mates?'

'Christ, it's not for hours yet. We're meant to be milling about, signing autographs. Soph's probably overseeing the cricket.' He couldn't keep the trace of bitterness from his voice.

'Big cricket fan, is she?' Western asked, surprised.

'Since The Roddy Eleven joined the yard!'

Western grinned. 'Then she'll be avoiding it, I'd imagine. You're not the only one who dislikes him.'

'Didn't you know? She and Golden Bats are an item.'

Western laughed at the nickname. And the information imparted. 'For about one day! Fuck, you'd never make a racing hack!'

'You mean they've split already?'

'If you can call a one night stand a split. He was sobbing into his beer in The Golden Lion all Saturday night! And he'd been no more than hopeful of his chances the Saturday before!'

'Not last Saturday?'

Western nodded. 'Sorry you missed it! I suppose you were still partying with the B-list celeb's at Sandown. Anyway, it must have done our Sophie the world of good, she's back racing again.'

'Are you sure this was last Saturday? They

were supposed to be in Deauville.'

'Were they?' He gave a short laugh. 'Icing on the cake!'

'You don't like the bloke?'

Western shook his head. 'Seb's fine – cagey, but polite. Roddy's a pain in the arse. And Roddy takes all the media calls.' He mirrored Pete's grin. 'She does tend to go for the wrong sort. Marchant was the Royal Pain of all Arses. If he hadn't been such a blinding jockey we would have danced on his grave!'

Pete laughed; but it brought home to him just why Sophie had sought him out nine long days ago. It may have felt like love, but for her it was no more than love for Dominic, protecting what little good name he had left. On the other hand, she had within hours ditched Roddy and avoided Deauville…

'No accounting for the female mind,' Western continued, 'and this show jumping that's not for hours yet, it's in just over an hour. So don't get on the wrong side of her. Hell hath no fury and all that.' He looked at the tape and saw that it was well past the point at which Pete had originally stopped it. He rewound it and held it out to Pete. 'Give the public a quote. I might as well gather as many as I can and hand this in to Sophie for her auction tonight.'

Pete said something to please his audience and Western hurried off on his spontaneous charitable mission to collect the spoken autograph, as he termed it. Pete decided to go in search of Sophie and his riding clothes, but bumped into Sebastian almost immediately, still in his cricket whites.

'How'd the match go?' Pete enquired, 'We

beat the Lambourn squad, I hope?'

'Foregone conclusion!' Sebastian agreed, 'I've to scoot down to the bank for Sophie, pop the takings so far into the night safe. She's doing very nicely, the day's a great success and we haven't had the auction yet.'

'That's good to hear. Is she around?'

'Up at the saddling boxes with the ponies. All your clothes are in the inspection box. The others are already up there, changing.' Sebastian laid a reassuring hand on Pete's shoulder. 'Tomorrow, by the way, we drive to Epsom together. I've booked us into a hotel in the town, to save driving back and forth for Tuesday's meet.'

'Seb, there's really no need...'

'No, no, I insist upon it. This business with the sprint tomorrow, it's a worry. You're not driving back to Newmarket. And certainly not on your own.'

Pete smiled, in gratitude; privately cursing under his breath. He was as determined as ever to confront the issue head on. But, at present, beating the National Hunt boys at their own game was much more of a pressing issue. He thanked Sebastian and continued across to the saddling boxes.

The parade ring itself had been converted into a jumping arena and, as he emerged from the inspection box, Pete looked across at the throng of people already pressing around the rails, trying to secure the best possible view. Flags had been sold to the partisan spectators, proclaiming their allegiance to the various teams preparing to meet in the ring, and the National Hunt and Flat support looked fairly evenly matched.

The Epsom Trainers were due to kick off the jumping, against their Yorkshire counterparts, and were already collecting their horses and mounting up as Pete wandered in. It was hard to take sides when all but the most successful of the Yorkshire trainers regularly employed him, and he wished each of them good luck in turn.

'Hello, Patches, can you jump, then?' he greeted one of the horses, recognising it from his visits to an Epsom stable. It was a large and heavy skewbald cob, belonging to its even larger and heavier trainer.

'Doesn't need to,' its rider quipped, winking, 'we'll just flatten the fences!'

'I did offer him one of the gymkhana ponies,' Sophie joked, joining them, 'but he was afraid he'd flatten that as well!'

Pete grinned and followed the riders across to the parade ring-cum-arena.

'The Epsom squad have a ringer,' he told Sophie, under his breath, 'Patches jumps like a Grand National winner!'

'Are you watching this, then?'

'Unless you're planning to send me back to our own ponies.'

She smiled. 'I'll do no such thing, I'm glad of the company. I seem to have spoken to a million people today and met no one!'

'The curse of the successful hostess! You know Danny Western's collecting good wishes from everyone on his cassette, to give to you for your auction?'

'Danny Western?!' Sophie was pleasantly surprised.

'You've melted even the toughest hearts!' Pete teased. 'Even mine.'

'Don't give me that! You were press-ganged, and you know it!'

They stood together and watched the cumbersome Patches soak up the laughter and attention from the crowd, while his team-mates and opponents competed.

'A natural clown, that one,' Pete told Sophie, 'they start the stable apprentices on him, for a laugh. He can clear ten paddock fences in as many seconds before they hit the deck!'

When it came to the big cob's turn, he backed Pete up by completing a clear round. But it wasn't enough to secure the Epsom team a win. Next into the arena were the teams from Newmarket and Lambourn, generating huge support from the many stable lads present. By dint of a home crowd, the Newmarket team had by far the loudest support, but unfortunately the most inept riders. Realising the depth of support and lack of talent, the Newmarket trainers played up to their audience and clowned around; which was what the day was all about, had it not been for the fierce rivalry between Flat and National Hunt. The fun and games ended in favour of Lambourn; then an air of intense expectancy fell across the gathered crowds.

'Nervous?' Sophie asked Pete.

'Very,' he admitted, with some surprise.

'You'd better get going.'

He sprinted back to his team mates, meeting them at similar runs from their own vantage points around the parade ring.

'Who's minding the ponies, then?' Pete asked.

'You mean they might nobble them?' Bob wondered.

'I wouldn't put it past them,' Terry said.

They found their ponies in the expert care of Angela Churchill and quickly mounted up, trotting them round the tree-lined pre-parade ring to warm them up. The National Hunt team were doing likewise, distancing themselves by half a lap.

'They look confident,' Marcel observed.

'We'll beat them,' Terry predicted. He eyed Marcel's ridiculously short leathers with a smile. 'They're underestimating us.'

'Slow and steady,' Pete agreed, 'they think that'll be enough.'

'Am I the only one taking this a bit more seriously than The Derby?' Marcel asked.

The others laughed, with a unanimous 'No!'

They were called into the parade ring and lined up neatly, while team captains Marcel and Eddie Donnelly flipped a coin to decide on starting orders. The silence around the arena was stifling. Marcel won the toss and elected to allow the first of the National Hunt team to kick off the contest. Leaving the chosen representative behind, the others filed back out to the pre-parade ring and listened anxiously to the commentary. The sharp intake of breath and relieved exhaling en masse of the gathered spectators told them more.

It was a clear round, in reasonable time. Nods of polite congratulations were exchanged; and Marcel left the group to take his turn. The successful National Hunt rider returned to his team mates, to hugs and pats. The Flat team looked on in nervous silence, their fate now out of their own hands.

The painful and erratic breathing of the audience virtually drowned out the commentary, as time and again Marcel obviously cut corners and asked too much of his willing pony. Each time, the risk was repaid; Marcel returning with a clear round and impressive time.

'Oh shit, this is worse than Derby Day,' Pete said, finally exhaling as the cheers rang out to signal the completion of a clear round. He was serious; and his team mates could only nod in agreement.

'We call it Grand National Day,' his rival remarked, with empathy, as he passed by to take his turn.

Marcel came back in to a joyous reception, before nerves and ears were strained once more by the next competitor. The agony of the crowd and rattle of a pole told the sorry story moments before the tannoy declared four faults. Despite themselves, the Flat team sighed heavily in relief, then glanced apologetically at their rivals.

Bob's clear round, albeit slow, lifted much of the pressure. The equally slow but clear round that followed only piled it on once more.

'Penalty shoot-outs,' Pete told Terry. 'Derby

Day doesn't even come close.'

'Still going last?' Terry asked.

'For glory or universal hatred,' Pete agreed. 'Good luck, mate.'

Terry trotted away; a few tense moments later matching the clear rounds, but taking a magnificent two seconds from the previous fastest time. This time manners and decorum were forgotten – the Flat team welcomed him back with all the fervour of a winning side.

The final National Hunt rider did his best, but the ultimate outcome rested entirely on Pete. A clear round and a better time than the last rider would ensure his team victory. One slip and it was gone.

There was no slip. Taking as many risks as an inexperienced Marcel, but with all the skill of a Junior Champion, Pete flew round to get within a second of Terry's fastest time. That it eluded him didn't matter; as last rider the success fell wholly on him and the home crowd of Flat devotees suddenly outnumbered the National Hunt fans. Be it penalty shoot-outs for the World Cup or Derby victory, Pete tasted a success beyond compare.

Amid the tumultuous congratulations and mobbing of fans, one person pressed against him and kissed the back of his neck. He knew the touch and swung round, ready to catch her in his arms, confess his love, crown the moment. But already she was slipping away, needed in a million places at once.

'Sophie-suds!'

She turned, and smiled, and he no longer cared about risking friendship or inviting rejection.

He stepped forward hurriedly, straight into the embrace of Su Jones.

'Pete Allen, you're my hero!'

'Put him down and give someone else a go!' Anne protested, squeezing in and taking over the hug.

'Come and get a drink, we're all in the champagne tent,' Su told him, as Anne released him, 'even the NH boys are with us – they bought the first Magnum!'

Pete smiled and looked searchingly over Su's shoulder. Too late; Sophie, and the moment, had gone.

He joined his friends in the champagne tent, the National Hunt team and their partners magnanimous in defeat. Before he could make inroads on the fast-flowing Bollinger, a tape was waved under his nose and his own glass swept up and emptied.

'Say something for your fans,' Western demanded.

'That was my bloody drink!'

'Danny Western, bringing to you, live, the theft of a glass of Bollinger from champion show jumper Pete Allen!' He pulled up a chair and pushed the tape across the table. 'Come on, girls, a toast, on tape. It's for charity.'

'To Sophie!' the table erupted.

'D'you get everyone?' Pete enquired, pouring himself more champagne.

'Everyone! Absolutely anyone who's anyone!' Western poured another drink. 'Except your guv'nor, actually. Seen Seb around anywhere?'

'Not since before the jumping.'

'Fuck. Still, I'll run into him, even if it's at the auction itself.'

'Still taping?' Pete asked with a grin, 'Good job kids can't afford to bid, eh?'

'You're no fucking angel yourself.'

'I'd be less of one if I could find Sophie.'

'Ha! Good luck to you in that one! The missus has left you a bit too long, even I'm afraid to turn my back on you and do up my shoelaces!'

'Piss off and get another bottle in!'

Western slipped away and returned, dutifully equipped, so that it was well into the late evening before they eventually left the tent and wound their way across to the weighing room, from where the auction was to be held.

'You after anything?' Pete asked Chris conversationally, as they stood alongside one another.

Chris shook his head. 'Marcel's after the stallion nominations, but you wouldn't be bidding for those anyway?'

Pete shook his head. 'I'm going for the tape.'

'The tape? Westy's?'

'Thought it would be nice to give it to Sophie. Sort of commemorate her day.'

'Bloody nice idea.' Chris nodded his approval and pulled out his wallet.

'What's that?' Terry asked, joining them; Su wrapped firmly round his shoulders, slightly worse for wear.

'Pete's bidding for Westy's tape, for Sophie.'

'Nice one! Count us in!'

To Pete's hidden consternation, Chris handed him a fifty pound note, matched by Terry. As Marcel, Anne and Maddy joined them, they were told of the less-than-personal gift and Marcel chipped in a hundred. Pete thanked them all and cursed his luck. The way things were going, it was only ever going to be an impersonal token of friendship anyway.

'If it goes over your limit, keep going,' Marcel said quietly, 'I will settle it.'

It was generous, especially as Marcel's own saddle and mementoes were up there, already donated. The stallion nominations were certain to raise tens of thousands, if not six figure sums. It wasn't all for Sophie alone, yet the sheer magnitude of support for what was her day hit Pete full force. Realistically, he didn't stand a hope in hell.

Marcel's saddle, carefully described as being that used on Derby Day the year he'd notched his first win in the famous Classic, fetched ten times its original purchase price; the stallion nominations each breaking through into six figures; the tape, eventually, an apparent bargain at six-fifty, as countless collector's pieces were knocked down for thousands.

Pete managed to slip away from his co-buyers, but Sophie was still clearly busy with the final arrangements, so he drifted away from the weighing room; from Terry and Su kissing on the steps as though they were the only ones on the racecourse; from Marcel and Maddy already planning which mare would avail of the newly-acquired sexual services of the stallions; from an evening populated by happy couples, flooding the exits.

'Pete.'

He swung round, his smile lifting him as though helium.

'Sophie! The very person!' Yet he knew at once something was wrong. He left the cassette and its precious tape deep in his pocket.

'Have you seen Sebastian anywhere?' she asked anxiously.

'Not for ages. Danny Western was looking for him, too. I last saw him heading off to the bank – that was an hour or so before the jumping. Westy would have seen him since.'

'No, he hasn't. No one has. And his mobile is turned off. We're worried sick, Pete. Dad's driven back and forth from the bank looking for him – no car, no nothing.'

'Well look, if his mobile's off, that's a good sign. Any problems and he'd be ringing you frantically.'

'He's got all that money, Pete. What if something's happened?'

'Any way of checking if the money went in safely?'

'Not till the morning.' She raised a hand to her throat in sudden anxiety. 'It's Bank Holiday Monday!'

'Look, don't panic, Soph'. This is Newmarket we're talking about, he's sure to have run into someone. Either en route, or on the way back. Christ, even a loose horse! He could be standing at the clock tower this very moment, holding the reins!'

Sophie smiled, laughing nervously.

'On the other hand, if his phone's off, he'll be in the pub.'

'Dad's been in the pubs. They're empty. The whole town's here.'

Pete considered it. 'There's no point panicking, Sophie. If he's still not back tonight, *then* we'll panic. But let the guy get drunk and stagger home first, eh?'

She smiled, desperately needing the reassurance.

'Can I help you get finished up here?' Pete offered.

'You were just on your way home.'

'Not through choice.'

'Oh God, then I'd love the help. Everything's more or less done, so many people are helping out. And I know it's silly to worry at this stage. But he wouldn't miss this...' she swallowed, trying to remain hopeful. 'The jumping, Pete. No one missed the jumping...'

'For all we know, neither did Sebastian. Come on, Sophie-suds, no one remembers seeing him – that doesn't mean he's not around.'

He thought of the tape, in his pocket. But this wasn't the time for gifts.

'Come on,' he said gently, 'we'll clear up what we can, then wait back at Seb's. You can tear into him when he rolls in!'

With so many helpers, it wasn't long before they were finished. Very little cash had changed hands during the auction, deals struck mainly by cheque and credit card. Sophie put what little cash there was into the bag for the night safe and Pete sat with her as she made one last drive to the bank. Of Sebastian, there was not a sign.

'Dad's a bit anxious about the money,' she admitted to Pete, as they parked outside Sebastian's house.

'So long as Seb's okay, the money doesn't matter,' Pete assured her, 'the charities have done blindingly from the auction alone. How much was there, anyway?'

'Thirty-two thousand three hundred and forty.'

She unlocked the front door and Pete followed her through to the drawing room.

'No one will tell me anything,' she complained, 'as though I'm still the youngest and need protecting. So I'm only picking up the gist, between Mum and Dad. And Dad seems worried Sebastian has *taken* the money.'

'Ah.'

'Ah?'

Pete cursed the involuntary reaction. If the Churchills had kept much hidden from Sophie, how much had Sebastian himself kept hidden from them? And he was hardly missing, not seen for a couple of hours. Only to return quite plausibly and discover his stable jockey had blown open every secret.

'There's a good cognac here somewhere,' Pete said, rifling through the bottles on a cabinet, 'we'll start with that, shall we?'

Sophie sat down, but only as far as perching on the front edge of the sofa. She accepted the glass and held it in both hands, twisting it fretfully and gaining more comfort from the action than from drinking.

Pete took a sip. 'It's a nice one. I thought you'd fetched it back from Deauville.'

'I didn't go.'

'No; I only found out today.' He took a second sip, no more than a chance to moisten his lips. Everything that he really wanted to say...

'I don't want to drop Seb in it,' he told her, 'you know we're all panicking needlessly. He's not been seen for a couple of hours, that's all. And when he gets in, he won't thank me for this.'

'Drop him in what and thank you for what?' Sophie pressed.

'He owes Casburg money.'

'Casburg should owe him!'

'Sebastian ran up a casino bill. A repayment arrangement has been made, Casburg doesn't pay training fees. But Casburg is running this yard for gambling alone and Seb wants out. With the right results, he could be free for next season. But he might also grab at a chance to repay Casburg in full a lot sooner.'

'With the gate money?' Sophie was horrified. 'He wouldn't do that! He's not a thief!' She took a large gulp of brandy. 'He's not an idiot, either. How would he expect to explain it away?'

'He hasn't pinched it,' Pete assured her. 'But with his track record, he's probably in London right now, borrowing it. Stake money.'

'Oh God. All those rows.' She lowered her

head, trying to recall past arguments between her father and brother; not wanting to believe what now sounded likely. 'He can't do that. Supposing he loses?'

'He won't expect to use much of it, before he achieves his aim. Gamblers are optimists – that's what keeps them going.' Pete sat down beside her. 'I've really screwed up here, Soph'; I'm sorry. We're jumping to rotten conclusions, just because we don't know where he is.'

She looked up at him. 'But so will everyone.'

He reached into his pocket; hesitated.

'I thought you and Roddy were a couple. I wish I hadn't, really.' He drew out the tape and handed it to her. 'Danny Western's tape, the memento of the day. Actually, I wanted it to be a special present, from me to you. But I screwed up on that, as well. When the others knew it was for you they all wanted to chip in. So it's from the whole gang.'

'Oh… Pete…' She looked at him, overcome; and then the tears fell in earnest.

At once, Pete hugged her and drew her in, safe and tight, his own eyes threatening to well at her distress.

'Soph'… I wish I could do something… make it alright…'

Instead, he just crushed her in his embrace; compensating for his inability to save her from this hurt; making up for all the longing and doubt he'd suffered; clinging to her desperately in case, in the end, she did say no, and this was all that he had.

CHAPTER ELEVEN

Sebastian didn't come in that night.

'He's at Aspens,' David Churchill said, with angry certainty, phoning at three in the morning and telling Sophie to go home, go to bed; thanking Pete for his concern, telling him to do the same. An anxious, loving parent feigning anger and once again clearing up his son's mess.

'Who's Aspen?' Sophie asked Pete, groggy from weariness and anxiety.

'It's a private club, in London. Casino.'

'Dad doesn't know he's there for sure.'

Pete hugged her apologetically, not needing to voice an argument. The hour and circumstances made it a safe assumption. David had clearly trodden this path before.

'I'm not going home,' Sophie insisted, 'I'm waiting here for him.'

'He'll probably go straight to Epsom from there, it'll be quicker for him,' Pete pointed out.

'Then I'll go straight to Epsom from here. You won't shift me, Pete.'

He smiled. 'Then you won't shift me, either. Seb didn't want me to go to Epsom alone anyway.'

She snuggled against him; so comfortably, so naturally.

'Why not?'

'Oh Christ, it's a long story. And not a good one, on top of all this.'

'The burns on your foot?'

'A loose connection, yes. That was a taste of things to come if I didn't follow orders. And the orders are to ensure Marcel gets beaten in tomorrow's feature race.'

'Whose orders?!'

'I don't know. And, of course, I'm not doing it. So Seb didn't want me left alone after the race. He was planning to look after me and he can't even look after his bloody self!' Pete sighed and ruffled her hair. 'It's darkest before dawn or something.'

'Planning to look after you? Protection – or money?'

'Christ, don't say that, Soph'. He's done a runner with your money just for me?'

'It's Sebastian all over. If he pays off Casburg, will it also stop the unwanted riding instructions?'

'Probably; I don't know. That's just another problem, another bloody headache.'

'Have you ever…'

'No,' he interrupted firmly, 'absolutely not. But someone's made a mistake, they obviously think I would throw a race. Although deliberately hampering another horse is in another league again.' He yawned and laid his head against hers, his cheek pressed against the soft silk of her hair. He could still feel her kiss from the afternoon on the back of his neck. 'Anyway, it'll all sort itself out tomorrow. What about you? Why did you blow off Roddy? What's a guy have to offer you, if Deauville's not enough?!'

'A tape.'

He kissed her hair, too tired for any outward show of the elation he now felt.

'You said I was putting him off for a reason,

just kidding myself,' she murmured.

'You don't want to believe anything I tell you!'

'Oh, it wasn't what you told me. It was what you did.'

'Put you off men for life, you mean?'

He felt her tremor of laughter, rippling through him. And her arm crept tighter around him.

'Put me off other men for life.'

They must have dozed intermittently, though they didn't remember it; waking stiff and tired and longing for the comfort of a bed.

'There are spare wash things in the guest rooms,' Sophie recalled, as they sat, bleary-eyed, wishing they were back in their own beds. 'Mum uses this house like an over-flow for guests. Sebastian wouldn't look after it, on his own.'

She picked up her phone and tried at once to call Sebastian, without success.

'I suppose his absence means he lost,' she sighed.

'Not necessarily. But we'd better start covering for him. The gossip could be worse than the truth.'

Sophie phoned her parents, while Pete did his best to freshen up in the bathroom. He felt no better when he rejoined her for breakfast.

'Roddy's overseeing morning stables,' she told him, 'I said you and Sebastian had left early for Epsom.' She shook her head. 'I just hope Dad leaves him barely enough alive for me to kill him!'

They ate cereals, then drove first to Sophie's flat, where she changed for the races, then up to the July course, where Pete had left his car. A complimentary copy of The Racing Post, conveniently folded open on Epsom's card, had been left on the bonnet, together with a packet of cigarettes and box of matches. Pete swept them off impatiently, anger long ago replacing fear.

'Litter,' he called to Sophie, sitting in her own car alongside, watching.

Back at his flat, he changed, while Sophie packed his kit bag.

'Overnight things?' she asked.

He shook his head. 'I'm coming back.'

They returned to Sophie's car and she drove, allowing Pete to catch up on some much-needed sleep. Her phone went off in the hands-free from time to time, her parents reporting no more than the continued lack of contact from Sebastian. The safety of the money dwindled by the hour.

Once at the race track, Sophie went straight through to the weighing room and took the precaution of allowing for Sebastian's delay, electing herself as stable representative. As she fulfilled her role down in the racecourse stables, Pete hovered outside the weighing room, avoiding eye contact with the disappointed band of girls and hoping that Western would be on the prowl for stories. Sure enough, Western emerged from the direction of the car park, recording the ever-patient Marcel Dessaint.

'He's on the winner,' Western told Pete, without satisfaction, as they stepped to one side for a quiet chat. He passed him a new cassette recorder. 'For you, sunshine. God bless expense accounts.'

'I've worse things than that to worry about,' Pete admitted, 'Seb's done a runner with the takings.'

Western was, for once, at a near loss for words. 'Fuck.'

'If you've any shred of decency, and compassion for Sophie, you'll keep it to yourself until they choose to announce it themselves,' Pete warned.

'He'll be at Aspens. Or Mattigans.'

'If he was, he's not back yet.'

'If he lost, he won't be back at all. Leave it to me, I'll ask about.'

'Discretion, Westy – if you hurt Sophie, I'll hire Mr Henchman myself.'

'Yeah? Well you'll be meeting him again soon enough.' Western gave a grin and headed off; and Pete didn't doubt for a moment that he could trust him. A month ago and he wouldn't have given him a quote. A month ago his job was secure and he was still pining for Barbara…

Sophie joined him on the steps and kissed him lightly on the cheek.

'The horses are here. No problems.'

'Still no Seb yet.'

'Dad says card games can go on till five or six in the morning.' She sounded cheerful, reassured by her father's excuses, the racecourse breathing new life into her. 'The only immediate problem is that I haven't so much as looked at the card for today, so if we need to go through tactics, we'd better sit and do it now.'

'Ah no, I'm fine. We ran through it Friday morning. The sprint I've just got to play by ear.'

Anne, Chris, Su and Terry chose that moment to arrive, delighted to see Sophie once more, and Marcel and Maddy were not far behind. The girls filtered off to the parade ring and Pete hung around on the steps, hoping to fill Seb in with any cover stories they'd invented by the time he turned up. But it was Western who turned up first.

'He wasn't at any of the clubs last night,' he informed Pete, his enquiries quickly completed. 'But your friend Mr Henchman's here. And I met a chap who knows him. Much dirt to dish, when we get a private minute.'

'What about Seb? What the hell has the silly bugger done?'

'My money's on the Deauville casinos. It's the height of their season and Casburg will be there. Seb can keep playing up his winnings until he has enough to hand over. Makes sense.'

'Can you find out?'

'Finding out now. The Post's French correspondent is happily trawling bars as we speak. My tape once picked up an interesting indiscretion, so needless to say his own discretion is assured.'

Pete grinned. 'What did he do?'

'Hey, fat bastard I may be, but evil bastard I am not. My word is my bond.' He grinned. 'And the question is not what, but who!'

'And the dirt?'

'Are you stopping in Epsom tonight?'

'No.'

'Then the Golden Lion tomorrow, if you can still walk by then.'

'Cheers!'

Pete returned to the weighing room, changed, and weighed out. Sophie herself came to collect his saddle and he told her an abridged version of events, in hushed tones.

'He's in Deauville? Are you sure?'

'Apparently so,' Pete assured her, without quite lying. It was better than allowing her to worry; but added to the queue when it came to killing the bloody idiot.

He joined Sophie in the parade ring, some ten minutes later, and their conversation centred more on Sebastian than the two-year-old filly walking past.

'Play it by ear, I suppose,' Sophie said with a smile, legging him up on the filly and standing back to watch him go out.

It was a typically fast five furlong nursery and Pete's filly was run off her feet, the low weight no advantage to her against such better company. Scrubbing along in an attempt not to finish last, Pete had hardly to worry about tactics or riding to secure the best possible finishing place. But he found himself worrying about it anyway, looking out over his rivals, getting a feel for the course and the positions and speeds of the sprinters. Wondering how he could stay clear of the favourite in the afternoon's main race, but still win on his own mount, if he could.

Standing back in the parade ring an hour later with Sophie, before the race, his chances looked slim.

'I was never going to outride Marcel

anyway,' he admitted. 'Try and give him a false lead and steal a march – like he hasn't done that to any of the rest of us six times a day!'

'There's no point winning, and losing the race in the stewards' room,' Sophie warned.

Pete smiled. 'They must have some high bloody opinion of me, to expect me to beat Marcel!' He tailored his words with care, as Sophie had done; the parade ring teeming with officials and press.

'Good luck,' Sophie said, legging him up. But he knew that even if he won, it would buy him only a temporary reprieve. The worst possible outcome was the one he craved most. Instant confrontation and a lid on the whole sorry affair.

And when Marcel won on the favourite a few minutes later, Pete no better than third and always on the opposite rails to Marcel, he got his perverse wish.

There were another three races still to be run, but Pete had no rides booked and Sophie was content to leave as soon as he'd showered and changed. She was too concerned with Sebastian's absence to be aware of the full significance of Marcel's win. Only Pete spared a thought for the room booked in an Epsom hotel for that night. He didn't even know which one. Couldn't have used it anyway, even if cowardice had won the day.

He rang Western, as they left the course.

'We're on our way home. Any word?'

'Not yet. I didn't know there were so many hotels in Deauville! He'll probably be home before Phil finishes them all! Look, I've got to dash, the race is going off. You watch yourself, Allen. Remember the tape and don't fuck it up this time.'

Pete returned the phone to his pocket.

'No news yet,' he told Sophie.

'Would you mind if we stayed at Sebastian's again tonight?' she asked, taking it for granted that their night would be spent together.

'Soph', I'm sorry. I have to go home. There could be repercussions from today. And you have to be at Seb's.'

'Dad can stop there. I'll come back with you.'

'I have to be on my own. It could get nasty, I don't know what to expect.'

She nodded in understanding, without protest.

'It has to all be connected, doesn't it?' she suggested. 'Do you think Casburg wants to use you for quicker returns than Sebastian can give him? And Sebastian's just avoiding you today, because of the demands?'

'We'll know tomorrow, when you check the bank.'

'Oh God, by tomorrow, we're going to have to think about calling the police, just for his own sake. But we can't let this leak out. Why won't he just call?'

'Wherever he is, he's fine. Still desperately trying to bail us out.' Pete smiled sympathetically. 'Trying desperately to win back thirty grand, so he can come home, poor sod. Coming home is going to take some courage, too. He doesn't need the police on his case.'

'And supposing he's lying dead in a ditch somewhere, a happy mugger thirty thousand richer?'

'Come on, Sophie-suds – one o'clock on a Sunday afternoon in Newmarket?! The only muggings we get are voluntary in William Hills and Ladbrokes!'

She smiled. 'I suppose it's taking quite a bit of courage for you to go home, too. Be careful, won't you?'

'Sebastian and I are a perfect team,' he assured her, 'we dig such bloody great holes for ourselves that we carry our own ladders in our pockets!'

When they arrived back in Newmarket, they drove straight round to the stables; Pete reluctant to allow Sophie anywhere near the flat. There was no need for excuses to be made for Sebastian, the staff expecting him to be remaining in Epsom, and instead Sophie and Pete shared a coffee in the kitchen before parting company.

'I wish I could stay,' Pete told her truthfully, holding her with an intense passion that would only bring him frustration for the rest of the night.

He felt her fingers curling around his flesh, in exquisite little pinches. She'd loved his build, the excess pounds he never quite shed off, such stark contrast to Dominic, who'd habitually wasted his five foot eight frame down to seven stone. Her fingers greedily explored every squeezable inch until she had unwittingly stirred him to the point of no return.

'We have to go to bed,' he told her as he kissed her, as though his life depended on it. And she merely pressed tighter against him, edging him out of the kitchen and into the hall without letting him go from her embrace.

They stumbled at the first of the stairs and remained there momentarily, the kiss too enjoyable, even for the calls of greater desire.

'If he comes in now, I'll kill him,' Pete said, finally letting her go and allowing her to lead him upstairs to a guest room.

There was no formal undressing, anymore than there had been the first time, just an intrusion of lips and fingertips, claiming layers of clothes as prizes, until they both lay naked on top of the sheets.

Pete promised her it would be even better this time; and it was. Each new remembered experience ensuring it would always be better and better, for ever more. And then they lay, exhausted, allowing the tumult of passion to ebb slowly away; until just lying there became a bore and they reached for their clothes once more.

'Stay for dinner?' Sophie pressed.

He shook his head. 'I can't let them think I've chickened out. I need to meet them, get it thrashed out. But I'll ring you, just as soon as it's all cleared.' He kissed her again, then reluctantly let her go.

It was a long walk home, even longer after such physical activity, and drawn out further by the constant need to watch shadows and doorways. No one leapt out from any of them, but he had learned through experience that his personal monsters shirked such crude elements of surprise.

His front door was securely locked and he relocked it safely from within, to await his visitors on his own terms. He set up the recorder on the hall table, in case he forgot later, and hoped it would surreptitiously pick up voices from the hall, living room and kitchen, if need be.

He checked his answer phone and returned calls and made himself dinner; and eventually wondered if Sebastian really had managed to bail him out. Until the car alarm went off.

This time it would be on his terms.

He went to the window and looked down. No one near the car, or hiding behind walls, or lurking on the balcony. He walked back to the hall and pushed down the record button on the tape. Moved a framed photo in front of it to keep it concealed. Ventured to the front door and braced himself for whatever lay outside. His own terms.

Opened the door and stepped out.

It proved a bad move.

It flashed through his mind that he had never been in any position to dictate terms to thugs, his sum experience of life starting at schoolboy, progressing to stable lad, peaking at jockey. As far removed from the street and normality as Star Trek conventions.

His brief fling with heroism ended abruptly as hands grabbed him from behind, hit him in the stomach, stuffed cloth into his mouth and pulled some form of canvas bag over his head, blacking out his world before he'd even seen his assailants. He knew only from the blows that there was more than one, in the same way he knew a horse had four feet when lying under it.

The lack of vision disorientated him, but

when he was thrust down onto a floor he knew it must be his own flat, simply because not enough time had swept by to enable them to take him anywhere else. He thought of the tape on the hall table and the demands listed in his head – now stuffed full of what appeared to be stable leg bandages, if the taste and texture was anything to go by. The hood was just that, he knew the scent and feel of the material, usually worn by horses reluctant to enter the starting stalls. Someone had been stealing from Seb's tack room.

He kicked and squirmed and fought and blackened shins in passing, but could do nothing to improve his position of flat on his stomach on a carpeted floor. Something wound around his face, tightening the hood, holding in place the length of bandage choking him and maintaining his silence. It wrapped around his neck and he recognised it at once as baling twine, the unbreakable nylon chord used to tie up bales of hay and straw. To leave a piece loose in a stable yard was a sacking offence. It could tangle round an equine leg and cut through to the bone...

He stopped struggling.

The twine seemed to be held firm. If he raised his head, it allowed no give. Without raising his head, he found, he was unable even to draw up his legs or roll over. And Mr Henchman didn't have to sit on him. Meanwhile, baling twine always came in pairs and his hands were securely bound, the nylon cutting into his wrists in warning against movement.

He lay in silent darkness, his illogical fear of baling twine slowing his pulse as his skin shrank from its touch. His breathing was slow, shallow, inadequate. *Never pull the chord from a bale, always cut it, never leave it looped. Knot it and re-knot it, until it becomes a tiny, harmless ball of nylon knots, then throw it in the bin. If not, it entangles legs and slices through to the bone.* These were things he'd learned in a stable yard as a school boy, feverishly knotting twine; not street savvy and retaliation against thugs.

Last time, it had been the threat. Then the demand. Now it was delivery time. He knew he could expect worse. Was prepared to cope. Was even marginally coping with the baling twine, which he'd not touched since signing his apprenticeship indentures. Just an illogical fear... only nylon string...

There were hands round his throat, pulling at his shirt, tearing it back. He felt the heavy press of the cotton as the buttons held momentarily before snapping. The cuffs were ripped through by the twine... he tried not to think; tried not to wonder at the necessity for him to be shirtless.

To be naked.

Trousers, socks, underpants, all yanked off with brutal force and lack of regard for the fabric. And this was now no longer bearable, no longer something he could cope with.

He writhed, only fractionally, until the twine bit at his skin and brought him to a sudden stop. Only the leg bandage prevented him from completing the humiliation by pleading for mercy. Instead he lay in silent terror, listening for the inevitable... scratch, fizz...

But, instead, someone spoke. Not Mr Henchman.

'Right now, the only thing keeping you in the saddle is your ability and usefulness. We couldn't afford to buy the Dessaints of this world, but you come cheap. You're well able to rig races when we ask. Last time, we had to leave you able.'

And then it came. In the silence as he paused. Scratch. Fizz. Sulphur, seeping through the hood.

Pete screwed up his eyes against the blackness of the hood. Bit down on the bandage.

The cigarette pressed down deep, between his shoulder blades. For too long.

'But if we can't use your services, why should we worry about your Medical Book?' the New Henchman asked, turning Pete's right hand over to reveal the palm and slowly pressing the cigarette into the first joint of his index finger. Then the second. 'Maybe you'll come round, see sense,' he continued, repeating the sequence on his middle finger. 'This is just a small taste. Next time, you'll do as we ask. And if you don't, there won't be another next time. There won't be another race for you.'

Henchman held Pete's left hand now, stretched it out as flat as possible, knuckles upward, tight against the biting twine. Held the little finger, slightly askew, away from any impending harm. And it wasn't a cigarette that pressed down, but a bone-shattering wooden club.

The hand sank into the flesh of Pete's left buttock, where it had rested, stretched to its limit for an easier break. And Pete knew at once that the knuckles hadn't broken, the impact absorbed by the soft flesh. He squirmed anyway, desperate to convince them of success, in case they smashed his hand a second time. The burns no longer hurt, the twine no longer induced terror, the fear of a broken hand over-shadowing all horrors and now relieved.

'Just to be certain,' the New Henchman suggested, 'one final reminder. It won't do you any harm. Not if you get it back in, in time. If not, it'll save us the trouble of using you again!'

And someone knelt across Pete's back, removed the twine from his face and neck, slit through the baling twine to release his arms, leaned into his right shoulder and snapped back his right elbow, dislocating his arm at the shoulder.

The New Henchman laughed. 'It's his party piece. You may want to ring for an ambulance!'

They laughed, as a small object thudded close to Pete's face, under his nose.

Pete knew from their taunt that it must be his mobile; a final wicked twist of the knife. Then they were gone; doors banging shut, voices fading.

Blind misery. Blinding agony.

Seb had warned him not to come home. Seb had booked him into a hotel in Epsom, before disappearing with the life buoy in the shape of stake money stolen from a charity. Seb was Casburg's silent partner, just as Westy had suggested.

Pete tried to shut out the thoughts; feverish nonsense rising from the pain. A pain that engulfed him in a myriad of colours, hazy rainbows, destroying reason. Yet thoughts crept in, alarm bells, cries for help, doubts.

The cries for help screamed the loudest. Westy. A million miles away in Epsom. Sophie.

Suddenly the prisms cleared enough for him to grasp the fact that he was naked on the floor. The realisation burnt into him more than the cigarettes. He couldn't let her find him like this. The vulnerability and humiliation...

He couldn't see. His eyes were open, staring at blackness; the spinning colours no more than tears. The phone, he knew, was near him, somewhere, offering salvation.

But he had first to get dressed. The urgency sharpened his brain, focused his thoughts on more practical tasks, locking out the agony. One good arm. Fingers not broken. The relief of that message was sufficient to obliterate their swollen condition, kid his body into thinking they were still usable, as he slowly raised his hand to his face and fumbled numbly for the hood.

It was removed; the sudden light equally blinding.

He recoiled mentally as unknown fingers brushed his lips. *His* fingers, unrecognisably swollen, too numb to register the contact. His heart had jumped, but mercifully no physical jolts. Any movement to his arm and he'd be gone...

He pulled helplessly at the cloth in his mouth, feeling its successful withdrawal with tongue and lips, not fingers. But they weren't broken. Not broken...

He could see clothes, just within his line of vision, but too far beyond it to be recognised. He didn't want to move. Couldn't move. Could only reach out a tentative hand and hope for trousers. Not torn shirt or jacket. Please not shirt or jacket...

He fetched the material up to his face – the jacket; and wept. The agonising twist of muscles in his shoulder raged across his whole body. Nothing could keep the pain from dominating every nerve, every thought... think of trousers, of Sophie; don't let her find him like this.

He stretched out a leg, hit the thick suit cloth, not shirt; pushed at it with his knee; grasped it in useless fingers that repeatedly presented thin air as his empty hand rose to his face. Then material.

After that, it didn't matter that he still had to get them on. He just lay in temporary satisfaction, winning. Besting them still, despite their strongest efforts. Unbroken, like his hand.

To get up, he would need to put weight on his right side. Or turn his head. Either option was impossible. Westy could come, and dress him, and say nothing of it ever again. And Sophie could come and undress him and make everything perfect. And Seb had done this. Had tried to protect him from it because he had seen it coming, and knew...

He realised that his thoughts were jumbled and fantastical. He was afraid to move in case he passed out, but had passed out anyway. For how long? How long did he have left? Might as well move and faint, move and faint, until it was done, than just lie here in delirium, achieving nothing. He couldn't go to hospital, face examinations, see his medical book handed over to officialdom. He couldn't let

Sophie find him like this.

He couldn't get up.

He slowly drew a knee up; somehow got a foot through a trouser leg, assured it was the correct one by the zip flies pressed to his face, to catch out the lying fingers. One leg in. Partially. A quick cry, not in pain, in victory. Get the tears shed before Sophie comes...

To draw up the other knee... every twist of the back, no matter how slight, sent shockwaves of protest flooding from his shoulder. Lots more tears. Had to be good; less left. And no pain from the burns. The bastards hadn't hurt him. And they hadn't broken his hand. And they hadn't left him naked; not any more.

He could just see his phone, just see his fingers and the keypad. Should have set up speed dial. Instead, fumbled laboriously through lists, hitting wrong buttons, two buttons at once, not pressing firmly enough; hearing it ring; and ring; and ring. And ring out. Trying again, same mistakes, then the ring.

'Pete?'

'I'm hurt.'

CHAPTER TWELVE

No more than minutes elapsed.

Pete heard the urgent fumbling at the door and was powerless to help.

'Pete?' Sophie called through the letter box.

'Across the hall,' he called back, 'she has a spare key.'

Again there came the noise at the door, this time a key in the lock, the door crashing open, banging against a wall. Pete managed to have the presence of mind to shout a plea to Sophie, just as she sprinted towards him.

'Don't touch me!'

He saw her feet stop dead, close to where he lay; his very own guardian angel. And there was another set of feet, she'd fetched her father; oh god, she was an angel...

'Go and put the kettle on, love,' David said.

A whole family, full of angels.

Sophie did as she was asked, without question, and David knelt down beside Pete.

'Now, don't, whatever you do, move,' he warned, unnecessarily.

He placed one hand under Pete's limp arm, at the shoulder, and firmly gripped the elbow. Pete closed his eyes and wished wholeheartedly for the foul-tasting leg bandage, but a sharp and loud '*SHIT!*' was enough to see him through. It may have been a first for him, but the Newmarket gallops had been littered with dislocations throughout David's lengthy career.

'Okay?'

'Ummm.' He couldn't quite speak yet.

David picked up the torn shirt and slipped it over the arm he still supported, helping Pete to turn and sit up and slipping in the other arm. Pete himself tested his newly-restored arm and did up his trousers, so that he looked dishevelled but decent by the time Sophie fetched in three mugs of tea. He remained sitting on the floor, in the middle of the living room, and Sophie and David merely sat down on the floor beside him.

'Next stop, Casualty,' David told him, 'get that hand x-rayed.'

'It's not broken,' Pete insisted.

'It hardly matters; I've seen your other hand and you won't be riding for a while, regardless of what your medical book says. So it's Casualty and x-rays.'

Sophie, listening, stole a glance at the other hand in question and wordlessly slipped back out to the kitchen; returning with a bag of frozen mixed vegetables. Pete took them from her, marvelling at the lack of fuss and total expertise of his personal, perfect, angel. Already, he couldn't live without her.

'I'll go and lay out some clothes for you,' David said, finishing his tea and making an excuse to leave them alone.

'Where are your medical things?' Sophie asked Pete calmly, 'bathroom?'

He nodded, about to tell her where and what was available, but she was already gone. She came back in with the tube of gel and some gauze and bandages, dressing his burnt fingers. And a glass of water and a pain-killer.

'Just one,' she told him, 'in case they give you something stronger at out-patients.' She held pill and water to his lips, with the skill and detachment of a hardened nurse; then set about dressing the burn on his back. There was nothing humiliating or degrading about being tended so divinely.

'Is your Mum an angel too?' he asked.

'What?'

He smiled at her; wanting her.

She smiled back. 'When you're ready, Dad'll take us to Adenbrookes.'

'I only need an icepack, to get the swelling down.'

'Then they'll give you an icepack! But let them be the judge, eh?'

He grinned, happy to lose just this one battle.

'And we're fetching you back home with us. Mum insists, so it's the law.'

'I won't argue, then.'

He finished his tea, a much-needed refreshment and a warm welcome back to normality.

'No word yet from Seb, I take it?'

Sophie shook her head, her face clouding with renewed anxiety. 'He didn't buy your way out of this mess, either.'

'So he's still busy playing up his winnings, or plucking up the courage to come home and face the music.'

'God, I hope so.'

Pete stood up. It wasn't so bad, after all. His hands hurt like hell; but they took his mind off the burn on his back and the dull ache of his shoulder muscles. His foot was already forgotten. He caught Sophie's eye, as she gazed up at him, smiling slightly quizzically.

'You're actually grinning,' she said, in some wonder.

His grin broadened. 'I was just counting my blessings. You'd be surprised!'

'That's the codeine kicking in!'

'Yeah, well, I feel like shit, but at least it takes my mind off other troubles!' He instinctively held out a hand to her, to help her up, but withdrew it hastily. 'Nearly! I'd better go and get dressed; you've enough on your plate, without spending the whole night at Adenbrookes.'

'Shouldn't be too busy, with luck.'

He walked, comfortably enough, to the bedroom, reflecting that his original Mr Henchman had inflicted more muscular damage, even if his friends this evening had been more specific in their cruelty.

David sat on the bed, loose cotton slacks and shirt carefully chosen and laid out alongside him.

'Sophie filled me in a bit, on the way over,' he told Pete, 'and I really ought to tell you to go to the Jockey Club.'

'But?'

'Well… Sebastian has already put himself in an horrendous position. And this can only make matters worse.'

'I wasn't actually planning to go the Jockey Club. I wasn't actually planning on this to happen, either. There's going to be a next time. But next time, I'm going to deal with it.'

David stood up, and helped him with buttons and zip.

'Also,' he said hesitantly, 'and please don't take this the wrong way, but Sophie seems... a bit keen.'

Pete took it exactly the way it was intended. 'I'm married and I have a lousy reputation.'

'Apparently, neither is true?'

'Barbara has left me, but I'm still married. And I haven't actually done anything to earn it, but I do have a lousy reputation.' He smiled ruefully. 'Thank you, for not taking those things into consideration when you put my arm back.'

David smiled. 'Sophie's a grown woman, independent. It really isn't any of my business; but I have to care.' He held out a hand. Pete raised his own, one bandaged, one blue and swollen.

'Sorry.' David grinned. 'Welcome to the family, anyway.'

Casualty was mercifully quiet and they returned to the Churchills' home still on the right side of midnight, no more than burnt fingers keeping Pete from riding. The hand had escaped even minor fractures, much to everyone's surprise bar Pete's.

There was no fussing, and no embarrassed silence on the subject of his injuries; removing any awkwardness from his already awkward position. It was enough to welcome in a prospective in-law who was married, non-Harrow, unsuccessful and a bit of a playboy. To have had to scrape him up off the floor first could hardly have compounded the situation any worse.

Sophie showed Pete up to his room, a large double bed thoughtfully fitted with a single duvet in the centre and an array of pillows around its perimeter.

'I don't know what else they did and I'm not going to ask,' she told him, 'but one way or another you ought to be able to get a comfortable night's sleep.'

He kissed her with overwhelming gratitude.

And she was right; despite everything, he slept well.

His fingers, on both hands, had benefited enough from the passing of seven hours to enable him to get dressed without calling for assistance. Last night, on top of all evils, it had hardly mattered; this morning it counted for much. Down in the kitchen, he found only Angela, opting out of morning stables to hold the fort.

'Breakfast?' she offered. 'If you don't mind waiting till they come back in off the gallops, I can do you a nice big fry up?'

Being out of the saddle for a few days had its benefits.

'Thanks, that'd be great.'

'Sophie will be back in with them. She saw to Sebastian's string first.'

'Still no word?'

Angela shook her head. 'We're out of our

minds with worry. Sophie told the yard he's staying in Baden-Baden with Walter Casburg. There are two horses going over for a race tomorrow, so it's not unreasonable. We seem to be the only ones missing him.'

'Has he ever disappeared before?'

'Never. A natural born ostrich – head in the sand, always. Right up to the point when the head man at some betting office knocks at our door looking for thousands. Sebastian would breeze around, still thinking nothing will happen, we'll never find out. The same hopeless optimism that lures him in in the first place. He doesn't run away from problems, he just ignores them.'

'How long will you give him?'

Angela pulled up a chair and sat beside him. 'The police already know. But they'll do nothing until tomorrow. Right now, he's officially avoiding us, in pubs and clubs. Tomorrow he becomes a worry. I get the impression it will be a week or more before they genuinely worry. People go missing every day of the week, I'm told.'

'With thirty grand?'

'We didn't actually mention that. Until the bank opens this morning, we don't even know that.' She sighed wearily. 'Which reminds me, you'd better phone Danny Western, he's been ringing you incessantly from about six o'clock this morning.' She pushed his own mobile phone across the table to him. 'You left it here last night. In the end, when we saw it was the same number coming up, we thought we'd better answer it. David told him you were out on the gallops.'

'Bloody hell, I forgot all about him. Thanks.'
Pete picked up the mobile and rang Western at once;
while Angela rose and loaded their cups into the
dishwasher, trying not to eavesdrop.

'Westy!'

'Allen, you bastard! So you're in off the
gallops?' His voice was heavy with sarcasm. 'I
phoned some work-watchers and you weren't out on
Seb's string this morning. And they were all on
Racecourse Side two minutes ago, watching the
Churchill string.'

'Yeah, well, the run-in didn't go so
smoothly.'

'Out of action?'

'A day or two.'

'Fuck. And the tape? Was it worth it?'

'Not exactly.'

'Oh for fuck's sake, Allen, are you a
complete idiot or what! Did you get *anything*?'

'Sore, actually, thanks for your concern.'

'But they won't bother using you again
because you're so unreliable and a total moron to
boot?'

'Wrong again. But don't worry, I have a
plan.'

'Do you now? How very reassuring! Are we
still on for tonight? Or are you laying in Adenbrookes
right now?'

'Still on.'

'See you then, sunshine.'

Pete was happy for him to ring off without

asking for details of the plan in question. Angela probably already believed he was a louse. But a violent, vengeful louse? Even the charm of the Churchills had a limit. He didn't even want Sophie to know…

About thirty minutes later, Sophie and David, and various assistants and work riders, flooded the kitchen and kept Angela busy over the stove. The fry-up was a happy compromise, the usual evils but reduced by an electric grill, yet no less enjoyable for Pete as the first eaten since February. Then the kitchen emptied once more, the staff filing back to the yard.

'I have to go back down to the office,' David apologised, 'now, Sophie, it's up to yourself, you can wait here with Mum while I saddle both our runners today – you don't have to represent Sebastian, you know?'

'I'll think about it,' she agreed.

As soon as David had gone, Sophie helped Angela finish loading the dishwasher, then took Pete down for a walk round the yard, introducing him to the eighty horses currently in residence. At the offset of Pete's career he had been in too high demand to ride for David; in more recent years, not good enough for the standard of animal David trained. He couldn't help wondering if his relationship with Sophie might shift the balance again; as he fed the stable stars polo mints from between his lips, his arm around their trainer's daughter.

'The bank staff will be in shortly,' Sophie said, glancing at her watch, 'we'll go back in and I'll ring them. If they can't help over the phone, I'll have to go up in person when they open.'

'He didn't bank it, Soph'. Why else would he do a bunk?'

'I know. But I have to know for sure, just in case.'

Back at the house, they sat anxiously in the living room while Sophie made her call, Angela studying her face intently, not wishing to wait for the words to end her suspense.

Sebastian hadn't, of course, banked the takings.

'We would have been even more worried if he had,' Angela pointed out.

'If he'd banked it, he'd be here now, sparing us this worry!' Sophie said hotly, suddenly feeling justifiably angry with her brother. 'He must know what he's putting us through. All his life he's been irresponsible. Never grown up, never damn well had to!'

'Look, love...' David began, trying to console her.

But Pete was already out of his seat, offering a sympathetic hug and words of wisdom.

'He's growing up right now, on his own, without any of your support or guidance,' he reminded her. 'That's why he's not here, where he ought to be. It's tough on all of you, but bloody tougher on him right now.'

It may have cooled Sophie's temper, but it broke Angela's composure at once.

'I'll go to Epsom,' Sophie told her father, 'you stay home here with Mum.'

No one offered any argument.

Pete reluctantly made his excuses, errands to run that he would rather not discuss in advance. He said instead that he had to get home, tidy up the flat, have a bath – the mundane chores sounding genuine and pressing.

He kissed Sophie goodbye, out in the hall; eyes closed, senses drowning within the embrace, never wanting to let go. Later, he wondered regretfully when he and Barbara had stopped kissing... the casual brush of lips in greeting, in farewell, meaning nothing. They hadn't needed to cling to such moments of passion, when passion could be had anytime, at their leisure, in the comfort of bed. To have that intense passion, without sex...

He thought only of Sophie, and not Barbara, as he tidied the flat, eased aching muscles in the bath, and dressed his burnt fingers to allow more movement and use. He also thought of Paul Smith and his colleagues, who liked to moonlight before going on duty at Seb's. When they set things up, it was on their own terms, no matter how ready and prepared he considered himself to be. So if he set something up, he would at last get his voice heard. How prepared could they be for the sudden, unexpected retaliation of a cripple with burnt and swollen fingers?

He walked across to Sebastian's yard, finding the three daytime security guards sitting around the fountain in the centre of the stable yard, lapping up the August sunshine and reading newspapers. They paid him scant regard, his presence only adding to their opportunity to relax, another set of eyes and ears within an unthreatened yard.

He wandered around the back of the main block of stables, to the tack room, feed rooms, inspection box, storage rooms left open and filled with stable sheets, wheelbarrows, brooms and forks. And portacabin, bearing the logo of the security firm. Inside, he found it to be no more than a small square office, as grey inside as out, with a sink and kitchen cabinet, a table and chairs, and a television set, which at night monitored the stable yard. At the far end, another door, which he found led through to a toilet.

Standing on the toilet, he found that he could comfortably reach the window, which flapped open only enough to allow ventilation. With much force and smashing of glass, it would allow the passage of a body, should that body require such urgent passage. Outside, there was a fairly high drop, down onto concrete.

Back in the main room, there were similar, larger, windows, one each side. And just the one door, in and out.

Pete unhooked the fire extinguisher from the tiny lobby between main room and toilet; also removing the extinguisher in the main room. He carried them out with him and stored them neatly with the barrows and brooms and forks. Back in the portacabin, nothing heavy enough to inflict damage. And the absence of the extinguishers unnoticeable.

Satisfied, he carried a grooming kit box from

the tack room round to the stables and nodded a goodbye to the guards as he passed them, depositing the kit box outside the stable office door. It had been an unnecessary diversion, the guards not interested in his movements or actions anyway.

And now there remained the rest of the day and much of the evening to kill.

The afternoon was dealt with in comfort, relaxing on the sofa in front of a brand new television set, watching Epsom races. Then ringing Sophie to congratulate her on saddling the winner his burnt fingers had cost him. Then making some dinner, killing more time.

After that, the passing of minutes ground to a halt. He wandered down the High Street and into The Golden Lion, far too early to meet Western, but needing some excuse to speed the passing of time. Already a few early arrivals were filtering back from Epsom; those, like Western, who had to stay for the dying moments, still en route.

Pete joined a group of lads from a yard he'd once ridden for and started the evening with a whisky, making it last long enough for Western's arrival. He didn't want to get drunk, anymore than he wanted to pile on weight with pints of lager. He wanted to be at home, with Sophie...

Before Western arrived, Sophie herself rang.

'I'm going to Baden-Baden tomorrow,' she announced, before the usual hellos, as though expecting an argument.

'Can't Roddy go?'

'Roddy is under the impression Sebastian's there already, with Walter. And with you out of action, I have to book a jockey.'

'I've got most of their mobile numbers, if you want to ring round?' Pete offered, a last grasp to keep her at home. He might need her...

'I checked the declarations, all the top riders are booked already. It's a matter of turning up early and catching someone in the weighing room in search of a spare ride.'

'What time are you flying out?'

'I'm travelling over with the horses myself. Our travelling head lad's going up to York, we've three runners up there. So I'll be going out in the small box to Stansted straight before morning stables, at five, I suppose.'

It was expected, but no less painful.

'I'm meeting Danny Western in a minute, I'm going to be too late back tonight,' he apologised, 'I won't come back to Seb's and disturb you. I really owe a big favour to Westy, I can't let him down. But tomorrow night, I promise you – Seb's, or your own flat, or my place, just say the word.'

He could hear her smile. 'One night won't kill us.'

'It's killing me!'

'Then come back to Sebastian's and disturb me. At least you can sleep in!'

It was oh so tempting. But if things didn't quite go to plan... it wouldn't be the first time the terms he'd set out had been brutally disregarded. He couldn't take the risk.

'Tomorrow night, Sophie-suds. Tomorrow night and every night. I promise.'

He returned the phone to his pocket, the table full of Newmarket stable lads now slightly rearranged, making way for an extra person.

'*Sophie-suds*? As in Churchill?'

Danny Western, sitting directly alongside him, grinning broadly.

'What, you don't know already?' Pete teased, 'You'd never make a hack!'

'Tomorrow night and every night!' Western mocked. 'Every night till Mrs Allen gets back! Bloody bastard!'

Pete said goodnight to the lads and stood up, signalling Western to follow him to a quieter spot. Western followed, still shaking his head incredulously.

'She's not coming back,' Pete told him. 'It ended months ago.'

'So this is serious?' He continued to shake his head. 'Please don't tell me she chucked Golden Bats, *for you*!'

'My wife left me, some sympathy wouldn't go amiss.'

'You pulled Sophie Churchill! Don't look to anyone here for sympathy, you jammy beggar!'

'Yeah, yeah, so what's this dirt you've dished?' Pete prompted.

'Aha, glad you asked.' Western leaned forward. 'Paul Smith is employed by anyone who needs a heavy from time to time. One crowd, an independent bookie out in Cambridge, already has its

197

own crew. But one of the team sprained a wrist...'

'Sprained a wrist?'

'Yeah, pathetic, eh? Maybe it's a euphemism for being sent down for GBH! Anyway, they were one short, and one punter too many at the dog track owing money, so they recruited your pal. They didn't take to him. He's a bit too serious, they say – a cruel streak. Wasn't one for supplying just a bit of muscle, as they put it.'

'The crowd with a sprained wrist?'

Western laughed. 'They're serious sorts themselves, they knocked back steaks and pints like Britain's Strongest Man. Expense account, but you can offer to pay me anyway.' Reminded, he downed much of his own pint. 'Anyhow, he bragged a bit. Seems his brother is even worse than he is, has a little speciality, a party piece they called it, dislocating arms for a laugh. Fun, eh? So you may count your blessings, sunshine, that it's Paul who stalks your yard and not Steve.' He finished his pint. 'What are you drinking?'

'Glenfiddich.'

Western crossed to the bar, returning armed with crisps and drinks.

'So where were we?' he asked, making inroads on both. 'Steve Smith. Works for an operation in Germany, drug dealers. Your pal Paul can get his friends anything they want. The Cambridge crowd were offered a few lines of coke for gratis, seems Steve Smith is swimming in the stuff, the amount he escorts round the continent.' He leaned forward once more. 'Now, here's the thing. I asked the Post's

German correspondent to dig dirt on Casburg's German connections, but there was no dirt. He likes to entertain prominent German businessmen, all very above board. Lots of names, such as one, Straubinger. Then I ran a few checks, elsewhere, on the Smith brothers. Steve Smith works for one Straubinger. Whether Casurg actually knows it or not, his business cronies include a Mr Big in the drugs world. And, by all accounts, a fucking dangerous one, too.'

'And they employ brothers.'

Western emptied the dregs of the crisp packet into his mouth. 'That's yet another coincidence. A lesser hack than myself, such as tabloid, would already be linking Casburg with Straubinger's drug activities and be asking who kitted out the casino's penthouses with cocaine.'

'Isn't there an outlet over there called South America?' Pete asked.

'I did say a lesser hack. But, maybe Casburg has a habit and needs a European dealer.'

'Meanwhile,' Pete posed the problem, 'my Paul Smith works for anyone with a pay cheque to offer. So you're basically none the wiser as to who is paying him to give me orders?'

'My money's on Seb,' Western insisted, 'trying to pay back Casburg. Incidentally, still no word on the young Churchill. Notably absent from Epsom these last two days, questions will be asked.'

'He's said to be at Baden-Baden with Casburg,' Pete told him.

'Good call and highly likely, too. Searched the Deauville gaming halls, but forgot all about the ones in Baden.' Western smiled, then turned his attention to Pete's left hand. The two sore fingers on the right were so discreetly taped that they escaped notice.

'Please tell me you did that on a chin?'

Pete shook his head. 'A deliberate blow to my medical book. With worse to follow, next time.'

'You said you had a plan? When?'

'Tonight.'

Western sat back in his chair and laughed outright.

'With that hand?!'

'I won't need it,' Pete said confidently, 'it's going to be my turn to set the demands and issue the threats.'

'I'm coming with you.'

It was Pete's turn to sit back and laugh. 'And you think my injured hand is a hindrance?! I'm an athlete, fit – you're an over-weight pen-pusher!'

'One step up from a fat bastard, which means we're making progress. I'm coming with you.' It was clear from his tone that he was not going to back down.

'Fine,' Pete agreed reluctantly, 'but I haven't told you the plan yet.'

CHAPTER THIRTEEN

The stable yard was in near-darkness. Some small solar lights lit the fountain and flower beds, the moon making a reasonable attempt at illuminating all else. It was sufficient to get Pete and Western safely round to the back of the stables without torches or accidents.

The portacabin itself was well lit from within, no blinds at the windows to block out the glare of interior lights and television set. The voices through the open windows suggested the three night watchmen were engrossed in a game of cards.

First, the threat. Then, the demand.

Pete crept silently up to the door and inserted the key he'd taken from the stable office, turning it gently until the door was locked; leaving the key half-turned in the lock, to prevent a key entering from the inside and pushing it out. Then he and Western peeled off either side of the door, the journalist to one window, Pete to the other.

Hopefully in unison, though neither could be sure what the other was actually doing, they each poured a tin of lighter fluid over a cotton duster, from the bottom of which dangled a hefty chunk of polystyrene, once the packaging from a television set. Lowering their respective dusters and polystyrene blocks through the open windows, they hooked them onto the fastening, struck a match, and pushed the windows shut. Then backed away rapidly, to view proceedings from a healthy distance.

Their actions had been spotted at once, even before the familiar scratch, fizz of the matches. But the polystyrene flared so quickly and repugnantly that it couldn't be approached, immediately filling the confined space with a noxious stench.

The occupants of the portacabin couldn't be seen from outside, the windows obscured by thick black smoke. But Pete was pretty certain they had only one place to retreat to, the smoking windows blocking an attempt for the door. They wouldn't be able to afford the time to endeavour to get a key in, once finding it to be locked.

Sure enough, amid yelling and curses came the sound of the toilet window being hammered at. Many bangs before the shattering of glass; but with the shattering of glass, Pete and Western made their hasty and total exit from the yard.

'We should wait, to see they all get out,' Western suggested, as he followed Pete at a run, out onto the road and across to the opposite side and the secure trails of horse walks that would get them back to Pete's flat.

'I tried it at home, it hardly burns for long, after the initial flare.'

'They might be overcome by fumes.'

'Serve the bastards right.'

They returned to the pavement and a more sedate pace.

'You'd want to be mad to fuck with Pete Allen!' Western said.

'You think we made that point, then?'

'Pretty much, sunshine.'

Before nearing the flat, under the assumption all three guards were now out and recovering their breath in the yard, Western rang the stable office, ensuring his own mobile number was locked as private. The phone rang for an agonising length of time.

'Don't ask them if they all got out,' Pete warned.

'Yeah, yeah, we don't give a fuck, we're thugs,' Western agreed; and the ringing stopped.

'Next time, you won't get out,' Western said menacingly, hoping he wouldn't hear a bemused Sebastian or Roddy in response, 'you tell your boss the Pete Allen account is closed and isn't to be reopened.' And he hung up.

'Was it them? Could you hear anything?' Pete demanded.

'My heart pounding in my ears. Other than that, fuck all.' He exhaled heavily. 'You know the worse thing? I thought I'd get a fit of laughter! All that next time business and I was struggling not to laugh.'

'You'd scare the shit out of me.'

'You can pay me the going thug rate, then.'

They returned to Pete's flat, largely because they had little choice. It was already two in the morning and too late to hide from retaliation. Pete dialled the local police and hung up before it actually rang.

'Hit redial,' he told Western, 'if anything happens.'

'Sprinklers, extinguishers and a fire escape?' Western asked.

'Got them all.'

'Then I'll hit the sack.'

Pete couldn't wind down quite so rapidly and made himself a coffee, sitting in the blackness of the living room, lights off, staring down at the outside street. He might have succeeded in forcing his would-be employer to look elsewhere for heavies, or to give up altogether in the issuing of riding instructions... or opened up a complete new can of worms altogether. The latter option hardly mattered. Any next time for him would take him out of the saddle, permanently.

Eventually, with no sign of life outside, he retired to bed, but not to the comfort of sleep.

The morning brought with it no repercussions from the late night activities. Western cursed heartily from the kitchen, bemoaning the limited breakfast options. The phone rang persistently, trainers looking to book Pete and enquire after his health. His health, battered as it was by nerves and lack of sleep, would see him back in the saddle – Jockey Club medical officer willing – within the week. Satisfied, the phone calls petered out. Western's abuse did not.

'For all its faults, The Golden Lion makes this place seem like the Black Hole of Calcutta,' he complained, staring into the fridge as though will power alone would magically stock it.

'There's toast, cereals, eggs...' Pete suggested.

'Cornflakes! And what shall I put on them – this watered down excuse for milk...' he picked up the small wax carton, the lack of weight a reasonable indication of its content, '...or some Lanson? It'll have to be the bubbly, won't it – seeing as how you haven't even got enough milk for a decent cup of tea!'

'Porridge,' Pete offered, deliberately winding him up, 'you make it with water.'

'No, *you* make it with water. The rest of us use milk.' He closed the door disdainfully. 'Fuck, I can't believe I'm even having this conversation! Who eats porridge anyway? Horses eat oats – we eat sausages and bacon and fried eggs.' He delved back into the fridge and retrieved a couple of eggs and some tomatoes. 'Have you even got a frying pan?'

'That drawer, under the cooker.'

He bent down and found salvation. 'Want some?'

'I'd kill for some, but I'll probably be riding Monday.'

Western gave him a sideways glance. 'You would, as well – I've seen you in action. No one fucks with Pete Allen!'

The kitchen was soon filled with the aroma of frying bread, eggs and tomatoes.

'Ever been to Istanbul for the Turkish Derby?' Pete asked Western, sitting at the table with well-buttered toast; Monday still just far enough off.

'Christ, yeah. It wouldn't kill them to use a frying pan in the morning, either! Cucumber for breakfast! You lot would have been in your element.'

'I won it, you know. I've ridden three Derby winners.'

'Turkish, German and Italian?'

'Turkish, Norwegian and Italian.'

'Not exactly Epsom.'

'No, not exactly. Life's a bitch, eh?'

Western buttered a slice of bread, mopping up the remains on his breakfast plate. 'Yours is. When exactly did you decide to flush it down the pan?' He ate the bread, his stare fixed firmly on Pete. 'Come on, the low-down, now – fast cars, fast women and a betting account, when did they hook you? Is it the price of fame and wealth?'

'The price of fame and wealth!' Pete laughed. 'You sound like a tabloid headline. Are you scratching for a story?'

'I'm always scratching for a story. And I'm interested. You really don't seem like the flash bugger we always took you for.'

'Cheers, mate. You're every bit the fat gutter pressman we always took you for. Just less of a bastard.'

'Can I quote you on that?!'

'Quote me on anything you like!'

Western laughed and sat back, sipping a nearly-black tea distastefully. 'I believed you, you know – the other evening at York when you protested your innocence. No one's ever deliberately stopped a horse, even though we chase the myth every day of the week. It would be the scoop of the century. But why did your career nosedive and how come you're topping the current most wanted?'

Pete smiled. 'You see – that's the journalist in you. You know it's a myth but you still dig for that connection.'

'Is there one?'

Pete shrugged. 'I suppose so. If I hadn't

blown it in the big league I wouldn't have needed to start gambling. And If I hadn't started gambling I wouldn't have got my name linked with bookies and players.'

'Did you blow it by selling info'?'

'Piss off, Westy! I didn't blow it at all. It was your lot, and the TV crowd. Too young for the responsibility. Wouldn't be a match for the top riders without the apprentice's allowance. Too inexperienced for such a big retainer. The usual hysteria. If the Marchant horses had been firing on all cylinders, the headlines would have come to nothing; I'd have gone from Champion Apprentice to Champion Jockey in a single season. Every jockey who rides for Nick Marchant wins the Championship.'

'Except you.'

Pete smiled ruefully. 'The Marchant horses were off-colour in the opening weeks and we didn't get the results expected. And I got the blame. Marchant got damning press, too. He should have gone for experience, not glamour. They made him out to be an idiot. So he got shot of me fast.' He smiled again, a grin in admission of guilt. 'I was also a cocky little bastard, which didn't help matters! But what the hell, eh? I was Champion Apprentice and I'd landed the Marchant retainer. Why shouldn't I be cocky?!'

'I wasn't in the game, then. But I'd have written the same headlines. It's news, isn't it?'

'Like race fixing,' Pete agreed bitterly. 'Trainers run their horses over the wrong trip to fool the handicapper, that's tactics. We ease a horse at the line, to fool the handicapper – that's your sensational race-fixing headline.'

Western shook his head. 'You ease it and get beaten, what else can we do but scream injustice? Mind you, you never actually have, have you?'

'I wouldn't dare.' Pete grinned more broadly. 'I'm still the star who landed the Marchant retainer, remember – I don't need to ease a horse at the line! I can set up the result long before the finish! Simple errors of judgement. If my horse takes a hundred yards to reach full pace, I don't ask him for an effort until eighty yards out. If he can only sustain his pace for a hundred yards, I ask him for an effort a hundred and ten yards out.'

'You stop it.'

Pete conceded defeat. 'In a word, yes.'

'And selling information?'

'I don't. I told Bisley I was on a loser, to clear my account.'

'And that keeps the Porsche in petrol?'

Pete smiled. 'If a happy punter gives me a fiver from his winnings, I fill her up.'

'You accept presents?'

'I stop horses, I accept presents. And I had a betting account. I lose my licence on three counts. But if you take out your leading, journalistic words, I've not actually done anything wrong. I don't physically pull a horse, I don't stop a horse, as you put it.'

'Three counts of a warning off, though,' Western pointed out mildly.

'So I look after a horse, go easy on it, if the trainer and owner ask? That's no more than the handicapper would actually do to it if it won – just weight the poor bloody animal out of its next few races. And presents? What the hell! Do you think I'm going to risk my licence for a few bob? Stop a horse on some Joe Punter's say so? I'll tell them what they want to know, if it's not a stable secret, and I'll pocket the present, if I get one. But we're lousy tipsters, you know that! I get more presents from Father Christmas!'

'But we're not exactly chasing a myth?'

'Your tabloid front page headline is just a broadsheet two line filler.' He looked at Western, wondering. If the tape had been whirring, his licence would be gone by the morning. At what point had he learned to trust a racing hack? At what point had he accepted Barbara's departure and fallen in love for a second time? Life was full of surprises.

'What are you missing today?' Western asked, 'Lingfield or York?'

'Baden-Baden.'

'Just as well, then, what with Straubinger and his party animal paying court on Casburg. You don't really want to be running into either of the Smith brothers for a while.'

'Sophie's there.'

'If her only vice is a bad taste in jockeys she'll be safe enough.'

Pete had his doubts. The constant and overwhelming need to be with her had been increased by an ominous fear. The Smith brothers and their party pieces in his flat, he could cope with. But their presence at Baden-Baden, with Sophie…

'I'm going over anyway,' he told Western.

'For Christ's sake, Pete, stay away. After last night… have you got a death wish?'

'Paul Smith's here in Newmarket. Steve Smith might not even be at the races – why would he be?'

'So why go?'

'Love.'

'You poor sucker!' He downed his tea and stood up. 'Lingfield beckons. Watch yourself, sunshine. Guten tag.'

They both vacated the kitchen; Western to gather up his things and set off for Lingfield Park, Pete to change back out of jeans and t-shirt and into a more appropriate suit for an afternoon at the races. He was already running an hour late against central European time and could only hope that there were seats available on the earliest flights. On the off chance, he rang the airstrip at Cambridge, hoping a taxi plane would be carrying over an owner or trainer for the German spa meeting, but without success.

As he drove to Stansted, he tried to convince himself that it was an unnecessary journey, but the feeling of unease could not be shaken. It was necessary, if only for his own peace of mind.

Had he arrived at the picturesque racecourse on the edge of the Black Forest purely for the racing, he would have been disappointed. The runners for the third race were already returning to unsaddle as he strolled through the gates, Sophie easily spotted in the wrong part of the winners' circle, greeting Sebastian's charge in the runner-up spot. Casburg was with her, mercifully alone.

Pete crossed the paddock and went straight to the weighing room, to wait for Sophie. In all his afternoons spent on German racetracks, he'd never seen the Smith brothers or indeed any of Casburg's associates. But he had rarely seen Casburg, for that matter, the owner hidden away in a private box. Who shared the facilities with him had never before been considered and was anyone's guess. This afternoon it might even be Sebastian, victorious from the German tables and ready to come home.

He nodded to his German colleagues and leaned on the rail beside the scales, his unexpected presence halting Sophie mid-stride as she followed in her jockey. He grinned and stepped forward to greet her.

'What on earth...'

'I just couldn't bear not seeing our runners.'

She smiled. 'You big softie.'

'I was bored at home. And I missed you.'

They leant on the wooden rail together, waiting for the riders to weigh out for the next race.

'I asked them which flight the horses were on,' Pete told her, 'but I couldn't get your flight back, I'm going to be half an hour ahead of you.'

'One of Walter's lads flew over with the horses, but he's not coming back. We've room for an extra flying groom.'

He gestured to his Italian suit. 'I don't think so. You won't be far behind me, anyway. I'll stick the kettle on!'

Sophie shook her head. 'All this way, just for an hour or so!'

'An hour of your company! And I'd hoped to get here earlier.'

Sophie glanced around cautiously. 'I'm glad you came. Walter knows nothing about Sebastian. He was surprised to see me. I told him Sebastian had gone to York.'

'Christ, it's not looking so good, is it?'

'Dad says there's a hundred clubs he could be in. For three days, Pete?'

'Three weeks isn't long enough for the Deauville crowd,' Pete pointed out, 'they've all moved on here.'

'But Sebastian hasn't. Walter would surely have run into him.'

'Your dad's right, Soph' – there're a hundred clubs. Seb could be anywhere.'

The jockeys filed through to weigh out. Sophie took the saddle and cloths for Sebastian's runner in the fourth race and Pete followed her out to the saddling boxes.

'What if he isn't at a club?' Sophie suggested as they walked through the paddock.

'He would have been in touch already.'

'Or the police would.' She shifted the saddle from right arm to left. 'Mum rings round the hospitals every morning. Every one of them. She downloaded a full list from the internet. And she never even goes on the computer.' She smiled, without humour. 'Amazing what you can learn when you need to.'

212

They approached the pre-parade ring, a number of people already crowded round the rails for an early view of the runners. Just a typical racecourse scene, only the many pet dogs present making it uniquely German. As Sophie slipped through the archway into the ring, she smiled in recognition and nodded to a spectator close by. Pete followed her through, his attention caught by Sebastian's filly, just walking past. He was about to remark on her well-being, when she took fright at a small dog by the rails and gave the girl leading her up an awkward few seconds before settling.

'Typical filly!' he remarked, 'we've a hundred dogs running round the yard at home and she spooks at that particular one!'

'She's had her fill of dogs today,' Sophie told him, 'the little customs spaniel at the airport barked its head off at her! Good job Steve, there, had hold of her,' she nodded towards the Steve in question, watching from the rails, 'Sally would have lost her.'

Pete followed her glance, picking out Steve.

'He's not one of our lads.'

'Walter's. German, I think. At least, he spoke to the customs guy in German. Sally said he always flies the horses across.'

'One way?'

'Umm.' It was meant as a yes, but already her attention was elsewhere, the job in hand of saddling the skittish filly of far greater interest than Casburg's flying grooms.

Not so for Pete. The flying groom's infamous party piece was too fresh a memory. He hadn't actually seen Steve Smith that evening in the flat; but he recognised the familiar features of sibling Paul, staring uncannily back at him.

Steve worked for Straubinger, here in Germany. Why was he moonlighting as a flying groom? Free flights across to Newmarket to provide extra muscle for his brother?

'Give a hand, would you,' Sophie called across to Pete, 'help Sally. The dog's stirred her up.'

Pete stood on the filly's off side, his hand reassuringly flat against her neck, as Sally struggled to maintain discipline and Sophie struggled with the girths.

'Your side?'

Pete slipped his fingers under the girth. 'Okay.'

Satisfied, Sophie went round the filly with the final finishing touches, as much to calm her as for appearance.

'I don't suppose you want to come into the ring with us?'

'I may as well,' Pete agreed, throwing the sweat rug over his arm, 'I'll play travelling head lad. Casburg can lump it, if he doesn't like it.'

They followed the filly through to the parade ring.

'That Steve's not travelling back with you?' Pete verified.

'Sally said he never does.'

'Was the spaniel actually barking at the filly, or Steve leading up?'

Sophie gave him a sideways glance. 'You

mean was he puffing on a joint all flight?!' She laughed. 'No one smoked or snorted! The little dog had probably never seen a horse before.'

'Did it bark at the colt?'

'The customs guy took him away, before the colt came by. What, you think the filly's a pothead now?!'

Pete grinned. 'You're well up on the lingo – you sure it wasn't you the dog was after?!'

They passed the time jovially enough, waiting for Casburg to enter; Pete successfully masking his anxiety. That morning, he'd booked his flight for no better reason than a dislike of the idea that Smith *might* be at Baden-Baden, with Sophie. The knowledge that Smith had actually flown over in Sophie's company was something he now had trouble taking on board. He reminded himself that Smith had no reason to threaten Sophie. But still, his shoulder encouraged illogical fear.

Casburg entered the parade ring, greeting Sophie warmly and paying such scant regard to staff that he failed to recognise Pete immediately. When he did so, he merely nodded perfunctorily. But when the horses left the parade ring, circumstances forced more cordial behaviour and he had little choice but invite Pete up to his box, having invited Sophie up for the earlier race.

'When will you be back in the plate for us, son?' he enquired, as they headed for the grandstand.

'Monday, if I pass the doctor.'

'Great! No offence to your substitutes, but we could sure use your services for Doncaster.'

Pete was tempted to ask which services; but bit his lip. 'Thanks.'

'Are you well represented over the four days?' Sophie asked the owner.

'In all but the Group races. That side of things will come, with time; your brother is a talented guy. We've made enough this season to aim a bit higher at the sales next year.'

'You can't pull off coups with Group horses,' Pete warned.

Casburg gave him a damning look. 'Who the hell's interested in coups when they've got Group horses? Hell, son, once the bookies have bought us a Classic winner, we don't need bother them again!'

Pete smiled politely, wishing he could believe the words. Even if the coups were a thing of the past and the pressure was suddenly lifted, what use were his services to a Classic stable? Casburg's heavies had made it perfectly clear that he'd been hired to lose, not to win. And Casburg couldn't see that it took talent, either way.

They joined Casburg's other guests in the box and Pete was introduced to various Bavarian dignitaries, Casburg clearly angling for favours in his choice of friends.

'Andreas Straubinger,' Casburg announced, as the final hand was held out in greeting.

CHAPTER FOURTEEN

Pete shook hands and thought of cocaine and dislocated shoulders, though Straubinger himself conjured neither to mind in his appearance. Tall, medium build, silver-haired and every bit the distinguished German gentleman; a valid business partner for any business other than a drug ring.

The handshake was brisk and formal, Straubinger giving no indication that he was aware of what lay under the discreet bandage. Casburg, for that matter, had neither shaken hands nor remarked upon the taped fingers, as though they had escaped his notice.

And Pete, it seemed, was unworthy of further notice. Almost at once the collected party moved off, leaving Pete and Sophie to watch the race alone, the filly finishing no better than fourth.

'That was a better run than I'd expected,' Sophie admitted, 'she handled the ground really well.'

'It was probably a better run than Seb expected,' Pete told her, following her down to the winners' enclosure, 'she never seems to move well on this type of going at home.' He made a mental note to warn Sebastian.

Casburg didn't bother to go down to greet his filly and she was quickly swathed in her sweat sheet and returned to the stables.

'I'll come down to the horsebox with you,' Pete suggested, the filly's departure closing their afternoon together.

'You'll only get mucky. You may as well stay on and watch the next race.'

'No; I'll get a taxi and head back.' He kissed her gently in farewell. 'Every night of our lives; I meant it.'

Sophie's mobile rang. She reached for it with great reluctance. 'Tom or Sally, probably, looking for me.'

She greeted her caller with a somewhat wearied 'hello?' and Pete raised a hand in a friendly wave, turning away. But Sophie was hanging onto his sleeve before he had even taken a step, still talking on her mobile and pulling him with force in the direction of the car parks.

'Sebastian's at the horsebox!' she told him, words still audibly pouring forth from the caller.

'What?!'

'Look, we're on our way down, we'll be right there,' Sophie told the excited Tom, whose voice was now audible even to Pete, 'two minutes, tops.'

She slipped the phone back into her pocket and dragged Pete at a run to the horsebox car park, still clinging to his sleeve. They arrived amid the rows of boxes, Pete clueless as to which they were heading for, a hired box ferrying Sebastian's runners to and from the airport. Sophie picked it out at once and Pete quickly recognised their own colt being led round beside it by Tom.

Sebastian, they soon saw, was sitting on the floor against the rear wheel arch, pointing at his colt in bemusement. He was dressed in the cricket whites he'd last worn at Sunday's gala day and their less-than-white appearance suggested he'd never changed out of them.

Sophie relinquished her fierce grip on Pete's sleeve and ran at once to her brother, kneeling beside him and burying him in her embrace. Pete joined them and squatted down on his haunches.

'He's drunk as a skunk,' he told Sophie, as Sebastian grinned back at him in private wonder.

'That's Brother Pipkin!' Sebastian said, pointing still at the colt.

'Well spotted,' Pete agreed, 'come on, let's get you into the cab.'

'He's supposed to run in Germany Wednesday,' Sebastian protested, struggling to form the words, 'what's he doing here?'

'It is Wednesday,' Sophie reassured him, 'and we are in Germany.'

Sebastian shook his head emphatically. 'No way! We can't be! It's the July course.'

'Baden-Baden, mate,' Pete assured him, slipping an arm round his shoulders, 'come on, into the cab.' He hauled the virtual dead-weight of his trainer to his feet.

'I was so lost,' Sebastian murmured sorrowfully, 'I couldn't see our box. It's not here. But I saw Pipkin.' He smiled lovingly upon the horse. 'Little Brother Pipkin! I would have been lost.'

'Oh, God, Sebastian, where the hell have you been?' Sophie asked in exasperation.

'Just here. Not been anywhere. I came with a horse. I remember coming with a horse.'

'I believe him,' Pete told Sophie, referring to the musty stable smell of the former whites. 'Which horse?' he asked Sebastian without interest, allowing him to ramble if it helped him walk to the cab any quicker. The weight was a burden he could do without.

'Don't know. Not ours. Not Pipkin.' He threw his arms tighter round Pete. 'I would have been lost, but for seeing Pipkin.'

'You were lost! We'd given up ever bloody finding you!' Pete smiled at Sophie, doing her best to add some support and get Sebastian up the steps into the cab.

Once in, the young trainer lay back on the bench seat and complained at feeling ill.

'I should think you do!' Sophie complained back.

'I don't think he gambled much at all,' Pete guessed, 'he drank it instead.'

'No, I don't drink,' Sebastian argued, 'I'm not drunk.'

'Just ill,' Sophie soothed, smiling.

Pete checked through his pockets. 'No money. No tickets. Just the usual IDs. How the hell did he get here?'

'A horse,' Sebastian told him, obligingly.

'He can come back with us as the groom,' Sophie suggested.

'You're kidding? They'll never let him on the plane. I'll bring him home. I can get him sobered up, stop overnight, even, if need be.'

'I'm not drunk,' Sebastian insisted, 'tell him, Sophie.'

'You heard the man!' Sophie said to Pete, with a grin. Tears streamed down her face.

Pete held her tight for a moment, until the tears subsided.

'Oh God, I was so scared.'

'I know... I know.' He felt an incredible sense of relief himself. 'You'd better ring your Mum and Dad. I'll help Tom load the colt and if Sally's ready she can fetch the filly across.' He turned to jump down from the cab.

'Look after the rugs,' Sebastian warned, 'they're not ours.'

Pete raised his eyes and blew Sophie a kiss.

Tom loaded the colt without difficulty or need for help.

'How's the guv'nor?' he asked Pete.

'He'll live.'

'He'll prefer not to, come the morning! Watch my horse, would you; I'll go and get Sally.'

Pete nodded agreement and wandered back round to the cab. Sophie was still speaking to her parents, Sebastian sitting up and rubbing his head.

'We've a flight to catch, if I can get you on it,' Pete told him, 'going to try to make a move?'

'I feel lousy. Is it really Wednesday?'

'It'll be Thursday at this rate.'

'Are we really leaving? Did they run already?'

'Pipkin got second, the filly was fourth and acted well on the ground.'

'I didn't meet Walter, did I?'

'Not to my knowledge.'

'Damn, I feel rough.'

Pete helped him down and waited for him to

221

get some sort of balance. In his favour, he reeked of horses, not alcohol. If he could walk straight and keep his mouth shut, he might make it onto the plane, seats willing. Hoping for the best, Pete rang for a taxi, reading carefully from the card given him earlier by the taxi driver and relieved to get the same person.

'We're heading off,' he called up to Sophie, 'I'll ring you when we're ready to board. We'll go straight to your parents'.'

Still on the phone, she could only wave and nod agreement.

Pete and Sebastian made slow but steady progress out onto the main road, to await the taxi. It seemed to Pete that Sebastian was sobering up rapidly, though he struggled to make sense of his surroundings. Never having drunk himself into such total oblivion, Pete couldn't begin to guess at the rude awakening now ensuing. He merely humoured his trainer and prayed silently for an evening spent at home and not at the airport.

'If it's Wednesday, why am I still in these things?' Sebastian asked, trying to dust off the dirt from his flannels.

'I have no idea,' Pete told him truthfully.

'Do you mean to say I haven't even been home yet?'

'There are some very frantic people waiting for you at home.'

Sebastian tried to take it in. He patted his pockets, lost and vulnerable. 'No phone.'

'That would explain why we couldn't call you.'

'Pete, you're telling me I haven't been home since Sunday and none of you know where I've been?'

'That's the sum total.'

'Christ.' He took out his wallet, checked it; replaced it. 'I haven't got a brass farthing to my name. And no phone. If I hadn't seen the horse…' His face clouded as a new horror surfaced. 'Pete! Sophie's money! I've lost it! I've lost Sophie's money!'

'Don't worry about it. *You're* not lost, that's the main thing.'

Sebastian frowned in concentration. 'I can remember losing it. The rest is just a blur.'

The arrival of the taxi spared him further puzzlement and he gazed out over the passing scenery, memory occasionally triggered by the sights. The Rhine edged their route, to their left; the aptly-named Black Forest to their right.

'I was in Baden-Baden,' he said hesitantly, 'and I walked… I saw the horseboxes. I was lost; and they were familiar. But they weren't.' He recoiled inwardly at the memory. 'I didn't recognise a single one. I was expecting it to be at home, you see. All the usual boxes. Not one.' He smiled. 'And there, like a miracle, Brother Pipkin.'

'So you were staying in the town here?'

Sebastian shook his head, more in confusion than denial. He thought it over for a while, until he apparently forgot the question.

'It was damned lucky, don't you think? Seeing the horse? And not even in one of our own rugs.'

It was lucky, certainly. Anyone in the horsebox car park would have recognised him. But only his own employees and sister could keep it from the press. Pete gazed out of the window, marvelling once more at Sebastian's ability to get into such massive trouble without ever actually getting into trouble at all. He'd lost a charity's thirty grand, drunk himself into oblivion, and no one would ever actually know; his career, his reputation, as always, unblemished.

And what was he rattling on about?

'What do you mean, not one of your rugs?'

'Ours are big padded things, tartan. Damned awful, if you ask me, but Walter's choice.'

'Oh.' Pete turned back to the window, uninterested. He wondered if he should ring on ahead, check if there were any available seats on his flight. 'It's a bit of an expensive jaunt for Casburg, then,' he remarked, 'a few grand to fly them over and then another couple of hundred for the rugs!'

'They always get returned. We must make on it, actually, because I don't recall ever returning the ones they come home in!'

Pete smiled to himself. Bloody Churchill good fortune, once again. He glanced around at Sebastian, but the trainer was dozing, the fight against the drunken stupor suddenly too overwhelming. With luck, he'd wake up with his memory restored, just in time to face the music.

By the time they reached Karlsruhe, some of the Churchill good fortune had rubbed off onto Pete, the airline happy to supply an additional seat on the same flight and allowing Sebastian's inebriated state to pass unnoticed.

'We're okay,' Pete phoned through to Sophie, 'same flight and about to board, so I'll have to turn this off in a minute.'

'I don't know what made you come over, but I am so, so grateful you did.'

'I've not done much,' Pete insisted, 'only spared him a trip back in cargo with the horses!' He smiled at Sebastian, listening in, who mouthed the words 'thank you'.

'That's enough on its own,' Sophie laughed, 'even that place has gone. The groom came back with us after all. See you back at Mum's.'

And she was gone.

Pete tried to remain calm. Steve Smith obviously used the flying groom service as a free means of transport. And the fact that he had arrived that morning at his destination, only to be unexpectedly summoned back to the UK that same afternoon – well, that wasn't any concern. Not to Sophie. Paul Smith, perhaps, sending out alarm bells after the attack on the portacabin? A welcome party back at his own flat? Complete with speciality party pieces...

They were being called to board.

'What do you know about Steve Smith?' Pete asked Sebastian.

'Smith? Isn't he that guard who delivered a threat to you?'

Pete shook his head. 'Another Smith. He's Casburg's flying groom. Escorts your horses on flights.'

'I wouldn't know – he does more than I do! I only escort their owner. Ask Jeff.'

Jeff was the travelling head lad. And Sebastian was recovering steadily from his earlier fuzzy state, which wasn't necessarily good news. The clarity of his surroundings and present situation threw him into sudden panic.

'How did I get here? And what was I doing here? How long?' The questions flowed rapidly and Pete could answer none of them.

'You said you came with a horse?' Pete suggested, trying to jog Sebastian's memory and inclined to believe him. He looked as though he'd slept in a stable; and possibly had, stumbling lost and drunk around the only other familiar part of the spa town he knew, when once the casinos had barred his presence.

'I was in a box with a horse. But that was at home. Gala day, the jumping ponies. Wasn't it?'

'I don't know, mate. Can't you think of anything you've done since?'

Sebastian stopped in his tracks, ignoring the protests from those behind, following him up the stairs into the plane.

'Nervous flyer,' Pete apologised, taking Sebastian's arm and helping him forcefully aboard.

'This is real! I'm actually here, at Karlsruhe! And that was my horse, so it really is Wednesday...'

'Look, just get on and sit down and we'll sort it all out.'

'Get me home, Pete. I've got to find Sophie's

money.'

'Don't worry about that right now, you'll only dig yourself in deeper.'

They took their seats and Sebastian calmed down once more. Though Pete tried quietly to dissuade him, he accepted all offers of drink and the Dutch courage merely added to his agitation.

Pete was heartily thankful when the tense journey ended and had only to convince Sebastian that they had no baggage to collect, as they walked out to the car park. He tried Sophie's mobile repeatedly as they walked, without success, which at least meant she was safely on the flight. And why wouldn't she be? Events of the past couple of weeks had left him paranoid.

'Look, mate, Sophie's only half an hour behind us,' he told Sebastian, 'would you mind if we waited for her?'

'I've just lost three days, how we waste the next thirty minutes doesn't really bother me. Wait for her, by all means.'

They walked back to arrivals and sat with coffees, watching the landings flash up on the electronic board. Sebastian lapsed into silence once more, rationale only surviving for intermittent bouts.

'They're in,' Pete announced, watching the details finally flip over to landed status, 'by the time we get the car and pull out, they should be through and following along behind.'

Sebastian followed him back outside and they walked without talking back to the car. As they made their way out of the airport, the young trainer merely stared vacantly out of the window, the prospect of returning home and owning up to the truth no doubt a daunting one. Once out of the airport and heading for the M11, Pete pulled into the first lay-by and sat back to await the horsebox. He'd tried Sophie's mobile two or three times without success, Sophie having forgotten to turn it back on after the flight.

Just as he made a further attempt to call her, the box itself passed them. He flashed his lights and waved to Aaron, the driver, then pulled out and followed it up as far as the motorway. No one signalled for him to pull over, which was a good enough signal that all was well. Once onto the motorway itself, Pete sped by and left the box behind.

Coming off onto the A11, Sebastian predictably stirred from his reverie and took some interest in his surroundings.

'I know this place,' he said, excitement replacing doubt even before he'd finished speaking.

'Six Mile Bottom,' Pete told him mildly, 'we only drive through it twice a day every day of our lives.'

But Sebastian sat forward, straining against the seat belt, trying to see out on both sides of the road at once.

'No, no,' he said impatiently, 'I actually remember this particular place. It's where I lost the money. I remember being here. *Turn here!*'

Pete swung the car rapidly down the road on the right, Sebastian's demand a little too late but insistent enough not to be ignored.

'Stetchworth?' Pete asked.

'Just further on.'

'Dullingham? Are you sure you really remember any of this?' Pete asked with concern. It was possible Sebastian had taken a severe bang on the head and was concussed, not drunk.

'I *do* remember it – that's the point!' Sebastian said adamantly, 'slow right down. Not as far as Dullingham at all. Somewhere around here… slower.'

Pete glanced in the mirror and pulled in to allow the car behind to pass.

'There's the box,' Sebastian pointed out, watching the road behind and the cars passing along the main road.

Sure enough, almost immediately the phone rang.

'Sophie! I thought your battery had gone!'

'Forgot to turn it on. Are you okay? Shall we follow you?'

'We're fine, just taking the scenic route. Have a word with Seb, would you.' He lifted the phone from the hands-free and passed it to Sebastian.

'Sophie, I remember where your money is! You go on ahead, we'll only be a minute or two.'

Sophie's voice rang out clearly, denying the siblings a private conversation.

'It doesn't matter about the money; really. We just want you home.'

'It matters to me! Anyway, I won't be long, I promise.'

He disconnected and handed the phone back to Pete.

'You can get going again now. I'll shout when I see where to stop.'

The car remained parked.

'Hang on a minute,' Pete checked, 'you couldn't have lost the money around here – there *is* nothing around here! And you couldn't get it back now, even if you had. What exactly are we looking for?'

'I lost the money here. I'm not entirely sure how, it's all a bit confused. I met boys from the yard, I remember that much, and we came here, I know that for a fact. I had the safe deposit bag; they took it; I saw them stow it away. I know, I absolutely know, that I'll recognise it. It's all I keep seeing in my head, when I think of the money.'

'Bloody hell, Seb! Are you saying you were *robbed*?'

'Well what do you think I mean by lost? Put it down and forgot it? Where the devil did you think I'd been for three days?'

'We hadn't a clue. But Baden-Baden was our most recent guess, seeing as how we found you there.'

'I remember as far as here. Then the car park at the racecourse. Pretty damn much zilch in between. Why would I go to Germany without telling you? Did you think I was with Walter?'

Pete pulled back out and drove slowly down the road. The collective lack of faith in Sebastian was something he hardly wanted to discuss; Sebastian was, after all, his employer.

'We were thinking up loads of different

scenarios. We were worried, Seb; we didn't know what to think.'

'Quick! Pull over!'

Sebastian was distracted by nothing more than a disused cattle feeder, rusting beside an equally dilapidated gate into a field. Pete pulled in, close to the gate, and Sebastian was out of the car almost before it stopped. Pete followed after him, intrigued.

'We passed this,' Sebastian recalled, standing beside the feeder, having pushed through the rusting gate. 'They were arguing, shouting.'

'Who were?'

'The lads. I don't know who. I thought I knew them, from the yard, but I just can't place them.'

'Would they be your security guards?'

'No, I know them.'

'The night ones? You didn't know Paul Smith.'

'Smith! I think it may have been him! The other two, I don't know. I thought I did, that's all. They saw me in the car park, called me over, I went across. I wasn't at all worried. They bundled me into their car, we got out here. And they had the safe bag. They were arguing about something, but I don't remember it. Just noise. They poked about at this.' He examined the feeder himself, as though hoping to find the money bag. 'Then we carried on.' He looked around, spotting an old stone barn some way off, virtually obscured by the hedgerow. 'That's it! That's where I was!'

He set off at a fierce pace and Pete had to run

a few steps to catch up with him.

'Pete, look! Do you see that little hut thing?'

It was a pump house or feed store, once a smaller version of the barn alongside it. Now the crumbled bricks merely suggested its former shape. Sebastian sprinted over to it and tore at the loose stones. Pete followed more leisurely, peering with interest into the cavity Sebastian unearthed.

'Bloody hell!'

'I knew it! I knew it!'

Sebastian withdrew the familiar night safe bag in triumph, looking as full as when he'd last seen it. He unzipped it, to reveal that, short of a full count, the contents were still intact.

'How do you bank stolen wads of cash?' he asked Pete, 'I knew they'd have to leave it here, at least for a day or two!'

Pete stared at the bank bag, and the pile of rubble to which it had been entrusted.

'Oh shit.'

'What?'

'We've got to get away from here. Now.'

Sebastian smiled. 'Don't worry, they've no idea I actually know this spot. I was out of it, they were carrying me. Drugged or something... I don't recall being hit.'

The recollection of being drugged was enough to confirm Pete's fears.

'We seriously have to go. Not back to the car.' He looked around. 'Through the hedge and back up to the road through the next field. Anywhere but here.'

Sebastian looked at the suggested route. 'You're being way too over cautious, you know.'

'You told Sophie you remembered where the money was. You know what those bloody phones are like, the whole world hears every word. And even if they didn't, they all saw us turn off to Stetchworth. And the Steve Smith who flies with Casburg's horses is in the box right now with Sophie. And I'm pretty certain he took the money in the first place. So, he's on his way this minute, now.'

'We'd better move pretty damn sharpish, then.' Sebastian hesitated. 'Maybe stow this away somewhere else? I seriously can't afford to lose it for a second time.'

He ducked through the hedge, after Pete, and looked for a suitable hiding place. Within a few yards he found a dead tree in the hedgerow, the roots opened up into various useful crevices. He availed of a hole, deep within the hedge, and hoped for the best, hurrying after Pete once more. They tried to walk as swiftly and quietly as they could, but the flaw in their escape plan soon revealed itself to be a lack of continuous undergrowth. From time to time the sorry hedge thinned out into a clear view straight up to the road.

'Still only one car up there,' Sebastian observed; and they pressed on hopefully.

The hedge thickened as they approached the road, the bulk of it brambles and hawthorn, as they discovered when they tried to push back through, onto the road.

'I told you you were being over cautious,'

Sebastian complained.

'Shut up and listen for a car!'

They emerged by the rusty gate, the Merc' still safely alone.

'Two points cross my mind,' Sebastian told Pete, picking thorns from his torn flannels, before getting back into the car, 'grooms travel in the back of the box, with the horses, and Sophie's phone is a better model than yours.'

Pete opened the door and climbed in. 'Yeah, yeah. But better safe than...'

'Than sorry?' Steve Smith leaned over from the back, as the door locks clicked down automatically.

CHAPTER FIFTEEN

'Nothing personal, lads,' Smith said with cheerful menace, jangling the car keys between their shoulders, 'I'm just the hired help, remember. Run to the police if you like, but me and Paulie have hard evidence we were elsewhere on any given date. So if you've made a mistake about names and faces, lads, you're pretty much unreliable, aren't you?' He grinned at each in turn, his face inches from theirs within the confines of the car. 'After all, you couldn't even remember where the bag was left, could you?'

Sebastian hoped his inward sigh of relief was exactly that, and not visible.

'The box must have dropped you off up the road, by the pub,' Pete risked a safe guess, 'so we've some hard evidence of our own. Four reliable witnesses can place you here, now.'

'Correction, they can place me *at the pub*. So, to business, lads. Here's the story. Churchill, you were saved a hiding.' He sat back in the rear seat, conducting his conversation via the rear-view mirror. 'I heard some lads were asked to deliver a message, rough you up a little, remind you it's owners who call the shots. Only, when they did, something else cropped up. So they slipped you some dope and left you to wander home and report a theft instead.' He leant forward and addressed Sebastian directly. 'But you didn't wander home or wander anywhere. You had people asking questions all through the next day, including the boss. Which was pretty awkward for the lads.' He delved into a pocket and produced a packet of cigarettes and a lighter, smiling at Pete via the mirror as he did so. 'Don't mind if I smoke? 'Course not.' He lit up and took a drag, never taking his eyes from the mirror. 'Anyway. Problem soon solved, they started asking for you round Deauville. So the lads dumped you in Baden-Baden.'

'Why?' Sebastian asked in bewilderment.

'Where else did thirty grand vanish, if you weren't robbed! And the small matter of you lying out of your head in a Suffolk barn for two days had to be brushed over. Fucking good shit, by the way.'

'I still...' Sebastian looked to Pete, questioningly.

'We thought you were in the casinos with Sophie's charity money, trying to play it up to pay off Casburg,' Pete explained apologetically.

'Oh, well thank you very bloody much.'

'The message from the lads is,' Smith interrupted, 'that if that story continues, so does Sophie Churchill's good health.' He casually reached a hand forward and tapped off the ash from his cigarette beside Pete. 'So no more searching, eh? Cheerio, then, lads – I've a pint waiting.'

He pushed the remote locking on the key ring and the locks sprang up noisily, Smith sliding smoothly out and sauntering back up the road.

'What are you waiting for?' Sebastian demanded, snatching up the keys from where Smith had tossed them, 'start her up and run him damned over.'

Pete said nothing, trying without success to quell the ever-rising nausea. He opened the door hurriedly and gave up the unequal struggle, together with everything he'd eaten that day.

When he did start up the engine and turn round to head back, Smith would have already been out on the main road and making for the security of the pub.

'A clean hit and run,' Sebastian said with regret, 'no witnesses.'

'We're not killers.'

'He's gone now, anyway. Let's pick up the money.'

'He could just be waiting for us to drive off,' Pete said dissuasively, 'he'll be desperate to move it now you remember where it is.' He drove back onto the A11. 'Christ, why did he have to bring Sophie into this? What's going to happen when he finds the money's not there?'

'Blame one of the others.' For all his misfortune, his optimism hadn't waned.

Pete said nothing, in no mood to argue.

'And you all thought *I'd* stolen it,' Sebastian said in wonder, 'thank God I can now prove otherwise.'

'You're not going to tell them otherwise,' Pete insisted.

'What? And let them think I'd actually gamble away charity money?'

'I didn't ride for you today.'

'And what has that to do with the price of eggs?'

'I didn't ride for you,' Pete said firmly, 'because the Smith brothers burnt the fingers on my right hand and smashed my left hand.'

'God, never! He was serious, then? About Sophie?'

'Deadly.'

They drove into Newmarket in silence.

Sebastian was slow to get out, even though Sophie ran to meet the car as they parked, outside the Churchill house.

'What am I going to tell them?' he asked Pete.

'The truth. You don't remember anything. You set aside the original stake money, that's all.' Pete watched him, with a twinge of empathy. 'They'll be too relieved to have you and the money back to get seriously mad. Chalk it up to experience.'

Sebastian shook his head and Pete made a move to get out.

'Lock the damned car, would you?' Sebastian said, withdrawing the keys from the ignition and tossing them over. He climbed out with some reluctance, into the embrace of Sophie.

'We stopped to mull over a few things,' Pete told her.

'It's best left forgotten,' Sophie advised, leading them in.

The warm welcome awaiting the prodigal son was mercifully free of recriminations. Pete had privately dreaded it, feeling himself to be no more than an intruder, despite Sophie's assurances to the contrary. In the end, it was the comfortable feeling of belonging, being just another family member, that won through. It took Sebastian a while to realise the significance of Pete's presence, no one thinking to fill him in, but his casual acceptance of the new relationship was no more than par for the course. It seemed to Pete little wonder that Sebastian could get away with murder and Sophie could fetch home any unsavoury character she chose.

The news that Sophie's money, at least, had been safely wired back helped to ease the situation. Yet it was the weight of what was left unspoken that hung in the air, as they all retired to bed.

That burden unfolded on Pete at around three in the morning, as Sebastian prodded hesitantly at his arm.

'Careful, don't wake Sophie,' the trainer whispered, as Pete groaned and woke and tried to pick out the shadowy figure disturbing him. Sophie slept on peacefully beside him.

'What d'you want? What's the time?'

'Get dressed, I need to talk.'

'Bugger off, Seb, it's the middle of the night.' But, nevertheless, Pete stumbled out of bed, pulled on shirt and trousers and followed Sebastian down to the kitchen.

'Tomorrow, the questions will start,' Sebastian predicted.

'Today, you mean.'

'And I can't answer any. Not unless I tell the truth. The absolute truth.'

'Seb, these people are serious. Our friend in the car – he dislocates arms as a pastime. Look.' Pete turned round, dropped the unbuttoned shirt from his shoulder, let him see the burn, left undressed, on his back.

Sebastian winced. He was quiet, for a moment.

'We can look after Sophie,' he persisted, 'round the clock protection. But I can't pretend I was in Baden-Baden gambling away her money. This is a police matter.'

'Police? I'll lose my licence!'

'I'm in danger of losing my family here, Pete.'

'Put the bloody kettle on.'

Pete sat down wearily, as Sebastian filled the kettle and readied two mugs for coffee.

'They seem prepared to forgive you anything,' he pointed out.

'Forgive this? Everything I've supposedly put them through?' Sebastian shook his head. 'Things will never be quite the same again. I have to tell them the truth, Pete.'

'Seb, you can't. Never mind my licence, if questions get asked and the Smith brothers find out, Sophie's safety is at stake. These are serious villains, Seb.'

'It's my reputation, damn it!'

'Pour the bloody coffee,' Pete told him. 'This was never in my contract.'

Sebastian smiled; and settled the coffees on the table.

'Marcel won on the favourite and you didn't stay at Epsom Monday night?' he asked, looking at Pete's hands, as the jockey reached for his mug.

'Pretty much. And all the time I thought you were bailing me out with the money.'

'I would never dream of doing such a thing. And I'm not in anywhere near as deep as you evidently are.'

'I'm in this mess because I refuse to do what they ask,' Pete protested, 'and who exactly gave them the idea that I would, when I first got this job?'

'Don't look at me! I asked Sophie for a jockey and she suggested you. Apparently high-class and affordable; although I have to question her motive now!'

Pete grinned, flattered.

'The best I could do on the retainer I was offering, were her actual words,' Sebastian corrected, with a grin, 'so you may wipe that smirk from your face.'

'Okay, so let's think this through,' Pete suggested. 'Casburg is plotting coups for quick returns and we refuse. He threatens me, which may or may not be over. I threatened Paul Smith and made it clear I wouldn't cooperate.' At least Steve Smith hadn't been aware of that gem. Yet.

'You did?'

'Hopefully. I locked him in the portacabin last night and smoked him out, through the toilet window. He'll either lay off me, or come at me all the harder.'

'Was that wise?'

'I don't know,' Pete admitted, 'but I've nothing to lose. Next time I refuse to stop a favourite, I'm out of the saddle permanently.'

'Jesus Christ, Pete! We have to go to the Jockey Club.'

'And have *them* put me out of the saddle permanently?' Pete shook his head. 'Only difference is, they won't break any bones in the process.'

'Extenuating circumstances,' Sebastian suggested.

'Jockey Club,' Pete answered simply. 'We're on our own. Which leaves your current dilemma. You stood up to Casburg, so he had you hauled in. But his men just stole the cash instead. And Casburg doesn't know that.' He sat back, thoughtfully. 'Which gives us something over them. Because they're not going to blame each other, you can bet on that.'

'And, meanwhile, all Walter knows is that neither of us is prepared to bend to threats!' Sebastian said positively.

'I'm too tired for all this,' Pete admitted, 'and I can't put Sophie through this. Sorry, mate.'

'Pete, if I told her the truth, she'd be relieved. We wouldn't need to tell her anything else.'

'Of course she would! She loves you!' Pete snapped. He held out his burnt fingers. 'They dislocated my shoulder, as well. Ask your dad about it. Then tell Sophie; if you still want to.'

Sebastian looked suitably remorseful. 'Will you come with me, to pick up the money?'

'Now?'

'They're likely to be watching for us in the morning.'

Pete smiled. 'You need to up my retainer.'

They finished their coffees and Pete headed reluctantly upstairs, to get shoes, socks and jacket.

'What's up?' Sophie muttered sleepily, as he

sat on the edge of the bed.

'Can't sleep.' He kissed her shoulder and watched her drift back off to sleep once more.

Sebastian wasn't going to lie for her.

Back down in the hall, Sebastian had his father's car keys ready and they slipped quietly out onto the drive.

'Torch?' Pete asked.

Sebastian patted his pocket in reply.

'You'll get us killed, you know that?'

They drove in silence to the rusted gate on the Stetchworth road and Sebastian locked up the car, with a rueful glance at Pete.

'Get on with it, it's bloody cold,' Pete complained, ducking ahead, through the hedge and into the adjacent field.

They walked slowly down the hedgerow, eyes scanning carefully for the dead tree and its wealthy roots.

'They might already have searched and found it,' Pete warned.

'Needle in a haystack,' Sebastian assured him.

'That's what I'm afraid of! All these trees look the same in the dark.'

Sebastian stopped and began to scrabble in the hedge. 'This one doesn't. And, bingo!' He withdrew the bank bag triumphantly. 'Let's go home.'

They trudged back to the car.

'When you tell them, you're certain they won't go to the police or the Jockey Club?' Pete checked, as they drove back to the house.

'I might tailor my story,' Sebastian relented.

Pete smiled to himself and relaxed back into the seat. He was half asleep as they pulled up outside the door a few minutes later and stirred only enough to get up to the bedroom and out of his clothes, flopping into bed alongside Sophie and falling at once into a much-needed sleep.

It was late, by their standards, when they woke the next morning.

'We've missed first lot,' Sophie noted.

'Seb's string must be home and hosed!'

'Home and hosed without him! That must be some hangover he's sleeping off!'

She went through to the bathroom and Pete stretched back out on the bed, trying to wake at a more sedate pace. He thought, fleetingly, of Casburg, though he would have preferred not to. And of Steve Smith's reaction to the disappearance of the money. And why Steve Smith had been recalled to Newmarket within hours of his arrival at Baden-Baden. And of brother Paul's reaction to attempted arson. Taken as a whole, he looked to be in a deeper mess than ever.

'Will you be able to ride out tomorrow, do you think?' Sophie asked, emerging from the bathroom.

'I'd best give it a go, if I want to get passed for Monday. Don't let Mike put me on anything that pulls hard!'

'Dad can put you on our rota, if you like? When you've finished at Sebastian's?'

Riding out for David Churchill. It was a hefty

step up the ladder.

'Saturday, maybe. If I don't get carted off tomorrow!' He flexed his fingers, reluctant to admit even to himself that they were still very sore. Such soreness, in the heat of a race, could be overlooked. On the gallops, not so easy to forget. And the high profile Doncaster St Leger meeting opened Wednesday...

He went through to the bathroom to wash and shave, Sophie perching herself on the edge of the bath, her presence as natural as their continued conversation. He watched her in the mirror, slightly incredulous that he could be this lucky and heartily grateful that he was.

They went down to get breakfast, the kitchen empty as the usual swarm headed back out onto the Heath for second lot.

'Scrambled egg?' Sophie offered.

'Make that double,' Sebastian requested, joining them, 'did Mum wake you up as well, crashing about with the dishwasher?'

'We slept blissfully,' Sophie assured him, 'how's your head?'

'Fine. I wasn't drunk, you know. One day I shall tell you all about it, but for now I have other people to consider, so I won't.'

'Case closed, Sebastian. Just as long as I can close the charity books up, I don't care.'

They ate their breakfast, Sebastian making no move to return home when the dishes were emptied and cleared away.

'For the record,' he announced, when David

and Angela were back in off the gallops and settling down with a pot of tea, 'I did not gamble with Sophie's money or have any intention of doing so. I merely needed entrance money and I set it aside the moment I was dealt in.' He directed his conversation to David. 'You told me long ago never again to run up a bill and I gave you my word. I bet with my own cash or not at all. Please don't think I have ever, or will ever, break my word.'

David smiled. 'I'm very relieved to hear it, but I'd rather hear how you managed to get in while still dressed in your flannels!'

'I believe that's a story he's saving for later, for the protection of those involved!' quipped Sophie, much to her brother's disgust.

'I changed to come home,' he said firmly.

'In other words, you lost the shirt off your back,' David suggested.

'The cash I had set aside specifically for gambling and no more.'

'I just wished you'd called,' Angela complained without rancour, putting an end to the discussion.

Sebastian finished his tea and said his farewells, the day ahead demanding his attention, catching up on work back at his own stables. For Pete, days off were so rare he hadn't yet worked out how best to fill it. There was always the likelihood that the Smith brothers were already arranging something for him.

He remained at the table, waiting for Sophie, who'd followed her mother upstairs.

'Did he tell you what actually happened?' David asked at once, as soon as they were alone, 'None of his story so far washes at all.'

'He was robbed,' Pete admitted, 'but we found the money. And it's entirely my fault, it took every effort on my part to convince him to lie to you.'

David mulled it over.

'A connection, then – between the robbery and your attacks?'

'Only loosely.'

'But you don't want the police involved?'

'I think Casburg's behind it all,' Pete told him.

David weighed it up. 'Not wise to involve the Jockey Club either, then. Bringing the game into disrepute and whathaveyou. But how is it to be resolved?'

'It may already be.'

David nodded, satisfied.

Optimism was hereditary, then, Pete reflected, wishing he had some. And, meanwhile, Steve Smith was searching in vain for thirty grand while mulling over an arson attack on his brother…

Sophie wandered back in and sat down on Pete's lap, enjoying the close contact previously denied her. He wrapped an arm casually round her waist, deciding, as he did so, exactly what he'd like to do with his enforced holiday.

'Fancy a couple of days on the Algarve?'

CHAPTER SIXTEEN

The honeymoon had to end. The brief flirtation with sand and sex was inevitably swapped for the Jockey Club offices and Newcastle races, Stansted welcoming them back after three days of bliss to the usual routine of racing life. Less welcoming was Pete's first port of call Monday morning, the feared visit to the Medical Officer to have the red ink cleared from his medical book.

'I rode four lots out this morning,' Pete told him truthfully, the late night flight from Portugal just about enabling them both to ride out for Sebastian that morning, before joining the Churchill string. The pleasure of riding David's above-average horses, even though it had only been in canters, was something he was still coming down from.

The Medical Officer seemed satisfied enough and duly noted down his fitness, merely warning him to keep the fingers taped and to wear gloves. The reminder was unnecessary, the mere thought of doing otherwise unbearable. Pete thanked him heartily and beat a grateful escape.

'Newcastle?' Sophie asked, meeting him on the steps outside.

'Newcastle.' He gave Sebastian a quick ring, to confirm his rides. The trainer, much like his own flat, had remained safely in one piece and unmolested during their absence. Neither he nor Sebastian were quite sure if that was a good sign, or simply ominous.

'A bloody relief, I can tell you,' he said to Sophie, as she drove to Sebastian's, 'I couldn't afford to miss Doncaster. And I thought you were going to make sure I wasn't on anything that pulled hard this morning? Or was that just your dad being sadistic?'

She laughed. 'Dad was particularly careful, blame the filly. They can be such little madams sometimes!'

'She picked her moment,' Pete agreed ruefully.

'Incidentally, are you going to Cologne tomorrow?'

'Probably not. I've to finalise things with Seb. We've two going at Lingfield and a nice maiden at Leicester that he'll probably want me on.'

'That's what I told Dad.' She smiled. 'He was wondering if you'd be available for his in Germany tomorrow.'

'Your dad's? You're joking!'

'Why not? You're pretty handy round the German tracks.'

'I'm pretty handy round any course. But your dad's owners won't want me up, surely?'

'It's a matter of booking the best available.'

'Well, if I'm there, I'll ride it, obviously.'

'Give him a call after you've spoken to Sebastian.'

They picked up Sebastian himself, then drove into Cambridge, for their taxi plane to Newcastle. The flight was spent in deep discussion, finalising riding plans. The obvious option for Pete was the maiden at Leicester, but Sebastian seemed to be fishing for an excuse to send his stable jockey to Cologne. Pete wondered if David had already spoken with him, and was willing enough to be routed abroad. Their own runner was hardly worth the journey, but the chance to pick up Group rides for David more than compensated.

But the purpose of Sebastian's fishing revealed itself when they were alone in the Newcastle weighing room.

'I'm not quite certain how much to say in front of Sophie,' Sebastian confessed, 'I hope to goodness you haven't told her every detail; it would worry her silly.'

'I can't hide my run-ins with Paul Smith, but there's no way I want her to know they're kidnappers and they've threatened her as well.'

'Good. But I need you to be with me in Cologne tomorrow. It's been a hell of a weekend, Pete. My nerves are in shreds.'

'What's happened?'

'Nothing. Nothing at all. And all the time, I'm sitting waiting for *something*.'

Pete fully empathised. 'We have to bring this to a head,' he agreed.

'Exactly so. And I've given the matter a bit of thought. The thought being, we confront Walter tomorrow. We tell him straight, not only are we beyond pressure, but his own men are up to no good behind his back. Cards fully on the table.'

'In the hope he'll call his men off?' Pete shook his head dubiously. 'And how do we deal with them, if he does? First we rob them, then we get them fired. We're not going to be flavour of the month.'

'They stole it from us first, remember! They're just hired men, surely it's not personal. That

250

Smith chap said so himself.'

'Hopefully. We can try anyway; and hope for the best.'

But Pete lacked Sebastian's optimism.

He also lacked winners, for that afternoon, at least. Neither of the stable's two runners could finish in the frame and he could manage only third on his outside ride. The silver lining in an otherwise cloudy day was that his sore fingers had been no inconvenience at all.

'I want to go to Cologne,' Sebastian told Sophie on the flight home, 'Walter's coming back with me for Doncaster. Roddy can saddle the Lingfield runners and maybe you'll take the colt to Leicester for me?'

'No problem,' she agreed, her two year absence from a racecourse already forgotten.

Back in Newmarket, Sebastian returned home, to sit and wait for hopefully nothing for yet another night. Pete took the more cowardly, but pleasurable, option of sharing Sophie's bed. They called in to his flat first, to pack a case for the four day Doncaster meeting and some overnight things for that evening, but everything appeared to be reassuringly secure.

'Doncaster already,' Sophie sighed, falling into bed an hour later for a welcome early night, 'the season has flown by.'

'I guess it has. What shall we do for the winter?'

'Madras usually, isn't it?'

'Sure, if you like. I was just going to stay on

for the All-Weather.'

'Newmarket, then. As long as there's racing and you're riding, I'm content.'

He smiled. 'Portugal was nice, though, wasn't it? I need the rides, but a bit of sun doesn't go amiss.'

'Plenty of English trainers in Spain. We could talk Sebastian into taking a few horses over for the winter.'

Pete laid down beside her, not really caring where his bed was, just as long as she was in it.

The morning brought with it the usual early start, with only just enough time to ride work before heading off to the various racetracks. A second piece of work for David was out of the question altogether.

'Scoot in and change,' Sebastian told Pete, catching his mount in the yard as they came in off the gallops, 'I want to head straight off... hey! Mind the suit!' This last part addressed to the horse, who sought to rub a sweaty face affectionately against its trainer's arm.

Pete jumped down and hurried off to the house, not seeing Sophie in the bustle of the yard. The box for Leicester was already being loaded, and the small box to ferry the foreign raiders to Stansted had pulled out of the yard before second lot. By the time he returned to the office, work clothes exchanged for a suit, the day's runners and their entourage had departed. And not even a parting kiss.

'You're clear on all the Doncaster entries?' Sebastian verified with his secretary, 'and Jeff knows the arrangements for the runners?'

'All written up on the board,' Valerie confirmed.

'God, I detest leaving the yard for any period of time,' Sebastian complained to Pete, as they walked out to the waiting taxi, 'It's as well I was stoned out of my head last week, or I would have been well and truly out of my head with worry!'

'You would have been impressed with the way we coped,' Pete assured him, 'you weren't even missed!'

'No, I noticed! You would expect a bit of concern from family and friends, wouldn't you? Gambling in Deauville! It's a wonder I'm even speaking to them.'

'You thought I'd backed that odds-on shot of Bob's at Newbury,' Pete pointed out, 'it's easy enough to think the worst of people.'

'Point taken. Incidentally, why did you lose the Porsche, if it wasn't to that Bisley chap?'

'Casburg's men.'

'You're certain?' Sebastian reconsidered their day's plan of action. 'I've never noticed these people with him at the races; he's not likely to have them within hailing distance, is he?'

'He did at Baden-Baden.'

'Damn it.'

It was Pete's turn for misplaced optimism.

'Don't worry,' he assured his trainer, 'what good are heavies against a well-known trainer on a crowded racecourse?' To a degree, he believed his words of hope. The danger was, they couldn't stay on a crowded racecourse forever.

They drove in thoughtful silence to the airport, Pete occasionally trying Sophie's mobile, without success.

'You may give up and turn it off,' Sebastian advised, as they were dropped off at Departures, 'she'll ring at half two when the colt wins!'

'I'd be on it, but for Casburg.'

'You've a nice ride for Dad.'

Pete smiled. 'I would have tried to beg off the Leicester ride,' he admitted.

'And I would have gladly released you,' Sebastian assured him magnanimously.

After a short and uneventful flight, they were met at the airport by Casburg's chauffeur and ferried in comfort straight to the suburban Cologne course. Pete wasted no time in trying Sophie's mobile once more, diverted repeatedly to her voice mail.

'Give me the damn thing, would you,' Sebastian demanded, finally losing patience and taking Pete's phone, 'I'll drag you out of the weighing room the very moment she calls!'

Pete relinquished it, with a sheepish grin.

They pulled into the owners' car park at the racecourse and the chauffeur unloaded Pete's kit bag, leaving their luggage for the forthcoming Doncaster meeting in the boot.

'Let's hope we don't have to make alternative travel arrangements,' Pete remarked grimly, as they headed into the course, 'and don't forget my bloody phone!'

Sebastian waited for Pete to hurriedly sign in, then they walked across to the private boxes, their path politely but firmly obstructed by an efficient security guard.

'Walter Casburg, please,' Sebastian requested.

'He has not yet arrived, sir.'

'Then we'll wait.'

'I am afraid that is not possible, sir, but I will see that you are paged when Herr Casburg arrives.'

It was a disappointing deferment.

'I had some very well rehearsed lines,' Sebastian complained, as they returned to the weighing room.

'First race is in less than ten minutes,' Pete pointed out, 'he'll be here any moment.'

He left Sebastian outside and went in to change for his first ride, a local horse in with a reasonable chance. Familiar with the owner and trainer and knowing that language was an awkward barrier, he went out to the parade ring earlier than usual; regretting the decision at once.

Steve Smith barred his way, smiling at him chillingly and holding up a mobile phone, much like any other.

'Fancy meeting you here! Looking for this, by any chance?' Smith turned on the phone and studied it momentarily. 'Ah look – a dozen missed calls. This your number?' He held the phone out to Pete, who saw his own name repeatedly listed.

Sophie's phone.

The where's and what's swamped Pete, preventing speech.

'Don't worry,' Smith assured him, 'she's

perfectly safe. Unlike poor Paulie. Did you hear, he broke his arm? Fell out a window. Could've been worse, though. Much worse.' That smile again; haunting. He studied the phone, turning it off. 'Bit careless of her… lucky I found it, eh?' It was hard to trust someone who smiled so much. 'By the way,' he added, tossing the phone casually to Pete, 'some bastard nicked our thirty grand.'

Pete held the phone, false courage failing rapidly.

'Still,' Smith continued genially, 'you can get it back easy enough. It doesn't have to be that particular thirty grand, does it?' His smile brimmed with goodwill. To any onlooker, two friends reunited at the racetrack. 'We give you the wink, you give your horse a pull and Bob's your uncle.'

'Which horse?' Pete asked numbly, no option but to accept his fate.

'Well, now… I'll have a look down the old Doncaster list and let you know. I wouldn't take any odds there yourself – the longer it takes us to get our money back, the longer Sophie Churchill remains at risk and the more horses you have to pull. Shall we call it a done deal, then?'

Pete nodded. He clutched tightly the grim reminder of his lack of choice.

'Good boy. Keep in touch, eh?'

And Smith sauntered off.

Pete stood for a moment, nerves unsteady, comprehension even shakier. How had Smith got the phone and how safe was Sophie right this minute? She was at Leicester races and couldn't be safer. Her phone stolen from the yard that morning, Smith travelling over in the box to Germany. Hunky dory, no need for panic. But panic mounted, regardless.

He composed himself as best he could and walked out to the parade ring, the composure too thinly adopted as his trainer enquired with concern over his health. He mimed dehydration, a pretend swig of drink that in reality he would gladly have killed for, and the wave of a hand in a definite no-no. It was an all too familiar answer and easily accepted.

The riding instructions were issued in broken English and similar mimes, but might just as easily have been spoken in slang German. Pete went out onto the course with a desperate feeling of having heard nothing. Yet the helpless inability to set his mind to tactics as they entered the stalls suddenly brought the words back with clarity. It was easier to ride to orders than think for himself.

He won, without much effort on his own part, his thoughts too far away to do his able mount true justice.

His next ride was for Sebastian. More to the point, it was for Casburg. They weren't expected to win the Listed event and if the unexpected looked like happening, Pete knew well enough what was required. Sophie may have carefully chosen Sebastian the best jockey available for the shoestring retainer; but Sebastian had only gone along with her choice because it suited his own needs.

He walked out reluctantly to the parade ring, timing his arrival neatly to coincide with the signal to mount. He had time only to touch his cap and get legged up, but there were no instructions to be issued anyway. He could ride the race as he liked, the filly wasn't good enough for a Listed race.

But only the trainer met him in the parade ring.

'Where's Casburg?'

'Still not here. Deliberately avoiding us, do you suppose?'

Pete shook his head. 'He isn't expecting any confrontation.'

'No, I suppose not. Just held up somewhere, no doubt.' He legged Pete up and wished him luck, without really meaning it.

As he trotted to post, the stalls for the ten furlong race directly in front of the grandstand, Pete wondered where, exactly, Casburg was. Yet it occurred to him that Casburg knew nothing of Sebastian's kidnapping and the threat to Sophie, so upsetting him would do no harm. A win would upset him quite nicely, the filly earning a penalty that would weight her out of all future handicaps. Not that the filly was good enough, but he could give Casburg a minor heart attack by trying.

The only thing he had never tried on the filly was making the running. With nothing to lose but the race, he jumped her out smartly and kicked for the winning post as though passing it for the final time, leading the field out to the back stretch. She seemed happy enough out on her own and settled well, so he set a strong pace and hoped for the best. She was untested over the distance and could either fade in the closing stages or leave her rivals with too much to do and unable to peg her back. With fingers crossed for the latter, he steadily picked up the pace and increased his margin, still feeling plenty of horse beneath him.

In his favour, the course suited a strong galloper and he realised, as they began the sweep into the home straight, that if his filly didn't run out of stamina before the line she wouldn't be caught. The winning post now loomed ahead for real and he could hear a race on in earnest behind him. If the strong gallop suited his own filly, it was certain to have played into the hands of several of his rivals. But had they waited too long for him to come back to them?

Approaching the stands, she was now in unknown territory and showing no signs of tying up. Pete kicked on again and felt her quicken. The filly who usually showed reluctance to quicken up from behind was now equally determined not to relinquish her first taste of being in front and stretched more gamely with each additional yard. Whatever battles were ensuing behind, Pete didn't look and didn't care; the finish comfortably within reach as the noise exploded from the stands.

Pulling up on his second winner from as many rides, the electric buzz of success momentarily eclipsed his thoughts of Sophie. But only momentarily. Yet success brought with it renewed confidence, a vibrant sense of invincibility and reckless courage. That same reckless courage that had seen him set a blistering pace on a filly of unknown stamina labelled ungenuine; that would always prevent him from caving in and taking the instructed pull, regardless of cost.

Saluting the crowd with his whip hand, he reserved his biggest smile for the winning owner, who stepped forward unexpectedly to greet his filly and lead her into the winner's spot.

'An inspired ride, son,' Casburg lied convincingly, apparently thrilled, 'our first Black Type! Well done, well done!' He slapped the filly heartily. Her Listed-class victory had at least earned her the right to have her win printed in the so-called black type of bold print on her pedigree when she retired to stud, increasing her slight value as a broodmare. But it also ruled her out of a more lucrative handicapping career.

'Wow! What was that all about?' Sebastian enquired appreciatively.

'Less judgement, more luck,' Pete admitted, 'she could as easily have folded on me.'

'Too late to supplement her for the Park Hill?' Casburg asked, referring to a Group race at the coming Doncaster meeting.

'We could find her something very nice at Longchamp for the Arc weekend,' Sebastian suggested, waiting for Pete to confirm or contradict.

'She'll get a stiff mile and a half,' the jockey agreed, 'but a step up to Group company… it's a big ask, isn't it?'

Still enjoying the present victory, Casburg switched his hearty pats from filly to jockey, slapping Pete neatly between the shoulder blades. Pete hid the wince and stepped away.

'You can stuff fashion, son,' Casburg told Sebastian, 'it comes and goes, by its very nature. Skill is inherent.' He gestured to Pete. 'That's the skill that won an Apprentice Championship. A retainer well spent.'

Pete turned away, to weigh in, unable to stomach the false delight. If it was Listed and Group race skill Casburg sought, he'd be replaced by a fashionable name overnight. And now his bloody back stung unmercifully. Bastard.

He weighed in safely and presently weighed back out for the Group Three sprint, David Churchill's travelling head lad giving detailed riding instructions before taking away the saddle. The race was there to be won, with no room for errors.

Sebastian leant on the wooden rails of the weighing room, listening.

'Worth a bet,' he remarked, 'the local horse is favourite on the pari-mutuel.'

'Can I have my phone?' Pete asked.

'Sure.' Sebastian fished it out of his pocket. 'She'll be calling in soon, our Leicester colt is due off when you go off.' He replaced the phone in his pocket. 'I'll give it to you after this, you've to go out now anyway.'

'When did Casburg stroll in?' Pete asked him.

'Joined me in the stands as you jumped out the stalls. Damned impressed, too. Well done.'

'Huh.' Pete tapped his boot casually with his whip. 'Listen, mate, take care of my luggage and sign me into the hotel tonight, would you? I'll make my own way over later.'

'You don't want to travel with Walter?'

'Just tell him I've picked up a spare ride in

261

the last on the card.'

'What if he offers to wait?'

'Yeah! Right! There's not time to wait, anyway.'

'He seems to hold you in high regard, Pete.'

'Why shouldn't he? I'm a regular goldmine,' Pete said bitterly.

Sebastian ignored the tone. 'I'll save our little chat for the plane. Try not to bump into us at Departures, won't you? Could be rather embarrassing.'

Pete walked out to the parade ring and got the leg up on his mount, a useful sprinter hopefully taking advantage of the lower quality of opposition in Germany. His confidence was further edged by anger and impatience; unexploded bombs common enough in a five furlong sprint, but usually beneath the saddle, not in it.

They cantered smoothly down the straight to the start, the colt little different to any other mount, any other day. But as they exploded out of the stalls, the quality surged through him; the ease of positioning, the speed of reaction, the extra gear when he asked the colt to quicken. It was like stepping back into the Porsche. Back onto the horses who'd paid for it. Back to what had once been. Three wins from three rides.

Sebastian was waiting for him outside the weighing room and he hurried straight back out after successfully weighing in.

'Any word?'

'Not yet. Still running, possibly. Here's your

phone.'

Pete switched it on, no longer expecting the long-awaited message. Sophie's phone was in his kit bag, turned off. But there was a message from her anyway.

'Technology, eh?' he complained to Sebastian, 'd'you know what time she sent this? Six bloody thirty this morning!'

'Between lots,' Sebastian recalled, 'it would have been quicker to find you and speak to you in person!'

Pete leant over the phone once more, reading through her message. His concern was apparent at once.

'What's wrong?' Sebastian asked anxiously.

'Shit! This can't be right! What was she on second lot?'

Sebastian tried desperately to recall. 'I don't even remember seeing her. It's usually Mexican Dream, but the boy, Eddie, was on her this morning.'

'Please don't tell me that, Seb – according to this, she was swapping to come to Cologne!' Pete re-read the message, hoping impossibly for a change in the fateful words. He read out the text verbatim. 'Maybe speak to you at races, but will try to swap and come over with filly. Something wrong with blanket.'

'Blanket? What blanket? She didn't swap, she's not here. Look, I've to shoot off, but I'll book you in no prob' and I'll call as soon as I hear from her and get a result.'

'Did you sack Steve Smith?' Pete asked.

'Which one is he? The chap in the car who's

not my guard?' Sebastian had so far managed fewer run-ins with the brothers. 'I asked for replacement night security.'

'But what about the flying grooms?' Pete asked urgently.

'Out of my jurisdiction. I didn't even know Walter sent his own man. And if I don't fly, I won't fly – literally!' He grinned in farewell, unconcerned; and unaware that Sophie's phone had arrived in Germany with Steve Smith.

Pete returned to his peg in the jockeys' room, changing hurriedly. He begged a lift from one of the trainers he often rode for and all but followed Sebastian and Casburg into the airport, but there was no danger of meeting them at the departure gate, as he had no intention of flying into Manchester. Getting up to Doncaster was tomorrow's problem. Tonight, he had more urgent problems to resolve.

CHAPTER SEVENTEEN

Pete arrived at Stansted in broad daylight and totally in the dark. He hired a car, opting for the cheapest because it was guaranteed to be something he wouldn't be expected to be seen driving. Then sat in the invisible little car trying to think of the next clever move.

He rang Danny Western.

'Where are you, Lingfield?'

'Home, actually. And you?'

'Nearly home. Was Sophie at Leicester today, do you know?'

'I wouldn't know, I was at Lingfield. But she wasn't, if that's any help. Word trickled back you rode a treble?'

'That's right. Look, mate, I'm lurking around the town, Stetchworth, Casburg's place, Seb's; just snooping. Check in on me a few times, would you?'

'And if you don't answer?'

'Try nine nine nine instead.'

'Just snooping?'

'Just snooping, just hoping. But watch my back for me anyway.'

Western was quiet for a moment. 'Will do. But watch yourself, eh?'

Pete started up the engine and headed for the M11, with two choices of destination. Possibly three. Possibly none. But he had to make one lucky call; had to...

He rang Jeff, the travelling head lad.

'Did Sophie go to Leicester?' he asked, after first asking for the maiden result. He hoped it sounded like any normal call.

'Well, no, she asked to swap for Germany. Didn't she ring you? There was a bit of trouble with the filly and the travel rug. Saw none of it myself, I was seeing to my lot, but Sophie got it sorted and asked to swap. That was fine. Then she had some argument with Casburg's man and disappeared off, so I had to re-organise everyone yet again.'

It all sounded so harmless.

'She's lost her own phone,' Pete told him, 'but if you do hear from her, tell her to give me a call. Thanks, mate.'

Pete hung up. Considered the options. Paul Smith had his arm in plaster. Steve Smith had flown over to Germany. But last week, with his head inside a hood, he'd heard a third voice.

He had three calls. And couldn't afford to strike out.

Coming off the motorway, he turned off for Stetchworth and parked at the first driveway; walking back to the rusted gate and cattle feeder. Seb would have moaned at him for being over cautious, but self-preservation told him he couldn't be cautious enough.

There were no sign of lights, torches or otherwise, emanating from the barn. It wasn't dark, but might possibly be inside the disused building. Which might possibly not be disused. Pete watched his step and approached as though the possibility was a certainty.

His mobile rang sharply and he fumbled for it with urgency, cursing his thoughtlessness. Should have switched it to silent. Stupid bloody bastard, him and the caller.

'Hello?'

'Good, you've not boarded yet. Listen, what the devil's going on, exactly?'

It was Sebastian. And distinctly not his usual charming self.

Pete drew a breath, to think of the least worrying explanation he could give, but Sebastian took the brief pause to be a lack of comment.

'You haven't exactly been upfront with us, have you?' Sebastian continued, not pausing for a reply, 'Sophie's at home in tears and Dad says he feels hurt, which means you've pretty much stabbed him to the core. We're none of us exactly straight, I know, but there's crooked and there's damn right crooked, Pete, and unfortunately you've over-stepped the mark.'

'Sophie's at home? What's the matter, Seb? What's happened?'

'A small matter of making certain Marcel's mount won the feature at Epsom. Which basically meant not winning on ours, didn't it?'

'But you know that. What about Sophie?'

'I know what you told us, the convenient get the favourite beaten threat. But Walter didn't have a clue what I was talking about! He doesn't even know these Smith brothers!'

'Christ, Seb, he's lying.'

'He really didn't give me that impression. You, on the other hand, sold stable information to Bisley's Bookmakers and Danny Western.'

'Seb, believe me, if that's what he's told you,

he's wrong.'

'Walter? He knows nothing of any of it. Sophie told me about Bisley, after she heard you assuring Danny Western about the favourite at Epsom.'

'But I never did! It's a mistake.'

'That's what Sophie thinks. A mistake. Yours is saying that you didn't, when she's just heard you doing just that on tape.'

The phone clicked off.

Suddenly the Smith brothers were the least of Pete's worries.

The word tape stung him sharply. He'd left a tape running the night the Smith brothers had paid him a call. After that, he'd no recollection. Presumably it had still been sitting in the hall when Westy stayed the night. Still within range of the kitchen when Westy had quizzed him about his shady career. Would Westy have seen it? And turned it on? And, if so, *what the hell had they said*? It had been damning, Pete remembered that much. 'That's three counts you'd lose your licence on,' Westy had told him. Shit.

Shit, shit and shit.

Pete walked hurriedly back to the car, trying Sophie's phone without thinking and soon finding out it was still turned off in his pocket. It was a brief reminder of why he'd come here, but Sophie had been found, never lost, and finding Paul Smith was no longer a priority. He called Sebastian instead, fearing that he simply wouldn't pick up.

'What now? We're checking in.'

'Look, I'm sorry. But check me in, would you?'

'Of course. I'm not vindictive…'

'No, I didn't mean… look, mate, I'm in Newmarket right now. I'll come up in the morning. Whatever you think, it's a mistake. I'm going to find Paul Smith and get it sorted.'

'Do what you like, I'm pretty put out with you right now.'

Pete hung up, a little put out himself. The lack of trust hurt, after all that he had done for Sebastian, which included much covering up, both on the racecourse and off. He wondered how much covering up had been done on his behalf. Without any, the morning would find his contract terminated and the Jockey Club issuing an appointment for disciplinary proceedings. Sebastian's attitude hardly inspired hope.

Feeling as battered as though he had run into both Smith brothers, Pete sat back in the car and drove at an unusually sedate pace to the Churchills. He considered the possible contents of the tape, convincing himself increasingly that he'd said nothing damaging. Warning off material, yes, but surely nothing that Sophie and her family didn't already know? And how could he have mentioned the Epsom favourite – it had surely all been taped *after* the event.

Cursing Westy and his bloody itchy trigger finger, he pulled in at the Churchill house and dragged himself out of the car to face the music. Maybe they weren't such angels, after all. Sebastian could freely commit murder, but prospective son-in-laws had to…

Tow the line.

Pete shuddered involuntarily and returned to the car, seeing Sophie futile. If his honesty was in question, why would they believe his protestations of innocence?

With no point in searching the barn, he was now left with just two options, which did little to improve his chances.

He drove round to Sebastian's yard and parked behind the house; walking through to the hostel, little more than a long narrow corridor off of which opened ten rooms each side, and tapping at the first door. To Pete, the lads' hostels always reminded him of monasteries, tiny box rooms equipped with metal bed, wardrobe, hand basin and nothing else, although the analogy couldn't usually be any further from the truth. He'd lived in one himself for eighteen months, until riding success elevated him to rented digs.

'Yeah? What d'ya want?' called a voice from within.

'Jimmy.'

'Second from the end, other side.'

'Ta, mate.'

If Jimmy himself hadn't heard the brief exchange, the others, who had, rectified it. The name 'Jimmy' was yelled at full throttle from various rooms, so that Jimmy appeared before Pete had even gone halfway down the corridor.

The lad smiled in recognition and ushered him into his room, a couple of the other lads joining them, out of interest.

'Want some tea?' he offered, flicking on a kettle on the floor beside the bed, then rummaging in the wardrobe drawers for the remaining ingredients, without success.

'You got any tea bags?' he asked of the spectators, who wandered off into any rooms but their own in search of milk, tea and sugar and returned almost immediately empty-handed.

'You rode a nice one on ours, I got twelve to one on the pari-mutuel,' Jimmy told Pete appreciatively.

'Did Steve Smith fly back with you?' Pete asked.

'That useless bugger? He did, as it happens. Doesn't usually, mind. I only went 'cos of him. He had a row with Tina about the rug, then Sophie tried her hand, but he'd have none of it, so she left him to it. The filly didn't need a rug that heavy. And the silly bastard disappeared with it again when we got there! I reckon he's got a tack shop over there and flogs them!'

'No, he brought it back,' one of the other lads corrected him, 'I saw him slinging it in the tack room when you got back in.'

'Bit bloody late, then,' Jimmy complained, 'she wore some old sheet we picked up in the racecourse stables to fly home in.'

'Does he ever mention where he stays, here in town?' Pete pressed, the news getting steadily worse. On the plus side, Paul Smith had his arm in plaster, which was at least one less fist to dodge.

'Never mentions anything. Only comes along for the free ride, if you ask me.'

'I'll find him around somewhere, I suppose,' Pete said, thanking him and walking down to the yard.

He headed past the feed room and tack room, to the portacabin, unharmed from its recent arson attack, the smoke damage cleaned away and the toilet window boarded up. Inside, three security guards sat watching a video, on the television supposedly monitoring the stable yard. They looked up, unconcerned, as Pete tapped at the door. Three strange faces, unthreatening.

'I was just looking for Paul,' Pete announced cheerfully, 'Paul Smith? Is he on duty tonight, d'you know?'

'No, mate, he's on another job.'

'Any idea where?'

'Couldn't tell you. Try ringing the office.'

'No, they wouldn't tell you,' another guard reminded them, 'security and all that. We'll pass on a message, if we see him? Can't guarantee when, though.'

Pete shook his head. 'Doesn't matter. Just wanted to ask him about a horse that got colic one evening.'

'You want that Mike chap,' the first guard volunteered helpfully, 'he gets in just before the night crew knock off and he writes all that sort of thing down.'

Pete thanked them and left them in peace to return to their movie. He had barely gone a few strides when he doubled back and called them out once again.

'Listen, can I have the tack room key? One of you can come with me, if you like? I just need to rug up the colicky horse, I'm a bit worried about it.'

'No problem,' the guard agreed, tossing over the necessary key, 'work away, we trust you!'

Pete was glad someone did; even though their trust was misplaced.

He unlocked the tack room and began sifting through the pile of rugs, not really sure what he was supposed to be looking for. The chances were it was nothing at all, but Steve Smith seemed to have an annoying habit of interfering with them, even if theft couldn't yet be proved.

Pulling out the first hideous tartan travel rug he found, Pete hung it over his arm and returned the key to the guards. Taking the rug round to the yard, he threw it straight in the back of the car and drove off toward his final port of call, a large Edwardian house out on the Bury Road, one of the few without a stable yard attached.

It had once been owned by Lady Markham, for the purposes of entertaining in the town during meetings, but had been leased for many years, the most recent incumbent being Walter Casburg. Casburg himself was absent – but had he left any security guards to protect his interests?

Pete drove slowly past, trying to detect any signs of life from within. To all intents and purposes the house looked deserted; yet who knew what dangers lay hidden out of view? Whatever the dangers, he had to find out. He desperately needed hard evidence of a threat.

He parked innocently further up from the house and walked back, making it up the drive unchallenged. Since it was confrontation he sought, there seemed little point in sneaking around the back and he simply pushed the doorbell relentlessly. If the Smith brothers were inside, they would have to answer eventually, if only to shut him up. He kept an eye on all the windows, hoping to spot a flicker of movement, but the house was definitely empty.

Which left only the whole of Cambridge and its environs, always supposing Paul Smith lived near to his job. Suddenly, the task of convincing Sophie of his innocence seemed less daunting.

He returned, deflated, to the car and was just climbing back in as his phone rang.

'Still able to answer, then?' Western greeted him, 'how's the snooping?'

'Not. Short of looking in every pub from here to Cambridge, I've drawn a blank.'

'Why the urgency? You'll be in Donny' all week, safe from harm.'

'Like York, you mean?' Pete smiled to himself. 'I met Steve Smith this afternoon and he wants his thirty grand back. He gives me the horse, I do as I'm told and Sophie comes to no harm. You think I can afford to sit and wait?'

'A Donny' runner?'

'I think so.' He wondered whether to mention the tape, but any cock-up had been his own stupid fault anyway. 'Seb's beginning to doubt me. If I throw a race this week then that's it, I'm finished. Once they've given their orders, I'm trapped. If I can only get to them before they issue the orders, I've a chance of recording their threat.'

'Are you even looking in the right place, then? Surely they're on their way up north as we speak?'

'I don't know, Westy, mate… I'm done for, aren't I?'

'Done up like a kipper, sunshine. Just head north and dodge the bullets. They've still got to get the message to you yet. Oh, and if you want some real advice, don't answer your phone again or pick up messages from reception, between now and Saturday night!'

'It might just come to that. Are you driving up tomorrow?'

'Morning train. You?'

'The morning, probably.'

Western laughed. 'You're tempted to go tonight?'

'Tempted to change hotels or move into the racecourse sauna!'

'Keep dodging those bullets, sunshine!'

Pete hung up and started the engine. There was one bullet he couldn't dodge.

CHAPTER EIGHTEEN

He pulled up outside the Churchills' and for the second time that evening braced himself to ring the bell.

David answered, looking about as stern as was possible for such a round cheery man. He dispensed with the normal greetings, no doubt finding the situation as awkward and embarrassing as Pete was finding it to be.

'Sophie's in the living room, you'd better go straight through.'

He stepped to one side, allowing Pete to pass, and called out to his wife, a semblance of heavenly manners still remaining.

'Angie! In the drawing room.'

Pete nodded to Angela as she passed him in the hall and counted his blessings that she was nothing like his own mother, still baying for Barbara's blood four months after first being told she'd left. He pushed open the living room door, the familiar line 'play it by ear' his only thought.

Sophie looked up as he entered, dry eyed and unable to disguise the fact that she was, at least, pleased to see him. He tossed her mobile over to her.

'Steve Smith gave it to me.'

'So that's where it went.' She put it beside her, on the arm of the sofa, the significance of his words slow to register. 'Oh, God – you must have been worried sick!'

'I was a bit. What happened?'

'Before or after I made the mistake of playing your tape?'

Pete smiled and sat beside her. 'Start anywhere you like, I'm just bloody relieved you're talking to me at all. Your bloody brother seems to have blown things up out of all proportions.'

'Possibly. Although it got a little heated earlier.'

'Why does he think I'm screwing him? I'll only look after a horse if he asks me to. I know I told Bisley about Breadline, but, for Christ's sake, Soph', it was no secret, he could have looked it up in the form book just as easily. If I could have beaten Marcel at Epsom I would have done. You must know that.'

'Of course I know that. I told them so. But Dad felt Sebastian ought to know.' She pulled a face. 'And you know his reaction. He'd just been given a roasting by Walter, apparently, so we didn't exactly time it well.'

'Ought to know what, exactly?'

Sophie smiled ruefully and stood up, going to the stereo and removing a cassette from the tape deck. She slipped it into the handheld player bought for her at the gala day, and fetched it across to Pete.

'Danny was running round gathering quotes, gala day. You must have spoken to him while he had this running.' She sat back down beside Pete and rewound the tape fractionally, as though very familiar with the necessary length. She pushed play.

'*If you and your mates have any money invested this Bank Holiday, the favourite for the big one at Epsom still looks a cert'.*'

'There you are, slap bang between Bob

277

Graham and yourself, as it happens.'

Pete sat back, remembering at once the conversation Westy had insisted upon recording over.

'That wasn't the gala day,' Pete told her. 'Seb himself let me use the office to confront Paul Smith about the Epsom threat...'

'So he reminded us, quite bitterly. And all, apparently, pure invention so his horse wouldn't win. Seb's words, not mine!'

'He's a bloody idiot.'

'So Walter had already told him. Your fault again, incidentally.'

'You can explain that to me in a minute. But back in Seb's office, I couldn't get Smith to admit to anything remotely incriminating. I just told him to return the message that I wasn't going to get the favourite beaten, no matter what the threat. That's what you've just heard. And when I gave the cassette back to Westy, he pointed out I'd only incriminated myself. So as far as we knew he went over it. I watched him do it, gala day. That's why I'm first on, saying hello. He had the bright idea to record messages from everyone.' Pete shook his head. 'Remind me to ram it up his backside next time I see him!'

Sophie laughed.

'You can actually hear the difference, now you mention it. Total silence, when you say that bit. We thought you'd met Danny in some quiet spot!'

'And what else did you think?'

'An elaborate hoax, that's how Sebastian described it! First of all, Dad and I were arguing in your defence, but Sebastian had us so convinced that I nearly turned turncoat myself!'

'Just because I told Westy the favourite would win at Epsom?! The favourite was always going to win – that's why it was the bloody favourite!'

Sophie smiled. 'On the flight to Manchester from Cologne, Sebastian confronted Walter. Accused him of threatening you, paying the Smith brothers and trying to set up coups outside the yard. Walter thought he'd flipped! He found it quite hysterical, by all accounts, and looked for the hidden camera! Then he got annoyed and branded Sebastian a total moron, at which point Dad rang Sebastian to see what his thoughts were on you telling the gutter press about the stable runners.'

'And his thoughts ran away with him.'

'A bit worse than that. Because Walter was within earshot and included in the discussion. It was Walter who suggested that if he himself hadn't hired the Smith brothers, someone else had. And then it all just snowballed ridiculously.' She smiled. 'It started to read like a Dick Francis plot! I told them you weren't that clever!'

'Thanks!'

'You're welcome! The rest of the tape was quite good, by the way.'

'I'm glad. It was beginning to look like the worst please-marry-me gift any would-be fiancé had ever given!'

'Is that a proposal?'

'Not yet. Call it the first down-payment.'

She laughed.

'So, what was this business with Steve Smith?' Pete asked.

'Oh, God, so long ago now, I'd forgotten. What with Seb's dramatics; Walter must have given him such a ticking off. It's about time someone did.' She stood up. 'Tea?'

'Gasping for one.'

He followed her out to the kitchen and embraced her from behind, clasping her round the waist as she put the kettle on. They moved across to a chair and Sophie sat on Pete's lap as they waited for the water to boil.

'It might be September already, but the weather doesn't know that yet,' Sophie told Pete, 'we were coming back in from first lot and the box for the airport was still there, so I went over to give them a hand and the delay was that Steve Smith arguing with Tina about the travel rug. Absolutely insisting the filly wore it, but the poor animal hates travelling and she was sweated up badly enough as it was. Tina absolutely refused to put the rug on her, which was fair enough. But Steve was just as insistent that it was to protect her in the box and was Walter's livery and therefore obligatory. They looked like killing each other, and the filly was ready to boil over, so I asked Jeff if I could swap.' She hugged Pete warmly. 'Quite looked forward to it, too. Surprising you in Cologne.'

'Is it nice to be surprised in Germany?!'

'Yes, very! Except I was too excited, so I text you to say I was swapping – sorry about that. Anyway, I rubbed the filly over and I told Steve I'd put the rug on at the airport, as it's cooler on the plane. But he just went ahead and put the rug on anyway! And he wouldn't let me take it off! Grabbed my arms and physically pulled me away, so I swapped again with one of the lads and went home. I did actually try to call you from mum's, but I only got the answer phone and there was so much interference I didn't bother to leave a message. It was Mum who said, have you listened to that tape yet?'

'Thanks, Mum!'

'Umm.' She got up and filled the teapot. 'If I'd just been listening at home, I would have ignored it. But, you know, telling Danny Western and his friends that it's safe to back a favourite doesn't sound so good to non-fiancé material. Especially as your whole game play for the race had been to get in the favourite's way and steal the race, if you could!' She poured four mugs of tea. 'Don't worry about Sebastian, Dad will smooth things over. And Sebastian can smooth things out with Walter. And all happy ever after.'

She handed Pete two of the mugs and carried the other two through to the living room once more, Pete following; calling out to her parents as she passed the drawing room.

'Tea!'

They settled themselves back down on the sofa.

'We'd best be leaving for Donny' straight after this,' Sophie suggested, 'it would have been a lot easier sticking to our original plans and leaving from Manchester and Leicester!'

'I'm going to drive up in the morning,' Pete told her. 'There's still the matter with Paul Smith and his brother. I didn't actually tell you what Steve said when he handed your phone over.'

As Angela and David now joined them, he felt it best not to tell her, and she tactfully didn't press. Instead, she explained to her parents what had happened and David rang the news through to Sebastian, who demanded to speak to Pete.

'I really can't apologise enough,' he said humbly, 'but I'd done my best to help you, I even booked you into a hotel for that Monday night. And then you rescued me in Germany and covered for me, even though you thought I'd pinched Sophie's money. I thought we'd reached the perfect level of trust. So it came as a real kick in the teeth to find that we hadn't.'

'That's okay, mate. I hear you got an ear-bashing from Casburg?'

'Ah, yes. Well, that as well. He made me feel such an idiot that I really felt I'd been played for one.'

'He was convincing, then?'

'Very. But he wasn't lying, Pete. I know lying. I play cards! No one bluffs that well.'

'He owns casinos, he's a grade above you, Seb.'

'Umm; I suppose you could have a point. So, you and Sophie will be up here tonight?'

'The morning.'

'Whatever suits. Sorry again and all that.'

Pete hung up and finished his tea.

'I'd best head off, I've some errands to run,' he apologised to his hosts.

'I'll come with you,' Sophie said, meaning more than just as far as the hall.

'It's dangerous, Soph', Pete insisted, when they were alone by the front door, 'stay here.'

'I can't sit at home waiting for phone calls,' she reminded him, 'I have to be there.'

'You saw what they did to me.'

'Whatever they do, it's not as frightening as sitting at home imagining it.'

She ended the argument quite simply by stepping out alongside him and closing the door behind them.

'What did Steve say when he returned my phone?' she asked, sitting alongside Pete in the car.

'He wants his thirty grand back. He's going to name the horse, I'm to do as I'm told. And you come to no harm.'

Sophie said nothing.

'I'll take you home, if you like?'

She shook her head, resolute.

'So, what are you planning to do?' she asked.

'Hide, actually. I've no idea where to look for the Smith brothers, so my only choice now is to just stop them finding me. If they give me the orders, I have to do as I'm told.' He suddenly remembered the rug. 'I've a rug in the back, by the way.'

Sophie grinned. 'Some kind of invite?'

'What, in this little box?! I'm an athlete, not a contortionist!' He grew sombre once more. 'Whenever anything happens, Steve Smith messes with the rugs. So I threw one in the back, for a look-see. You never know.'

'A distraction, maybe,' Sophie mused, 'to stop me going to Cologne, to stop Sebastian recognising his horses at Baden-Baden…'

'I wasn't thinking along such subtle lines. Steve Smith couriers drugs.'

'*In our rugs*?!'

'Maybe. Where can we go to check it out?'

'Home first, I need my case. Then off up to Doncaster. If we stop somewhere en route, Newark, maybe, or Grantham, you'll be well hidden from Smith and we won't have so far to go in the morning.'

'Do you have to go home? Can't you borrow some things from your mum?'

'Pete! What do I tell her? I can't go to my own flat because your hit men are waiting to kidnap me?!' She smiled. 'You're not making things easy on yourself with the prospective in-laws, are you?!'

'To your place, then.'

They drove carefully, alert to any danger, but the flat looked safe enough and they made it inside without harm. Sophie hurriedly grabbed her case, already packed, and they returned to the car.

'I was going to drive up with Dad in the morning, when I missed Leicester,' Sophie told Pete, as they set out on the long drive north, 'the fact that you'd fallen out with Sebastian was irrelevant. If it ever comes to taking sides, I'll take yours every time.'

'Sebastian seems to be taking Casburg's.'

'He must be a convincing liar.'

'So far, he's pressuring me into fixing races. That's all. It was the Smiths themselves who jumped Seb and took the money. So he doesn't have a great deal to deny, anymore than I have a great deal to accuse him of. Certainly no evidence. But if we can just raise the stakes a fraction...'

'The rug?'

'Well, hopefully. He can still bluff if he likes, but it's got to make him more nervous. Less convincing.'

'More dangerous,' Sophie observed, 'an animal backed into a corner.'

'Very reassuring, thank you.'

They drove on in silence for a while.

'Sebastian had better name me as his representative,' Sophie said at last, Suffolk and Cambridgeshire a long way behind them.

'Why? It's you they've threatened, not him.'

'The weighing room – out of bounds to everyone but trainers, jockeys and officials. You've got the perfect bolt-hole. And I can't get in.'

'Christ, Soph', you shouldn't even be here at all.'

'If I'm at home, I'm a sitting target. As Sebastian's rep', I can just sit in the weighing room.'

'We'll have to change rooms at the hotel,' Pete suggested, 'keep that room, as a decoy, and book another under assumed names.'

'St Leger week? And they'll have a spare room, I suppose?'

'A different hotel, then.'

'Unless it's in a different city, you still won't get a spare room!'

'Somewhere out of the city's fine. Racing doesn't start till two and we've the car now.'

'We can't just run away.'

'I've already tried meeting them full on, and look where it's got me.'

More miles passed, in silence.

'At what point do you go to the Jockey Club?' Sophie asked.

'When enough evidence points to Casburg and his men, instead of me.'

'You will go, then?'

'I probably won't have any choice in the matter. Even if we skip over their heads and go straight to the police, they'll hold their own investigation. I'm no saint, Soph' – it's scary.'

Sophie smiled. 'You're a saint to me. I never thought I'd be back at the races again, with someone I felt... comfortable with. Complete, again.'

Complete. Pete smiled inwardly, hearing what he had already recognised, the breach in his own life healed, too.

The sun set, the miles passed; they had no need to speak.

They pulled in just before Grantham, choosing a small country house-style hotel and enjoying a late dinner before retiring to their room. Only then did Pete fetch the rug up from the car.

They stretched it out on the floor and knelt beside it, examining the seams.

'You couldn't keep stitching these up,' Sophie pointed out, 'anyway, they're undamaged.'

'Flip it over, there must be something on the

inside.'

They turned the rug over, the tartan lining just as hard on the eyes, but revealing nothing within its busy pattern.

Pete ran a hand over the rug and struck gold almost at once.

'Bingo! A seam!'

Sure enough, running perfectly along a yellow line was a split in the material, fastened by some hefty press studs that took a degree of pulling before popping open. Sophie mirrored his move and found a second secret pocket on the opposite side. One each side, just in from the shoulder, perfectly placed to escape detection. The padding within the rest of the rug was discernibly thinner within the pocket, masking perfectly any contents.

'Try just below the back,' Sophie suggested, feeling along the line, 'they'd want to even out any weight, or we'd feel it, throwing the rug over.'

They both found the third and fourth pockets, no longer so well hidden when one knew what to look for.

'Okay, so how do we prove these pockets are for smuggling drugs?' Pete asked.

'The dog at the airport,' Sophie recalled, 'we take them to a police station where they have sniffer dogs and ask them to check.'

'Does every station have a sniffer dog?'

'I don't know. The big cities must. Doncaster.'

'Maybe we should just press on, then. We're only another hour away.' Pete looked at the rug, doubtfully. 'Although it might not be drugs. Diamonds, documents, you name it.'

'I'll ring Dad,' Sophie decided, 'if we stay here now and do nothing until tomorrow, we don't want to leave the rest of the rugs to get stolen. They're evidence. This one isn't. You stole it and possibly tampered with it.'

'Right! I'm a dab hand with a needle and thread!'

'I don't know how the law stands, Pete. At least if Dad picks up all the rugs tonight and locks them in his tack room, they'll be safe from the Smiths.'

She rang him, without further debate.

David was mystified as to why he should urgently retrieve all of Sebastian's travel rugs, but Sophie refused to tell him any more than that Paul Smith was probably stealing them, to sell.

'You must have heard Sebastian moaning about the rugs always going missing?' she insisted.

'Yes, but he blamed the German racecourses!'

'The lads blame his own security men, Paul Smith and his brother.'

'What about the stable rugs and paddock sheets?'

'Worthless,' Sophie convinced him, 'all initialled. Just the travel rugs. And before the night security come on duty.'

'Tell him to say he needs a rug for a colicky horse,' Pete advised, 'that's how I got this one.'

'Dear God, how many people have you got

stealing these rugs?!' David demanded, hearing Pete, 'I shall simply say I'm borrowing them, which is perfectly acceptable.' He sighed audibly and promised to go straight round to the yard.

'He does everything he's told,' Sophie assured Pete, with a grin, as she hung up, 'bless his heart!'

'Okay, then. Hopefully we've got some evidence. We still don't know what it's evidence of, mind you.'

'No one would go to such lengths to hide anything legal,' Sophie assumed.

'Enough, then, just to shove this in his face and cause major panic, you think?'

'Pretty much,' she agreed.

He smiled. 'Bed, then.' The gentle smile turned to the familiar seductive grin, complete with the usual desired affect.

Complete. It was a nice word to take to bed.

Pete was aware of the phone ringing, a hazy warning not to answer it competing with the more insistent plea to return to sleep.

'Who is it? What time is it?' he muttered, as Sophie said a far too cheery hello.

He needn't have bothered asking, Sebastian's voice pounding back at him as audibly as Sophie's.

'Why the bloody hell have you kidnapped all my rugs?'

'We'll tell you when we see you, they're just

in safe keeping.'

'Safe keeping? Jeff's blowing a gasket, trying to get the horses boxed up for Donny'. We thought they'd been pinched, until I rang Dad to borrow a couple of his.'

'Did he tell you he had them?' Sophie's disgust at such betrayal only seemed to add to Sebastian's.

'So he's got them! He told me to speak to you!'

'Why the fuss? It's too warm for rugs anyway! We'll be up there by eleven, we'll tell you everything then.'

'Where are you, then?'

'That little hotel near Grantham. We stopped there for dinner once, on the way back from York, when Mum won the ladies' race.'

'You could be here in an hour!'

'Why would we want to be? Racing doesn't start 'til two! Go and have some breakfast and read your Racing Post, we'll be there in our own good time.'

She hung up and snuggled back down beside Pete.

'Flipping heck,' he complained, 'we don't often get to lie in. What time is it, anyway?'

'Six. They've just found all their rugs missing.'

'So I heard. At least Seb got blasted out of bed before us!'

He wrapped himself tightly around Sophie, all thought of sleep gone. Together, they killed the time in a way that he and Barbara never could, the passion somehow elevated to a different plain. So much was still new and experimental, and he was grateful for the difference, relieved not to have to let go of not-so-old memories just yet.

Eventually, they got up and showered and wandered down for breakfast, both electing for fruit juice and cereal. It took the amoral strength of a racing hack to eat egg and bacon in front of a jockey. Remembering Western, Pete borrowed Sophie's phone.

'You took me at my word, then?' Western observed, noting the new phone number.

'I'm taking no chances,' Pete agreed, 'Steve Smith doubles as Casburg's flying groom – and all Seb's travel rugs have got secret pockets stitched in.'

Western's response was predictable. 'Fucking hell! You've stumbled on the mother load!'

'I did wonder as much. Now to tell Casburg.'

'Fuck that, sunshine! These are drug dealers, not bookies! Get the fuck out of there and tell the police! You owe me an exclusive, there's no way I'm fishing your body out of the river!'

'Relax, I'm covered. The rugs are at David Churchill's. Casburg's already cooked, mate.'

'Relax? When pulling horses is just a little sideline?! Where are you now, anyway? Still in HQ?'

'Grantham. We drove up part way last night.'

'I'm getting the nine o'clock train. I'll be in Donny' at twelve.'

Pete hung up and returned Sophie's phone. As he handed it back, he visualised Steve Smith handing it to him. Steve Smith had Sophie's number.

'Check the caller IDs before you answer that,' he warned her.

But she was no longer paying any attention, staring past him at the open doorway, leading out to the reception area.

Pete turned around.

Sebastian was walking toward the breakfast room.

And with him, Walter Casburg.

CHAPTER NINETEEN

It would have been a heart-stopping moment, had there been time. As it was, Sebastian had already pulled up a chair and joined them before the shock of his appearance registered. Casburg was slower, taking his time, selecting a chair, assessing the room, the company.

Pete watched him, warily.

'So – what's your problem, son?' Casburg asked, genially enough. His bluffs were too good for Sebastian.

'You tell me,' Pete fired back.

'Okay;' Casburg conceded, 'how about you pour some of that tea, Sophie, hun', and we'll see if we can't just talk this through?'

Pete looked across at Sebastian, trying to gauge the situation. Sebastian appeared unconcerned; certainly not a man under duress. A man in cohorts?

'Talk this through?' Pete protested, 'your men have attacked me, robbed and kidnapped Seb, and threatened Sophie!'

Casburg looked suitably amazed, which infuriated Pete still further.

'Choke on this then – we've got the rugs!'

'Whoa! Now hang on there, son,' Casburg protested, 'wind back a little to the start. This is just more of Seb's nonsense and some!'

'Which start? Torturing me? Kidnapping Seb? Smuggling drugs?'

'*Drugs*?!' Sebastian looked at Sophie, Pete's sanity openly questioned in his expression.

Casburg had nothing to say. He looked from

Sebastian to Pete in bewilderment.

'Is he for real?' he asked Sebastian eventually.

Sebastian shrugged helplessly.

'Cut the crap, we've no time for denials,' Pete warned, 'they've threatened Sophie. You've to put an end to this now.'

Casburg sat back in his chair.

'These guys, would they be the security guys Seb told me about?'

Pete studied him. Thought of casinos and bluffs and the silver-haired, silver-tongued Straubinger. 'You didn't know?'

'Don't panic, son, I believe you. I didn't, when Seb first came up with this kooky story. I thought you were inventing some cover.'

'Shit!' Pete declared with sudden realisation, 'they're working on their own.'

'The first sensible thing you've said,' Casburg agreed, 'so now can you start from the beginning?'

Pete stared into his tea, demoralised. The emergency stop button had been snatched from his fingertips.

'Steve Smith and Paul Smith? Ever heard of them?' he asked.

Casburg slowly shook his head, considering the names.

'Christ, you must know Steve Smith!' Pete insisted, 'he's your flying groom.'

'I don't employ stable staff, that's Sebastian's jurisdiction.'

'I didn't employ him!' Sebastian protested.

'Would Andreas Straubinger have recommended him?' Pete asked.

'Why should he?'

'Steve Smith works for him. Couriering drugs.'

'Drugs? Are you for real?'

Pete nodded.

'Does Andreas know?'

'That's exactly why he's employed.'

Casburg's eyes narrowed. 'And just how do you know all this?'

'Donkey work. They started messing with me, I started digging for information. Paul Smith was piling on pressure to get me to throw races. I had to try and get him off my back.'

Casburg considered the words. 'Smith would be the guy's real name?'

'Brothers. Steve works for Straubinger, Paul was on Sebastian's night security staff.'

Some light clearly dawned, but Casburg was careful to betray little more.

'You paid Paul Smith to apply pressure?' Pete guessed.

'If that's who he is,' Casburg admitted. 'But not on you. You made it perfectly clear you wouldn't give any of my horses an easy ride and Seb backed you up. So I hired some Smith guy to test the water, see if Seb might come round. There's money to be made, knowing the right information.'

'I had the charity day takings,' Sebastian told him bitterly, 'the Smith brothers stole it and drugged me up. I was abandoned in a Suffolk barn, then dumped in Baden-Baden, without a penny to my name.'

'Now, son, that wasn't any of my doing. If you want me to come forward to the police then I gladly will. Those boys want locking up.'

'None of this is tracing them or helping Sophie and me,' Pete stepped in. 'Have you a contact number for Paul Smith? Can you get one off Straubinger, without raising suspicion?'

'I could certainly ask. But the drugs – tell me more?'

'Your travel rugs have secret pockets sewn into them,' Pete explained, 'Steve Smith always travels with the horses across to Germany, disappears off with the rugs, returns them later to the tack room, if at all. It seems he's using the horses to courier the drugs across, presumably for Straubinger.'

'Pour me some more of that tea there, hun',' Casburg asked Sophie. He looked back at Pete. 'And the threat to Sophie?'

'They've tried to give me riding instructions,' Pete told him, 'but so far I've not complied.'

'You should see what they've done to him,' Sebastian volunteered unnecessarily.

'The hand you hurt on the gallops?' Casburg suggested.

Pete nodded. 'Yesterday, Steve Smith told me to ride to orders or they'd hurt Sophie.'

'Well then you ride to orders, son! And the orders?'

'Safely dodged, so far. That's why we're here

and not Donny' or HQ.'

'HQ?'

Pete smiled, forgetting Casburg was a foreign visitor. 'Newmarket. Headquarters of British racing.' He added more milk to his tea and sipped it gratefully. 'Your turn, now. How do you know Straubinger and why are your horses being used?'

'Damn, son, this is all news to me. But I met Andreas in Vegas. I was looking to set up in Deauville, but I couldn't get a foot in the door. Andreas suggested Baden-Baden.'

'Any idea how the horses got involved?'

'I've always had horses. I've a small string at home with Dean Hadley. Seb joined us for a couple of seasons as Dean's assistant. Impressed me enough to send him over a few. A big string, as you know. Your courses here are so varied, easier to fool the handicapper, I figured we could run a profitable yard. Andreas has a few horses in Germany, he told me to bring a few over. Just social. Keeps them out of sight of the handicapper, too.' He paused, thinking things through. 'He also put me off buying here. He made a point, you know. Why buy European, when the Europeans are buying our horses by the plane load? And I know our breeding.'

Pete saw the point. 'You ship in forty horses from the States and God knows how many kilos of South American coke, then ferry it across in batches to Straubinger.'

'Sure looks that way, son.'

'Just a minute,' Sebastian interposed, 'we must be talking big bucks here, surely?'

Casburg nodded. 'It ain't cheap, son.'

'So why mess with a few piddly bets?'

'Straubinger doesn't,' Pete reminded him, 'and the Smiths are only on his pay roll. Let's face it, punters and bookies, it's an age old war. Even you two go into battle, and neither of you exactly need the extra cash.'

Casburg smiled and leaned back comfortably.

'When Seb told me you'd taken his rugs, I thought it was time to pay you a call and give you your marching orders. You're a great jockey, son, but I can do without eccentrics, we've enough of them in Vegas. As it is, I'll just tell you to go to the police. Right this minute. The racing can wait. There are more important things than horses.'

Pete shook his head. 'Not for me. I need those rides.'

'Televised handicaps? If I told you my budget for this year's sales, you'd drool! Next season you'll be on Group horses, son. No need to put on a show for the cameras. Go to the police, miss this afternoon, if you have to, I'll just go home and buy you a Park Hill winner, a Champagne Stakes winner – hell! A St Leger winner!'

Pete smiled. 'I'll ring the police. They should be through by one anyway.'

'One other thing you'd better mention,' Casburg added, 'Andreas is on his way over. He's my guest for the meeting. Or, should I say, was.'

The police were through by ten, taking down

298

the details meticulously, removing the travel rug with care and treating all witnesses with the utmost respect. The impression they gave was that they were dealing with obsessive children with over-active imaginations and that they actually believed none of it. Grantham was no more a hotbed of drug smuggling and kidnapping than Newmarket.

As they closed their notebooks and thanked everyone again for their help, Pete glanced at his watch in relief, only to be quickly crushed.

'The details will be sent down to Newmarket. I'll let them know you're on your way and they'll arrange to interview you,' the constable told them.

'On our way?' Pete queried. 'We're on our way to Doncaster races.'

'And now you're on your way back to Newmarket,' the constable told him firmly.

'That's no problem at all, officer,' Casburg assured him. He had already had to give his own assurance that he wouldn't be leaving the country during ongoing enquiries.

'But I've horses to saddle!' Sebastian protested, 'And a jockey to book.'

'Are we all needed?' Sophie asked. 'I could saddle for you.'

'Miss Churchill is free to go,' the constable agreed.

'No way!' Pete stepped in, 'not until the Smiths are under lock and key! Phone your dad, Seb, let him see to your runners. Soph', you're coming back with me!' He looked across at Sebastian and grinned. 'Tell him we've all been arrested –

something to do with rugs!'

Sebastian laughed.

'Don't forget to send him to the hotel for your things,' Sophie reminded him, 'save you having to turn round and go back.'

'Raid the hotel as well? He's becoming quite the burglar!'

'No, leave the gear,' Pete advised, 'we'll all be back up tomorrow, surely?'

'I damned hope so,' Sebastian agreed.

He made his call, while Sophie and Pete took their bags out to the car.

'Dad's organised a lawyer for you both,' Sophie told Pete, as they drove back down the A1. 'He thinks you'll need a good one, when the Jockey Club hold their own investigation.'

'Listening to the police, we come out squeaky clean.'

'And looking at it from the Jockey Club's point of view, why didn't you go to them when the very first threat was issued? They're going to look at every race you've ridden in this season.'

'I know they won't find anything,' Pete admitted, 'but it still scares the shit out of me. I've an ingrained fear of stewards. And medical officers. And baling twine.'

'Baling twine?!'

'Yeah, but I'm learning to overcome that one!'

'Well, it can't exactly snatch away your

licence at any moment!'

'It's a bugger losing those rides this afternoon.'

'Only the two. And not really winners.'

'Possible places.'

'Maybe on the first.'

They argued the merits of the horses, and the prospective results over the coming three days, until nearing Huntingdon and home turf. Cambridge; Newmarket; the horrors of the past weeks had been left behind as they pulled in at the Churchills' yard. Sebastian and Casburg followed them in.

Having notified the local police of their arrival, again there were the same questions, the same repetition of statements, the same meticulous gathering of evidence. Tedious after similar repeats to Angela.

'Aren't you going to use sniffer dogs?' Pete asked, watching the officers file past with armfuls of rugs and load them in a van.

'Forensics are more reliable. We'll find traces of anything carried in the pockets.'

Sebastian was taken away, 'to assist with enquiries', the polite disinterest of the police still succeeding in stirring discomfort until it was hard for Pete and his trainer, under the weight of irrational guilt, to remember they were victims.

'I'll be glad when this is all over,' Pete told Sophie with feeling, his turn at the station fast approaching. 'We'll stay here tonight and drive up again in the morning.' He glanced at his watch. 'I'd better give Westy a call, he'll be at the races already and wondering where the hell we are.'

'You certainly owe him an exclusive!'

Pete grinned. 'Let him fish for it! It's what he does best!' He tapped in Western's number. 'Hi, mate, still alive. Want an exclusive?'

'It's worth more from a better name than yourself!'

'Take what you're given! Straubinger's going to be in the private boxes this afternoon and he's going to have a visit from the boys in blue.'

'The drug racket?'

'All speculation, but we think the stuff comes in with Casburg's horses from the States and then over to Germany. Casburg knew nothing about it.'

'So he says!'

'No, it's true, he's clueless. And he's investing in his UK string big time for next season. Classics are on the agenda.'

'Nice one! Who's he got lined up to replace you, then?'

'Piss off! My contract's being renewed.'

'And your friends the Smiths?'

'Paul will be traced from the security firm. That's one contract that won't get renewed!'

'I'll meet you in the bar, you can fill me in.'

'Not today, mate, I'm back home, helping the police with their enquiries.'

'Do you want me to bake you a cake with a file in it?!'

'Save it for the Jockey Club hearing!'

Western laughed. 'Look out for tomorrow's Racing Post. There'll be a full page profile of a former Champion Apprentice in there.'

'It'd better be complimentary!'

'Fuck off, I don't write fiction!'

Pete laughed and hung up.

Eventually, the police interviews came to an end; a little too late for Pete to relax and watch the televised racing. Casburg returned to his own house, to catch his horses on TV; Sebastian took control of the telephone and bombarded David with instructions, none of which mattered, in the end, the two horses finishing unplaced.

'Fancy the pictures?' Pete asked Sophie, bored by the afternoon's inactivity.

'Why not, what's on?'

He glanced down the uninspiring listings in the paper. 'Action, action, teenage dross or Disney?'

'Disney, then!'

He smiled, remembering the last film they'd watched together.

They took separate cars into Cambridge, Pete returning the little hired car, no longer in need of its anonymity. After the movie, they settled down in a restaurant, Pete ordering the salad starter as his main course.

'When Sebastian stops trying to get his horses in at the bottom of the handicap, you can stop wasting,' Sophie pointed out.

'Just one of the many advantages of stepping up in class,' Pete agreed. 'Shall we get a bottle of bubbly, to celebrate?'

'Have you still not got any in the fridge at home?'

'I think I have, as it happens. We'll just go home and get sozzled! Want a dessert?'

She shook her head politely.

'I'll get the bill, then.'

They turned their phones back on.

'Which home?' Sophie asked, as they headed out to her car. 'Yours, tonight. But we don't exactly need two.'

'Is that a proposal?'

She laughed. 'Call it a down-payment.'

'How about neither? A new place, fresh start.'

They settled into the car, Pete's phone immediately shattering the peace.

'First of many,' he grinned, counting his blessings. Who but one of their own would tolerate a salad main course, five-am starts and busy mobiles? 'Pete Allen?'

'Pete, shit, where have you been?' It was Western, sounding subdued and anxious. 'Your phone's been off half the evening.'

'We were at the pictures. What's up?'

'I can't say. Just get up here, would you.'

The phone clicked off.

'That was Westy,' Pete told Sophie, concerned. 'He wants us up in Donny'.'

'Tonight?'

'He just said get up here.' Pete checked the phone, only to reveal a private number. 'He didn't even say where he was.'

'He'll be in the same hotel as us. He always

uses the same hotels, he can pick up snippets from the bar after racing. Is he in trouble, do you think? He didn't try to interview Straubinger, did he?'

'Christ knows, I hope not. We'd better forget that champagne. If Steve Smith's paid him a call…'

Pete tried Western's phone, without success. Turned off.

Sophie pulled out into the traffic.

'My case is in the boot, your things are already up there. We'll head straight up, will we?'

Pete nodded grimly. 'If you don't mind.'

CHAPTER TWENTY

It took little more than two hours to reach Doncaster, during which time imaginations had worked overdrive.

'I wish Dad had stopped over,' Sophie said, locking the car and following Pete into the hotel.

'Chris and Terry are here. We've cavalry to hand if we need it.'

They picked up their own key from reception and asked for Western's room number, stopping in at the bar in the vague hope Western might be there.

He wasn't.

'The gang's in the far corner, if you want to join them?' Pete pressed.

'I'll come with you.'

Pete didn't argue, not so sure of his own ability in Florence Nightingale mode.

They took the lift up to Western's floor and located his room. A tentative listen at the door gave the impression the room was empty, but when they tried the handle and stepped inside it was anything but.

Dave Bisley sat in a chair by the desk. Western sat slumped in a chair at the foot of the bed. The Smith brothers were lying back comfortably on the bed, reading papers.

'Go back down and get the boys!' Pete said quickly, Sophie already backing out of the door.

'No one's stopping you, sweetheart,' Bisley assured her, 'but lover boy might not thank you for the audience.'

She hesitated, uncertain.

Western shook his head and she waited.

'We had a horse for you today,' Bisley told Pete, 'but you let us down. The boys are just finding one for tomorrow. I done five hundred grand at Newbury. The boys are only looking for thirty. But don't worry, we're in no hurry. If we spread it over the rest of the season, a couple of races a week, the exchanges'll never pick it up.'

'Spread it how you like,' Pete told him confidently, 'there's a warrant out for those two.'

'I don't need them,' Bisley assured him. 'They'll be out the country tomorrow, straight after your race. I don't need heavies to twist your arm, I've got leverage you can't run away from.'

He picked up a tape from the desk and smiled at Western.

'I'm sorry,' Western said simply, 'the party piece; I had to.'

'He's a good lad, our Westy,' Bisley told Pete, 'I knew he was snooping on your behalf, so I told him nothing. Let him have a no-lose account when he found out about your governor's account. He's a better window than Sebastian Churchill ever was. It's worked out better for us both. Better than I could have ever hoped, actually.'

He smiled and played the tape.

Western closed his eyes and lowered his head, as his voice rang out from the cassette player.

'Come on, the low-down, now – fast cars, fast women and a betting account, when did they hook you? Is it the price of fame and wealth?'

'Are you scratching for a story?'

'I'm always scratching for a story. Can I quote you?'

'Quote me on anything you like!'

'Did you blow it by selling info'?'

'Too young for the responsibility. Too inexperienced for such a big retainer. If I hadn't blown it in the big league I wouldn't have needed to start gambling.'

'And selling information?'

'I can set up the result long before the finish! Simple errors of judgement. If my horse takes a hundred yards to reach full pace, I don't ask him for an effort until eighty yards out. If he can only sustain his pace for a hundred yards, I ask him for an effort a hundred and ten yards out.'

'You stop it.'

'In a word, yes.'

'You accept presents?'

'I stop horses, I accept presents. And I had a betting account.'

Everything Pete had said, one morning in the kitchen. Expertly edited. Three clear counts of a Warning Off. Banned from riding, banned from racecourses, banned from racing stables.

'I can run off a copy each for the boys,' Bisley continued. 'This one, of course, for the Jockey Club. And another for my own records.'

'I'm sorry,' Western repeated uselessly, 'I never…'

'You bastard,' Pete cut him short, 'you bastard. I trusted you.' He looked desperately at Sophie. 'That's not what I said! They've edited it!'

'I stop horses, I accept presents, I have a betting account?'

'You didn't hear what he said! They've cut him out, Sophie!' He looked at her pleadingly, but she avoided his gaze, catching Western's eye instead.

He turned back to Bisley, defeated. If the Jockey Club Warned him Off, it wasn't only his livelihood he'd lose. He felt Sophie's hand slip into his own, squeezing it resolutely, the overwhelming relief enough to break him, on top of Bisley's threat. He swallowed; took in a breath; waited.

'Found any horses yet, boys?' Bisley enquired.

'He's in the Listed tomorrow. Marsh's on the favourite. Only five runners, it'll go off long odds-on.'

'Very long odds-on. Although I think I can afford to be a little more generous than most. If I opened at just three to one on, I should attract all the big backers looking for easy money. Fifty grand a piece to win sixteen and a half, I should easily get two of the players snatching up my odds.'

'I can't fix a five horse race,' Pete said quietly, his mouth dry.

'You don't have to be discreet. You can afford to let the stewards haul you in for a ten day ban for reckless riding. Better than being Warned Off for life. Just put Marsh over the rails. Bring him down. Do what you like, but don't slip up, like Newbury.' He picked up the tape and waved it at Pete. 'I won't post it straight to the Jockey Club. Not when I can sell it to the tabloids. I'll get my money, one way or another. The choice is yours. Tow the line. Or get Warned Off.'

Tow the line. Put Chris over the rails. Bring him down. Down on the turf amid the forty mile an hour half ton hooves; like Dominic.

Dave Bisley. The third voice in his flat.

'You can lay Marsh's horse,' Pete agreed.

He looked at Western, but Western turned away. He felt Sophie's grip tighten round his hand, but he couldn't quite face her just yet. Couldn't face anyone. Couldn't do this.

Couldn't not do it.

'Make sure you turn up tomorrow,' Bisley ordered, as Pete turned to leave, 'if you step down from the ride, I'll sell the tape anyway.'

Outside, in the corridor, Pete leant weakly against the wall, the familiar warnings of nausea rapidly rising. He slid down the wall, drew up his knees, and lowered his head.

'Danny nodded to me frantically, when you said the tape had been edited,' Sophie told him.

'Did he really? Too little too late.'

'If you go to the Jockey Club first…'

'What? They'll only Warn me Off for five years? Right now, Soph', I just want to go home and slit my wrists.' He buried his head once more, trembling and sweating, as much in rage as in panic.

'Who in their right minds would say those things!' she protested, 'not even the Jockey Club can seriously believe that tape!'

'Sophie, I can't seriously deny it, either.' He looked up at her. 'What does it matter if it's out of context, that they edited it? At the end of the day, I only told him the truth. And he taped every bit of it. The bastard.'

'The lift's coming. We'd better go back to our room, it's nearly midnight.'

'I can't just walk away, Sophie. I should just let him do his money tomorrow, when Chris wins. But I need it finalised.'

He opened the door to Western's room. If he was going to lose a night's sleep, he wasn't going to let Bisley go to bed thinking he'd won. He heard the lift bell ring as they walked back in.

Western was still slumped miserably in the chair, the Smith brothers now standing beside him, waiting to leave. There was no sign of Bisley, but he could be heard, in the bathroom, washing his hands.

'What? You forget the name of the horse or something?!' Paul Smith laughed, surprised by Pete and Sophie's reappearance. His grin fell away almost instantly, as the door clicked shut behind them.

'What is this, safety in numbers?' enquired a crisp, clipped German voice.

Pete stepped out of the way, amazed to see Andreas Straubinger behind him. Straubinger himself failed to recognise either Pete or Sophie and he ignored them, his interest fixed purely on the two brothers.

As was his gun.

'Am I not paying you enough, that you have to set up your pathetic little extortion schemes?' he demanded. 'Do you know where I have been for the past five hours?'

It seemed apparent they did not. As they stared at the barrel of the gun held on them, Western fumbled on the desk behind him, grasping the tape and succeeding in slipping it into his breast pocket. He didn't have to worry about discretion; Straubinger held all attention.

'I have been helping the British police with their enquiries.' The German spat out the words with such venom, the Smith brothers drew back a little.

Western saw Sophie glance across at the desk. He caught her eye and patted his breast pocket; then lifted up a cassette recorder from his jacket pocket, enough for her to see the buttons. One was pushed down. She nodded, hopefully in understanding.

'Hey, look, we didn't turn you in, man,' Paul said nervously.

'Oh, but you see, you did,' Straubinger corrected him. 'You robbed the trainer, you threatened his jockey – they found the rugs, you stupid little person!'

They were too shocked to respond, though there was little they could have said in their defence.

'They cannot yet link the rugs to me. They cannot yet link you to me. But they will. And since I already face a long prison sentence, why should I worry about adding to it?'

He turned the gun away, momentarily; looked at it, lovingly. Aimed it once more.

'You think I won't use it? And why should I not?'

In the momentary silence, something clicked.

Bisley, perhaps, had tried to lock the bathroom door. Straubinger turned round, unconcerned. He hardly seemed to care about his audience.

In the brief second the gun was turned away, Steve Smith sprang to one side, unable to reach the door, but grabbing Sophie instead. Straubinger turned on him in an instant, smiling at his stupidity.

'You think she is a shield? The bullet will pass through both of you.'

It was Paul's turn to run, diving at the bed, hoping, perhaps, to roll over and out towards the door. But the room was too cramped to dodge even the small hand gun. A loud report, cries of shock from all in the room, and the gun was pointing steadily once more at Sophie and Steve.

'There, you see how easy it is?' Straubinger announced calmly. 'I may as well hang for three murders as for one.'

Things suddenly moved far too fast, though for Pete time seemed to stand still. He recalled hanging upside down beneath a horse; the seconds slowing to minutes as adrenalin speeded his reactions, trying to save him. The seconds slowed again for him now, as he screamed Sophie's name, powerless to help, powerless to save her, despite all the time in the world. Time enough to cry 'no!' as the second report blasted the air. Time enough to watch her, as though in freeze frame, drop to the floor; Steve Smith falling, like a shadow, in her wake.

Perhaps time had been suspended for them all, that same innate self-defence mechanism that had somehow given Western enough impetus to react.

Just as it had beneath the flashing steel hooves of the horse, time kicked back into overdrive once more.

Pete ran to Sophie – already sitting up, stunned; confused as to what had happened, expecting to be dead, to be hurt, and finding herself to be neither. And the awful weight across her legs was suddenly too awful, yet she couldn't scream, though she felt it rise within her.

Pete held her tightly, pulling her face into his chest, desperate to shield her from the sight he knew she had already seen.

'It's alright, it's alright,' he repeated softly, feeling her sobbing into his chest, her fingers digging into his flesh, unable to hold him tightly enough. He looked down, momentarily, and couldn't contain his own tears, the shock and grief too overwhelming.

Danny Western lay sprawled across Sophie's legs, his eyes wide, his mouth gaping. A hole, surely too small to do damage, pierced his breast pocket.

It was the massive exit wound in his back that had killed him.

And Straubinger – who now sat casually on the bed, awaiting arrest beside his first victim – had been correct about the bullet. It had been enough to kill Steve Smith as well.

By the time the police arrived, Dave Bisley had come out of the bathroom. He didn't bother to look for the tape, the carnage facing him pushing it out of his mind totally. In any case, it was irretrievably shattered in Danny Western's breast pocket. Instead, he sat quietly beside Pete and Sophie, the violence witnessed unlike anything he had ever falsely termed with the word in his own life.

Sophie thought of the other tape; slipped it, undamaged, from a lower jacket pocket and handed it to the female officer who now plied her with tea.

'He taped it all,' she told her, shakily, trying not to cry again. 'That man, Dave Bisley, he was trying to threaten us. Danny taped it all.'

Bisley didn't flinch. Couldn't flinch. They were all too numb to care much for their own troubles.

'I didn't know,' Pete said softly to Sophie. For a minute, wished he hadn't known. But it didn't change anything. Westy had still taped his confessions, sold him out to Bisley.

The police officers, though patient, were anxious to get Sophie, Pete and Bisley out of the room. As soon as they were steady enough on their feet they were helped up and ushered out.

Only death remained, neatly recorded and photographed, as though just in case the lifeless figures might suddenly stretch and move as if in sleep.

On Western's desk was his final copy, already emailed for the next day's Racing Post; the careful results of stopping and starting his tape painstakingly to get just the quotes he needed. It had been the quotes he didn't need that had made Bisley prick his ears and think of more than just the cheque he was delivering.

"Presents?" Western had written, within his interview, "What the hell! Do you think I'm going to risk my licence for a few bob? Stop a horse on some Joe Punter's say so? I don't physically pull a horse, I don't stop a horse, as you put it. I get more presents from Father Christmas!"

He'd credited the words to Pete Allen, "Champion of the past, likely Champion of the future, and a jockey undeniably loaded with both talent and integrity."

Only Danny Western would never get to read his final article.

ALSO BY LISSA OLIVER

CHANTILLY DAWNS
Marcel Dessaint stands alone in the deserted
Longchamp racecourse, an outcast in the only world
he knows…
Sealed within an inescapable world of hatred,
the comforting blanket of Chantilly becomes a
claustrophobic prison as the demons of his past return
to torment him.
And so dawns the battle for personal
salvation...

Available from The Book Republic
ISBN 978-1-9072210-8-5

TALES OF THE TURF...
A host of entertaining characters take the
reader on a humorous tour of their unique world.

...& OTHER WORLDS
Introduces the reader to such diverse yet
loveable characters as pop stars, vampires and serial
killers!
All of whom are guaranteed to raise a smile
and make this the ideal bedside and travelling
companion.

by
Lissa Oliver

Available from The Georgian Rose Press
ISBN 978-0-9534167-0-7

NERO – THE LAST CAESAR

His childhood stolen by politics, Nero is
emperor at sixteen.
Dominated by his mother, controlled by the
senate, manipulated by his Commander, he fights to
retain his enthusiasm and dedication, only to be worn
down by the politics of Rome.
Adored by the people, revered by foreign
statesmen, loathed by his peers, Nero ended his short
life in suicide, a sad and lonely outcast.
But his reputation lives on, epitomising the
wealth and decadence of ancient Rome...
A modern story set in an ancient world;
shocking, erotic – and ultimately moving.

by
Lissa Oliver

Available from The Georgian Rose Press
ISBN 0 9534167 1 2